TRUE LIES SERIES

UNTRUE COLORS

VERONICA FORAND

Helping him could be fatal...
She's on the run...

Brilliant art appraiser Alex Northrop's ex used stolen art to fund his nefarious activities. Now he wants her dead. But it isn't just herself she's worried about – if he discovers who she really is, he'll kill her family.

Professor Henry Chilton is shocked to find a beautiful stranger passed out in his bed, and even more so when she reveals the priceless painting in his house is a forgery – the painting he'd planned to use as collateral for a woman's shelter. She's mysterious and frightened, and he's determined to discover why.

Alex's knowledge of art is undeniable—just as Henry's attraction to her is irresistible. But in order to help him recover the real painting, Alex isn't just risking exposure...she's risking everything she cares about.

Praise for *Untrue Colors*

"This book was full of adventure, mystery, action, fear, anger, pain, hope, loss, family reunions and so much more...I was a little sad when I finished it because I wanted the story to continue."
   - 5 Star Top Pick, Night Owl Reviews

"The plot is filled with globe-trotting intrigue, stolen art, secret identities, and dangerous villains, and Forand balances the suspenseful mystery with a passionate romance. Alex is an intriguing heroine--a linguistic genius and a master of disguise with an uncanny eye for appraising art. She's complemented by Henry, a dashing anthropology professor and earl who's dedicated his life to helping abused women and children. Their romance unfolds in scenes that are both tender and erotic. The supporting characters are also strong, including Simon, whose sexy swagger conceals an unrequited love***Detailed settings and references to real stolen art, including Henri Matisse's 1901 painting The Luxembourg Gardens, enhance the story. A briskly paced romance featuring breathless suspense."
   - Kirkus Reviews

"Untrue Colors is one of the best Romantic Suspense books I have read."
   - Ellesea Loves Reading

"Seriously, one of the better contemporary romances that I've read in a while. The plot was very well written. It was equal parts mysterious, suspenseful and romantic."
   - Christine Marie's review for Lulo Fangirl

"Gripping, fast-paced, and wickedly unique."

"WOW - a superbly written roller coaster ride that keeps the reader on the edge of their seat from the very beginning."

For Deb Wiseley

The sister I never had,
the friend who always has my back,
and my sanity in this insane world.

CHAPTER 1

lex looked toward the Louvre for possibly the last time and grieved the loss of everything she'd taken for granted. She wrapped her arms across her chest and tried to steady her breath. Overhearing Luc's plan to celebrate their four-month anniversary by murdering her had set off her own plan of running as far away from him as possible—not an effective plan, considering the monster currently sat six inches away from her in a car on the way to her death.

What began as a fairy-tale romance had morphed into a traumatic descent into hell. A glamorous job, a handsome client, a little romance. They appeared perfect for each other, a rich art collector and the young art appraiser who had fallen head over heels for him. Rugged good looks combined with an enormous amount of wealth made him an ideal catch for a woman who didn't mind being beaten into submission.

Alex had objected to every broken bone and every bruise on her body. And then she uncovered his deception. Luc was a crook, and she'd been his gullible appraiser used to dupe art collectors and even small countries out of their valuable assets.

While his main henchman, Pascal, drove them through Paris,

Luc held her hand in the back of the Mercedes like they were still lovers.

Dressed in a thousand-dollar suit and wearing a sophisticated five-o'clock shadow across his chiseled features, he seemed headed for a night at the theater, not on the way to eliminate his girlfriend. Alex leaned away from him. She needed to get away. His free hand caressed her arm, rubbed her shoulder, and pulled her back toward him. Moving slowly, seductively, he wrapped his fingers around her neck and started to squeeze. He stared at her, observing her reaction.

"I promise I won't tell anyone. I swear it." She pleaded for her life, speaking French, the only language they'd ever used with each other. As his hand tightened, she gasped and struggled for breath.

Luc drew her face closer to his. His lips pinched together, causing the muscles in his neck to tense. "Liar."

She struggled to pull away; his grip tightened. No longer able to inhale, her eyes watered and her vision faded. With nothing left to lose, she struck out at his face. He released her, but slapped her ear so hard, her head flew into the door. The pain ricocheted through her skull, leaving her numb for a moment.

She glanced out the window and saw salvation. As Pascal slowed for a turn, she opened the door and jumped. Her Chanel suit acted as her only protection when she hit the ground and bounced onto the road. Asphalt scraped her skin with each rotation until she slammed into the curb. Pain rebelled in ribs not yet healed from the fall down Luc's marble stairway. Car brakes screeched nearby. In seconds, they would be on her. She hobbled to her feet, sucking in huge breaths. Bystanders pressed around her, trying to assist, but she twisted away, her hands poised to fight anything that touched her.

She merged into the manic crowd entering the Gare du Nord at rush hour. Men and women in suits, groups of schoolchildren, and what felt like hundreds of tourists slowed her escape. With her passports tucked in a travel belt under her skirt and several hundred euros in her possession, she boarded the high-speed train for London and prayed he wouldn't follow her.

CHAPTER 2

Two months later

Alex sat in her favorite booth in the back corner of the Yellow Dog Pub with a Coke and a cup of pumpkin soup and pulled out the book *Matisse, Father & Son* from her backpack. One of the students she'd met offered to check out books for her from the library, and she devoured every one she could lay her hands on. She'd created a comfortable yet temporary life in Oxford. She dressed as one of the students at the university, lived at a youth hostel, and earned money by helping a pub owner clean up after closing. Still, she felt far from safe.

"Gabe, how's the soup?" Matt, the owner, asked.

She'd become used to being called Gabe West. Gabrielle, her mother's name, had been the only name she could think of when she'd arrived in Oxford. West reminded her that her family was across the ocean in Boston. Since moving to Europe eight years ago, Alex had kept in sporadic contact with her family. Since meeting Luc, she'd had zero. They didn't need to become mixed up in her problems. Luc was too dangerous.

She took a spoonful and savored the first taste of her main meal for the day. "You outdid yourself."

"Glad to hear it." He sat across from her, his wise blue eyes framed by laugh lines. "Listen, love, some bloke's been asking around the local pubs about an adorable undocumented French art lover. Never did hear you speak anything but English, but thought I'd give you a heads-up."

Her spoon dropped into the bowl, splashing some soup on the table. Her body tensed, ready to run away from this sanctuary. Had they found her? She scanned the room. The crowd contained only familiar faces, students and locals. Most of them had welcomed her without any questions.

"French?" She laughed. "I can barely understand your brand of English, never mind an entirely different language."

Matt's expression relaxed. "American English is just a weaker version of the real thing." His smile faltered, though, and he clasped her hand. "I enjoy your company and your work ethic, Gabe, but I prefer you safe. If you need to leave, I've got your back."

She nodded. Tired of living in constant fear, she craved a hug from anyone who would call her by her real name. Instead, she had to run. "Can you return this book to Fred? I don't want him to get a late charge."

"Absolutely."

They stood at the same time. She took two steps and froze.

Dressed in black with arm muscles the size of telephone poles, Pascal pushed through the entrance and glanced around the room. He hadn't noticed her yet, so she ducked behind the bar, grabbed her pack, and crawled into the bathroom.

She climbed on top of the toilet and waited, listening. Glass shattered, as did her nerves. Angry words between Matt and Pascal escalated into a full-blown argument. Several other patrons joined in, and then a gunshot.

Horror clawed through her composure, and her legs nearly gave out. She couldn't go back out there. He'd kill her for sure. After a quick prayer for Matt, she smashed the bathroom window with her boot to make her escape. The backpack fit out the window with room to spare. It wasn't large, but big enough to shimmy through. She pulled herself up with relative ease, but her left hand slipped and rammed into the ragged edges of the glass sticking up from the frame. The glass sliced into her palm and her thumb and made several gashes in her wrist. She bit through the pain, climbed out to the alleyway and ran. Again.

Keeping an eye out to see if she'd been followed, Alex walked for an hour until she had no choice but to stop and tend to the blood dripping from her hand. A white sock from her bag soaked up most of the mess, but the blood continued to flow. Her vision clouded for a second, and she shook her head to stay alert.

A few blocks later and she was in one of the outer neighborhoods surrounding Oxford University. Faculty houses lined the streets. Dressed in a faded black leather jacket with long pink hair, she blended into a group of students moving toward an elegant brick house.

She had to get off the street.

She climbed the front steps to an open red door. The two female students entering in front of her were dressed in cute dresses and high-heeled shoes. She hadn't worn heels since leaving Luc. Combat boots and sneakers were more practical, and she could run fast in them.

Smirking faces and rolled eyes greeted her as she maneuvered through the crowd toward the main salon. Boys sporting silk ties and arrogant grins stood around pontificating on the plight of the less fortunate of the world as they drank Chianti from lead crystal glasses. A few artistic types, dressed like Alex, stayed together and mocked their better-dressed counterparts for mocking them. She could pass for one of them as long as she stayed in the periphery of the conversations. All she needed was five or ten minutes to find a bathroom to rinse off her wounds, and then she could figure out how to move on to a new location.

A quick stop in a small bathroom provided her with a few moments of privacy. Cleaning the bloody hand with soap, she dried it off with a very nice towel she hid in the back of the cabinet so no one would notice the bloodstains on it until after she departed. Hiding the towel was preferable to stealing it. She pulled out another somewhat clean sock to wrap her hand. Perhaps no one would notice if she kept the hand in her pocket as she walked around. After she finished, she tried to wash off the heavy black eyeliner and black lipstick she'd used to hide her features. The makeup smeared, but didn't disappear. She almost took the safety pin out of her ear, but it wouldn't draw any more attention than cotton-candy hair, so she left it.

When she returned to the crowded foyer, Alex noted the beautiful oak paneling in the hallway, carved by a master almost one hundred and fifty years ago. The three oil portraits by George Frederic Watts, two of distinguished men and one of a lady, also caught her attention. Art soothed her mind, but now wasn't the time to appreciate Watts's brilliance using color to capture detail.

"Dr. Chilton, I'd like to introduce my flatmate Jenny." The formal introduction pulled her from her thoughts. A boy, no older than nineteen, was introducing his date.

The older man, a faint smile on his face, shook the girl's hand and welcomed her to his home. He didn't look like any professors she knew. He seemed too young and handsome, and his expression carried more confidence than anyone she'd met since Luc, but in a different way. The man wore the brown tweed jacket and beige pants of a Hollywood English professor, though his tan indicated he spent a lot of time outside. Rugged, yet preppy.

She remained standing in the hall staring at those eyes. Green, framed by dark-rimmed glasses and brown hair with enough length to curve, but not curl. In the past, she would have fantasized about a man like that. Now she preferred to be left alone.

The girl, wearing a short red dress and high heels, gazed up at the professor, leaving her hand lingering in his for a moment longer than necessary with her boyfriend standing at her side. Alex watched as the girl shifted her hips, plumped her lips, and batted her eyelashes. The professor didn't seem to notice. He turned his attention to the boy, and Alex refocused on finding food. She wasn't sure when she might get to eat again.

She roamed toward the study, admiring the exquisite art and furniture around her.

When she turned the corner into the room, her breath hitched at the reader's paradise. Huge windows overlooked the lawn, two leather recliners faced a large fireplace, and on the wall between two oak bookcases full of novels, journals, and knowledge hung a seascape by Gustave Courbet from the 1860s.

"Are you lost?" someone asked with a condescending British accent.

Alex turned toward a junior aristocrat, wearing a striped bow tie in the blue and white colors of Harrow.

She slipped her bandaged hand behind her back. "Looking for the bar."

She put on a confident grin as she edged around him toward the bar, her heartbeat racing. She ordered a Coke and picked up a few nuts from a cream-colored Wedgwood bowl. When she turned to leave the room, the boy followed.

"Why don't you join us?" He and three other guys in suits surrounded her before she could leave.

"No, thanks."

They all glanced at one another with big smirks.

"American? I don't recall seeing you in our class. I'd have remembered you." He brushed his hand through her pink hair, resting it against the bare skin of her neck.

The caress reminded her of the last man who thought touching her was his right. The memory sent chills through her veins.

"Who did you come here with?" another asked.

By the look on their faces, they knew she was an outsider, a party crasher.

They were blocking the exit, so she backed up toward the bookcases. Her legs barely held her up, and her nerves squeezed her throat, preventing her from speaking.

A trespassing charge against her would be disastrous. She'd end up back in Luc's custody before her arraignment.

"I wager you'd be quite attractive without that makeup," someone to the side of her said.

"Gentlemen," The professor's voice boomed across the room, genteel, yet firm. "I think the lady would prefer to dine with people closer to her own class and caliber, so I must request that you boys head to dinner without her. We will discuss your behavior after the spring recess."

Her tormentors' faces fell from smirk to grimace, and they backed away. The easygoing manner she'd seen on the professor earlier had faded a bit, revealing a side of him intent on lifting each of the boys up by his neck and throwing him out the door.

"Sorry, Sir, we thought your guest would want to meet everybody," one of the instigators called out.

"I'm sure she appreciates your hospitality. If you'll excuse us." The professor stood a few inches taller than them, and his solid physique made it clear that he could best each and every one of the little snots in a fight. Not that he would, especially over a trespasser.

Her mouth dropped open to say something as her body began to sink to the ground. The professor stepped forward and clasped her elbow. The knot that had twisted her insides all afternoon subsided a bit, and she was tempted to lean into his arms and absorb some of his strength. He never spoke, but his possession of her caused the boys to back away.

Without a word, the boys strolled out of the room, leaving her standing in the corner with an empty glass and a pounding heart.

The professor released her. His eyes softened. "Are you all right?"

How could she find trouble so quickly after leaving the pub? He'd throw her out when he realized she didn't have an invite.

"I just need a minute." Holding back tears of frustration and hiding her injury, she plastered on her brave face and smiled.

"Take your time." He gave her a slight bow before he

departed, like an actual English lord and not a schoolboy who pretends to be a gentleman and then harasses women when he thinks he can get away with it.

Alex returned to the bar on trembling legs and asked for another soda. She'd make it through the night. She had to.

***

Several hours after his last guest departed, Henry pushed aside a pile of ungraded exams and three articles to be reviewed for the *Journal of the Anthropological Society of Oxford* to make room for his glass of scotch. The newest lecturer in the department, he'd been roped into three introductory courses and two seminars for the current year. Most of the other faculty were nearing retirement age, not thirty years old with a brand-new PhD. They'd earned their lighter workloads. Or so they claimed. He took another sip. Tonight, he didn't want to think of the work burying him. He wanted a good book and his pillow.

At least the dinner with his students had been a success. Except for the pack of wolves circling the lady in his study. She'd worn an expression seen in people who had nothing left to lose. A desperation born of hard times and bad choices. A look he'd observed in many of the people he'd helped over the years, yet something about this petite woman with pink hair tugged a bit differently at him. Maybe his thoughts stayed with her because she'd disappeared before dinner. Was she okay? Did she need help and hadn't been able to ask? He couldn't save everyone, regrettably. With luck, she'd made it home without any problems.

The clock chimed once, signaling Henry's bedtime. He finished his drink and rose. Straightening his favorite beige cardigan and securing his glasses on his nose, he ambled down the hallway and paused outside his bedroom. Something wasn't right. Perhaps it was the light from his bedside lamp, beaming through the open door.

He padded into the room in silence, until the old wooden floor creaked.

The girl from the party, still sporting a worn leather jacket and black combat boots, stirred and then jumped up, poised for a fight. Her hands clenched into fists, and she swung into a martial arts stance, one foot forward, the other slightly back.

She mumbled something in French about bathroom windows and bloody socks. The warrior image faded as her body swayed backward. Her face turned white where it wasn't streaked with black, and her eyes opened wide and flashed him a vivid blue-green glare. Scanning the room for another exit, she crossed to the opposite door, but it only opened to his bath.

He needed to calm her down. "Easy does it, Sunshine. You're going to break something."

Ignoring him, she opened a window, but she was too high up for an easy escape. Why was she panicking? He wasn't going to harm her.

Henry remained in front of the doorway. "You're safe here. Please calm yourself."

He leaned against the doorjamb to assure her he meant no harm. Why would this young woman remain in his house after the party? She swayed and then leaned on the wall. Her eyes seemed disoriented. Did she even know where she was?

She'd been unable to stand straight when he'd spoken to her earlier in the evening as well. Perhaps she was drunk. That happened with an open bar.

When he stepped toward her to help, she wobbled to a table containing a seventeenth-century Rouen vase, acquired by his grandfather. She paused, and Henry's heart paused as well. Thankfully, her hand reached over it and grabbed a tacky Venetian glass statue his cousin had sent him from Italy. The statue flew through the air toward his head. He ducked, and it smashed on the wall. Pieces scattered across the floor and his oldest Aubusson rug.

This was ridiculous. She'd end up smashing his room to bits.

"Her aim is almost as good as yours." Simon approached from behind.

"Not quite. I never miss." Henry kept his focus on the girl in case she decided to break something valuable.

"Your skills are rusty." His half-brother loved to mock Henry's transition from Royal Navy sniper to boring academic. "Need backup?"

Henry shook his head. "Miss, please stop. You've already caused quite enough damage. I'll have to call the police." That would be unpleasant. Young female university student in a lecturer's house after hours. He'd be retiring before he had truly begun his new career.

She squeezed her eyes closed for a second and bit her lip. Henry remembered the torment she'd endured from a few of his students in the study. *Poor kid.* He lifted his hands in a show of forgiveness.

She hesitated, then took a step back and glanced at her hand, wrapped in a bloodstained cloth, before tucking it behind her.

"I'm sorry, please don't call the police," she said with a soft American accent.

A grungy brown backpack sat on the bed. The girl picked it up and retreated into a corner. Her eyes darted side to side and landed on Henry and the open door. She staggered into a lamp, but saved it before it fell over.

Henry stepped toward her and onto several jagged pieces of his cousin's gift. Shards of glass dug into his heel. "Bugger." He'd be ripped to shreds by the time he made it to her. "We need to get her out of my bedroom and into a safe location."

"That won't be necessary." Simon stepped through the glass in his shoes and pointed toward the corner.

Their visitor lay in a pile on the floor, unconscious.

CHAPTER 3

─────────────── ✑ ───────────────

lthough Henry had left his uninvited guest at the hospital with the utmost trust in the facility, a gut feeling had wrapped itself around him and prodded his conscience throughout the night. His instincts rarely lied. Up at 7:00 a.m., he headed to the hospital, more than a little apprehensive.

The voice of the American woman echoed down the long blue hallways of the hospital. Henry trotted toward the sound. He balanced more on the ball of his left foot to avoid reopening the minor cuts on his heel from the night before. A slight commotion came from the corner room. A constable stood in the doorway, holding a familiar backpack while facing off with the petite woman attired in a patient gown. Several nurses and a woman in a plum suit gathered nearby as well.

"Unless you're here to arrest me, you must release my pack." Her face, makeup free and more inviting than the night before, pointed up at the tall officer, who was holding her bag behind him. She never touched him, but she appeared quite threatening despite being dressed in nothing but a loosely tied hospital robe.

"We'd like to ask you a few questions before you leave." The officer spoke in a composed, reassuring voice.

The woman, clearly agitated, eyed the pack. "I answered every question I was asked by the doctors and the nurses and the very pushy woman bringing me a tray of gruel and tea." For a woman terrified of something or someone the night before, she had a surprising amount of grit in the face of the authorities.

The officer's voice continued to remain unruffled despite the woman's open hostility. "We understand. It's scary to press charges against the person who abused you, but in most cases, it's the right thing to do. If you won't do it for yourself, then perhaps you'll help the next woman crossing that individual's path."

Abused? She did act scared when she'd first awoken. She'd been desperate enough to throw one of his possessions at his head. Her story just became a whole lot more interesting to Henry.

She shook her head and stepped back again. "I'm not pressing charges, because I wasn't abused. I fell down the stairs, smashed my ribs, and broke a window when I tried to catch myself. Is clumsiness a crime?"

Definitely abused.

Her painted hair and grunge clothes contrasted with her articulate speech. The woman was a complete mystery. Those types of injuries, combined with a defensive tone, more often than not indicated someone had beaten the hell out of her. He sucked in his breath long enough to simmer his rage. Abuse would never become commonplace and mundane to him. His father had broken the spirit of his mother, and Henry vowed long ago to protect any woman he could from living the same miserable existence.

The woman in the suit, possibly the social aid worker, reached out and held her uninjured hand. "Please, we want to help you." Her voice lowered, perhaps in an attempt to keep the conversation private. It was too late. The entire wing of the building had been privy to their discussion.

The girl's mouth lifted into a slight smile, transforming her pretty face into something indefinable, yet incredibly appealing. "I appreciate your assistance, but it's unnecessary. I'll be fine.

What I really need is a bathroom and my bag for supplies. Monthly girl issues." She held out her hand, expecting to receive the backpack.

Although the officer didn't look too keen on giving it back, he handed it to her. She thanked him, backed into her bathroom, and shut the door.

When the door lock clicked, the crowd dispersed, except for one nurse, the police officer, and the woman in the suit. They stood together whispering back and forth. Henry couldn't make out the details of their discussion.

He approached the group cautiously. "Excuse me. I'm Henry Chilton, I brought the young woman in last night."

The woman in the suit glared at Henry. Did she suspect he'd beaten her? Terrific. The cop just waved and turned back to talk to the others. Obviously to him, Henry wasn't a suspect.

A pretty young nurse led Henry away from the group. "I'm Clara Dawes, Ms. West's nurse. I'm afraid we can't explain her medical condition, privacy and all that."

"No problem. I was just checking up on her."

"Is she a student of yours?"

He had no idea. Probably not, as he'd never seen her in any of his classes. He would have remembered the hair, at least. "She was a guest at a dinner party I held last night at my house."

The nurse leaned toward him and spoke softly enough to keep her words from traveling. "Her main injuries are the cuts on her hand, but she has enough scars and old bruises to make us concerned. If only she'd tell us who did this to her, we could help." She stood so close to him, the floral scent of roses displaced the antiseptic scent of the hospital. "I'll tell her you stopped by."

"That won't be necessary." She probably wouldn't remember him.

If he returned in an hour or so, she might be more relaxed, and he could determine if she needed his assistance. He got into his car and started for home, but slowed at the sight of the brown backpack displayed like a homing beacon on someone's back. No hospital discharged patients in under ten minutes. She must have escaped through the window.

She walked down the road wearing jeans and a black T-shirt with her leather jacket tied to her pack. Without the jacket over her shoulders, she'd shrunk two sizes. Without the layers of black makeup, she appeared softer, less hostile toward the world.

He pulled alongside her. "Need a ride?"

"No, thanks." She moved to the other side of the sidewalk, and her hand tightened on her bag.

"I'm Henry. Henry Chilton. I brought you to the hospital."

She stopped moving, but remained at a safe distance from the car. "Was I in your house last night?"

Henry smiled. "Yes. I teach anthropology, the dinner was for my students."

The pack slid down her arms and she readjusted. Her hand remained at her side, hidden in white gauze bandages. "I'm sorry for breaking the statue. I wasn't myself last night."

"Perfectly understandable. I'm just glad you didn't throw the Rouen vase. It's been in my family for generations."

"I'd never harm such a beautiful piece." She shut her eyes and then shuddered. "Thanks again, for your help." She started down the road again. He followed in his car. If she wouldn't allow the police or hospital to assist her, maybe she'd allow him to help.

"Are you a student here?" he yelled out his window, trying not to sound like a stalker.

"No." She increased her pace.

Thank God she wasn't a student. But had she passed the age of majority? He could protect her if he could remove her from Oxford.

"Can I ask your age?"

"Looking to get lucky? Because you won't with me."

"Actually, I want to help you. Where are you staying?"

"I'm not sure yet. It depends how far out of town I get."
Perfect, but would she trust him?

Pulling up a little ahead of her, he stopped. He reached into his pocket and produced a card for the Ripon Women's Group. He paused before handing it to her. She'd either believe he was in her life as a lucky coincidence, or she'd think he was a con artist taking advantage of her situation. Coincidence or not, she needed him. "This is a place for women who need a safe haven."

A few seconds passed before she reached through the window and took the card. A small acorn tattoo marked the inside of her wrist. Her rebel appearance didn't match her personality. Instead of fighting with the boys at the party or the hospital staff, she tried to remove herself from the situation. She acted cautious and intelligent. And here she was running away from something again.

"We protect families who need a temporary place to stay. No cost, just a promise to give back someday when you find someone else in need."

She hesitated, as any woman in her situation should do, and glanced behind her. A police officer exited the hospital, the same one who had taken her backpack. Her body shrank down behind Henry's car, and then she opened the door.

"I could use a place to sleep for a day or two. I'm Gabe." She tossed the bag to the floor of the front seat, jumping in after it. Her avoidance of the police marked her as a fugitive from something.

"Nice to meet you, Gabe. How's your hand?"

She glanced at the clean white bandage and shrugged. "I'll survive. Thanks for taking me to the hospital."

"It seemed the prudent thing to do after you passed out."

"Not everyone is prudent or kind."

He drove away, and Gabe shifted in her seat as though she'd need to duck out of sight any second. "By the way, I'm twenty-four," she whispered to him. Something in the way she carried herself told him it was the truth.

Eventually, she crouched down low and rested her head on the armrest of the door. He wanted to ask her a hundred more questions, but he had to earn her trust before a further inquisition. He'd take her home and keep her protected until he could get her up to Ripon. She'd be safer there, away from her abuser and Henry's traitorous thoughts.

A few blocks later, she lifted her head a few centimeters and peered over the dashboard.

"Are you hiding from the police or someone else?" he asked, unable to stop himself.

"I just need a place to crash for a night." Her voice harbored hesitation. She didn't trust him yet, but she would. "I understand. I won't give your location away to anyone."

The contorted way she tilted her neck to remain hidden appeared painful.

"If you truly want to hide, get down on the floor. Or lean on me, I'll try to cover up that hair of yours." Henry opened his arm.

After a slight hesitation and a glance at the floor of his car, she slid closer to him. He brushed her hair back from her face, covering as much of the exposed pink strands with his hand as he could. A jolt of electricity went through him the moment he touched her hair. Her sea-siren eyes widened and met his. Her muscles tensed, and then she relaxed into his arms. They both looked away at the same time.

Probably the incoming rain.

***

Alex's constant feeling of detachment and isolation lifted off her shoulders when Henry wrapped his arm around her. Hidden under his conservative button-down shirt and navy wool sweater was a strength she hadn't expected.

She didn't need a man's protection, but for one small moment it was nice to feel like she wasn't alone. Most of the men in her life failed miserably in their protector roles. She needed to be her own superhero to survive. If she ever allowed another man into her life, he'd have to be the sidekick.

Arriving back at his house, Henry led Alex inside from the

garage. She hadn't noticed it at the dinner party, but he was favoring his right leg.

"You're limping."

He continued to walk into the kitchen. "I stepped on some glass last night. My fault. I should have been wearing slippers."

No. My fault.

She'd thrown the statue. Smashed it on the wall. And now he was injured. She paused. Could he be lying about helping her? Her track record for placing her faith in the wrong people was fairly perfect, although Matt had helped her for nothing more than a few swept floors. She'd been very lucky he'd assisted her when she first arrived in England. She'd have to send him word that she'd found a temporary place to stay. The memory of the arguing and the gunshot made her uneasy. Was he okay? Pascal could be cruel without a splinter of remorse for anyone or anything.

Henry turned around and reached his hand out to show her in. "I recommend you stay inside for your own safety. You'll have your own room here with a lock on the door until we leave for Ripon tomorrow, and then I won't have to return to Oxford until after spring recess."

His kitchen had a large island in the middle with an assortment of copper-bottom and stainless pots and pans hanging from hooks in the ceiling. A huge gas range with an ornate copper hood embossed with a grapevine pattern stood majestically as the focal point of the room.

"Do you remember Simon, my assistant, from last night? Simon, this is Gabe."

Simon took a sip from a large coffee mug and looked at her, smiling. She didn't remember ever seeing him before, and he was definitely the kind of man a person didn't forget. A beefy pinup with a hard-edged face, he seemed stuck in intimidation mode despite the killer smile and the blue apron that read *"Chefs do it in the kitchen. I'll do it anywhere."*

He then turned away to drop bread in the toaster, fry eggs,

and, if her nose was accurate, make cinnamon rolls. Hard to be intimidated by a guy who made baked goods. Even a guy the size of Pascal. The memory of him arriving at the pub fizzled some of her optimism until Simon walked to the table, poured a cup of coffee, and handed it to her. She thanked him fervently. Black coffee fueled her in ways water, juice, or wine never would.

She rested the mug against her chin so she could take in the aroma before her first sip. "Sorry about ruining your evening."

Simon smiled again as though he found the entire incident amusing. "Henry's never had such a spirited lady in his bed, it was a nice change for him."

"You're overstepping your position." Henry raised his eyebrows toward Simon, but he couldn't suppress his own smile.

"Sorry, sir." Simon winked at Alex and then headed toward the refrigerator.

"Ignore him, Gabe. He doesn't appreciate all I do for him." Henry escorted her past the island to a breakfast nook with a small table covered by a blue-and-white-checkered tablecloth. She looked out the window to the backyard. The view of the small garden she'd seen from the study was even nicer in the daylight.

Simon poured three glasses of orange juice and filled a carafe with coffee. He set the drinks on the table, then followed up with three huge plates of food.

The fried eggs with real butter tasted wonderful on her empty stomach, but the warm cinnamon rolls transformed her entire attitude. If she could manage to lift herself from a dirty, youth hostel to a beautiful house filled with handsome men, decadent pastries, and fine art, she could find a way to protect herself from Luc.

Henry sat down and allowed Simon to wait on him as though he was lord of the manor. His mannerisms, however, didn't display the arrogance or self-importance that had characterized the usual men in her life.

"Have you been traveling a long time?" Simon poured her more coffee.

They wanted to help her, but still, she had no idea who they were and if they had connections to Luc's world. "Just a few weeks."

Simon paused for a moment to eat his eggs, and then continued with his questions. "Get into London at all?"

"No."

"You sound like you're from the States?" Simon didn't stare, but he watched her reactions. He also drank his coffee with the benign expression of a man trying to look like her answers didn't matter. They mattered. Every scrap of information she handed out could be used against her someday.

"I'm from a small town in Indiana. The most peaceful place in the world." Her eyes purposefully wandered to the window. Could she miss a place she'd never been? Probably not. But she could yearn for the rhythmic sound of the ocean waves rippling across the long stretches of sand near her family's summer home in Martha's Vineyard. Her heart thumped at the thought of all she'd lost. A magnificent life exchanged for no life at all.

Sighing, she pulled her gaze to the breakfast table. Her reverie caught the attention of Henry and Simon. Both stared at her, as if looking for a clue or a hint about who she really was.

Sorry guys, not today.

Henry leaned back in his chair. "Oxford must be a nice change from a small town. Ripon isn't a big city, more like a large village that wants to be a small city. I hope it won't bore you."

"Trust me. Ripon will be perfect." She turned toward Simon. "I can't thank you enough for breakfast."

He waved her off. "It's no bother. I have to cook for Lord Henry anyway."

"Don't you have places to go?" Henry motioned Simon to leave.

"As soon as I finish the clearing-up." Simon stood and picked up a few dishes. "Don't get up, fair lady. You had a rough evening." He waved his arm in front of him as though a courtly knight, forcing Alex's smile to break free.

Henry stood and assisted him. "Can you bring back some beer when you're out? The students drank us dry."

"As you wish, my lord."

Their continued banter lightened her mood. The men moved around the kitchen as though they'd lived together forever. They towered over six feet tall, but Simon had Henry by at least two inches. Simon seemed military, with his cropped hair and GI Joe muscles. Henry, on the other hand, appeared athletic, yet sophisticated. His house fit his personality. The old carved wood, the darker, more somber colors. After years of living in a black-and-white modern apartment in Paris, she appreciated this warm, elegant environment.

When Simon left, Henry escorted her to the main stairway.

"Come. I'll show you to your room." He didn't attempt to carry her bag, probably sensing how important it was to her.

She followed him, slowing down in front of several paintings. "Are these pieces yours?"

"Every one. If you like art, I can show you my collection after lunch." He continued up the stairs, whistling.

She not only liked art, she loved it more than she liked eating a piece of crispy bacon.

Maybe Simon the brawny chef would make some the next morning. She licked her lips in anticipation and glanced up at the paintings again.

Hot breakfasts and quality art. This place was too perfect to be real.

"I'd love to see your collection," she called after him. She'd enjoy looking it over, but she'd never again share the depth of her knowledge with a stranger. At least, she'd try to keep her opinions to herself. Her typical enthusiasm when looking at masterpieces bubbled out of her without a filter. Had she kept her opinion to herself about the provenance of the art in Luc's gallery, she wouldn't have a death threat hanging over her.

CHAPTER 4

A fter escorting Gabe to her room, Henry poured himself more coffee and carried it to his study. The smell, infused with a hint of vanilla, soothed his nerves even before he tasted it.

He sat in a leather chair and thought about his guest. Gabe fascinated him. She reminded him of the women at the shelter, stoic regardless of the abuse thrust upon them. And in a testament to her mental strength, she hadn't stayed with the person who had battered her. She'd run.

Two hours and eight graded exams later, he sensed a presence behind him and turned. Gabe stood in the doorway, looking into the study with a half-smile and her fingers tapping together. For a moment, he was captivated by her eyes, the exact color of the ocean off the coast of Santorini. She shifted slightly, glancing around, and a few strands of neon hair fell into her face, breaking the spell.

"Am I disturbing you?"

"Not in the least. Are you ready for the tour?" He stood, walking next to her. A tiny pixie of a thing in bare feet, the top of her head barely reached his shoulder.

"Can we start in this room?" She pointed with her bandaged hand to the framed masterpiece above the fireplace.

"It's a Gustave Courbet." He showed her several smaller pieces that complemented the seascape. She stayed silent, but her gaze took in her surroundings as though cataloging everything for use later.

They continued through the house. Her comments, although infrequent, gave him pause. For some, art was simply decoration; for others, an investment. Caressing heirloom tables and chairs, Gabe eyed details that only a representative from an auction house would know. She noted the location of a hidden drawer in the John Guilbaud cabinet and the unusual lack of a cabriole leg in the settee in the drawing room.

The more rooms they entered, the more excited she became. After discussing one of Henry's favorite portraits in the upper hallway, she stepped to his bedroom door, the scene of her break-down. She probably wanted to forget she'd ever been there. He hesitated at the door, but Gabe entered. She crossed the room and touched her fingertips, to the top of his late eighteenth-century George III dresser.

"This is beautiful," she said. "See the brass swan neck handles and the mahogany cross-banding? I only know of two cabinet-makers who mixed the wood types with such an eye for detail."

"You recognize the cabinetmaker?"

She immediately withdrew as though she'd stepped over her bounds, revealing too much of herself perhaps?

He pointed to a side table. "Can you recognize the wood in that piece?"

SHE TILTED her head so her hair moved away from her eyes. With an exaggerated squint and the quirking of her mouth to the left, she answered, "Pine?"

He laughed. "Seriously? Even I wouldn't guess pine. Don't tell me you can't figure it out."

"It might be oak." She shrugged her shoulders.

It certainly was oak, but was stained to look like mahogany.

"Are you familiar with the designer?"

"Are you testing me?"

Yes, I am.

He stepped in front of her. A challenge radiated from her bright blue eyes. He'd watched her face off with obnoxious university boys and huge police officers. She didn't seem the type to back down from a challenge.

"I can't imagine you really know what you're talking about," he whispered so softly, she moved a centimeter closer.

"William Kent," she whispered in response.

***

Alex leaned away from him; his breath had smelled a little too tempting. And she didn't intend to run from one mansion into another. Men with money had secrets, usually bad ones. What did she know of Henry, anyway? Nothing.

Based on the easy smile he offered, he seemed to care for her. Luc had been romantic once, too. She needed to remind herself of him and why she was running, even when this man didn't seem as cruel. In fact, he acted more protective than controlling. They descended the main staircase, chatting nonstop about their preferred artists.

He paused on the landing and bent toward her. Their proximity was one inch too close for her comfort. Alex took a step away from him. Too much, too soon.

"Who's the architect of the house?" she asked, trying not to appear overwhelmed by Henry's presence.

"John Dover." His eyes were intense and mesmerizing. She needed fresh air.

"It's really beautiful." She began to descend the stairs again and pointed to a few of the pieces. He obliged her by explaining how he acquired some of the paintings. They were in wonderful shape. Not many people appreciated art the way she did. Not many people could see art the way she did. Henry may not have an appraiser's eye, but he genuinely cared about the pieces he owned.

The art in his house revealed high value and depth in the quality and the range of the works. He seemed to exist comfortably with such riches surrounding him. Imagine living side by side with these pieces, greeting each new day staring into a two-hundred-year-old mirror or reading a book while perched on a chair that existed at the time of Queen Victoria. And not just any chair, but a chair of such exceptional workmanship, the temptation to lock it away for its own protection would be overwhelming.

All her thoughts dissipated when she approached the final room. Henry, walking close to her and causing her heart to beat too fast, guided her inside a large space with paintings on all of the walls and statues interspersed with several small sitting areas. A personal art gallery. Amazing.

"What do you think?"

"You certainly saved the best for last."

A black-and-white charcoal portrait by Camille Pissarro hung on one wall along with several other lithographs and landscapes from some of her favorite artists. Henry remained near the doorway as she walked slowly by each one, savoring the textures, the colors, and the emotions.

Turning to the next wall, she paused and stepped closer to the large portrait hanging there. Why would he have a newer imitation mixed into his fabulous collection? "Everything is impressive, I'm not sure about the Sir Thomas Lawrence reproduction though. It's a quality piece, but I'm unaware if Lawrence ever painted anything involving a blonde aristocratic lady sitting on a chestnut mare."

Henry came up beside her and placed a hand on her shoulder. "It's not a fake."

"Of course it is."

Henry leaned his gorgeous face directly in front of hers again. Those eyes could hypnotize and seduce the most virtuous woman into his bed. She breathed him in. His breath tasted sweet, like vanilla mixed with one of Simon's cinnamon buns. His tone, however, contained an acidic edge. "That painting has been in my family since the early eighteen hundreds. She's my ancestor, Lady Elizabeth Gillett."

Lady Elizabeth Gillett smiled down on them with the bluest of eyes. Her hair, parted in the middle, had tight curls gracing each side of her face. Although her yellow dress seemed one decade before a true Regency style, the wider waistband and lower neck-line made Lady Liz a very sexy ancestor. Studying the paint, Alex observed barely visible cracks throughout the oil brush strokes, an expected characteristic of an oil painting older than the advent of locomotives or a flaw intentionally created with paint additives to make a new painting appear old.

"I'm sorry. I overstepped my bounds. You didn't ask for my opinion. You need somebody from one of the big auction houses. They have experts on staff who can give a professional opinion." She would know. She'd taught many of them.

He shoved his hands into his pockets and stepped back while continuing to stare at the painting. "You think I need an expert appraiser?" His Adam's apple became more prominent in his neck, although he seemed to be trying to rein in his emotions. "Your claim doesn't seem plausible."

She paused, haunted by the disbelief in his expression. As always, her need to prove herself overpowered her need to protect herself. She studied the painting again, reconfirming her initial assessment. "Her eyes. It's a reproduction because of her blue eyes. Cerulean blue."

Henry walked closer to the painting and stared at Lady Liz's eyes. "I don't understand."

"The pigment. There was no way to create cerulean blue in paint until 1860."

He laughed, but his face stayed somber. "The painting is a fake because of the color of her eyes?"

Why didn't I keep my mouth shut?

"How can you identify that specific color?" He faced Alex and looked at her as though she were a specimen in a laboratory. She'd seen the same look in her parents' eyes.

Although she hid most of her gifts because the sum total made her seem more witch than savant, she wanted to explain herself to him. "A sommelier can distinguish between very similar wines. I discern colors and tints most people can't. I also recognize most types of wood and gems. If I'm having a particularly good day, I can even tell if the finish on a piece of furniture was done a year ago, a decade ago, or two hundred years ago."

She pointed with her free hand to a raised brushstroke in Lady Elizabeth's bodice. "The paint's been altered as well. See the slight amber line in the crack? Whoever did this added resin to the paint to make it harden and crack like an authentic antique oil painting. An old trick, but effective against untrained eyes."

She ended her speech with a shrug and a mound of regret for revealing herself too intimately with this stranger. Too bad silence wasn't her gift.

Henry paced back and forth for several minutes, his eyes never leaving the canvas. Alex left him to his thoughts and stepped toward the foyer.

He ended up directly in front of her, blocking her exit. "How accurate are you?" The lighthearted and sexy Henry had been replaced by a very serious and powerful man.

"I could be wrong."

Although I've haven't been wrong yet.

"Damn it." His fist clenched, and his forehead creased with the type of deep lines only revealed by extreme tension.

"Are you okay?" She backed up, nervous. She didn't think he'd hurt her. Would he?

He looked back at the painting, still strained. "I've been

better." His voice seemed to wrestle back a range of emotions, including a hint of anger and frustration. When he turned toward her again, his emotions had faded like the tide after a full moon. He gave her a grim smile, but his eyes remained clouded and impenetrable. "I'd like to spend more time with you tonight. Regrettably, I've committed to go somewhere with Simon."

"You're going out?"

"The security in this house is first-rate as long as you don't open the doors for anyone. Trust me, this is the safest location in Oxford." He stared into her eyes for an uncomfortably long time, probing for something, until his smile finally returned, but it wasn't his full smile. "Make yourself at home. There's leftover chicken marsala in the refrigerator. We can meet up for breakfast. Good night."

He's going out? Why would he leave me in the house alone with all his valuables? He doesn't know me. Not really. Even I wouldn't trust me in this place.

He left her standing alone in the art gallery with small master-pieces on one wall, one very large fake on the other, and a tight knot in her stomach.

His house no longer felt like a sanctuary. Alex made her way back to the study and turned on the television, sitting on one of the leather recliners. She flipped through the channels, trying to find a local news station so she could learn the weather forecast, traffic reports, and any other information necessary to leave this place.

Her stomach dropped when she saw a picture of Matt Shaw. *No.* Beginning to shake, she turned the volume up. The bland voice of the newscaster confirmed her fears: in an apparently random act of violence, Matt had been shot dead defending the patrons of the Yellow Dog Pub.

Tears streamed down her face as she struggled to listen to the news. The illegal import of firearms into Great Britain dominated the discussion. They should be talking about the sweet man who had always offered a smile and a cold beer to whomever walked through the doors of his pub. Instead, they focused on the gunman. The police would never find him. Luc's connections ensured his subordinate's anonymity with the law. Her tears turned to sobs. Would anyone be safe around her?

CHAPTER 5

Henry looked in the mirror, straightened the tie on his tuxedo, brushed his fingers once through his hair, and then spun away from the image.

Gabe, with her unbelievable intelligence and inquisitive eyes, liked his collection. Except the one piece that mattered. The devastation of possibly losing his most precious belonging faded when he thought about her appraisal of the work itself. The pink hair and black leather façade had given way to a confident and capable professional as she ripped his world apart.

Simon, dressed in a similar tux, strode in and seated himself on a chair in the corner. His dark hair stuck up a bit longer than a buzz cut, but he still looked military. If he had an ugly face and lost those blue eyes, he'd be scarier than hell.

"You're on time." Henry slipped his feet into shiny Cole Haans.

"I said seven o'clock. Reliable is my middle name."

"Your middle name is O'Rourke. I think it means untrustworthy and insolent."

"It means ruggedly handsome and well hung."

"Right." Henry laughed. "What do you think of Gabe?"

"She's very pleasant for a girl with a safety pin in her ear."

"I thought the same thing, but she possesses an unusual understanding of art and furniture. She even knew the maker of several of the pieces."

"Interesting."

Henry stood and took his topcoat out of the closet. "Strange, though, she believes the Lawrence portrait is a reproduction."

A rare frown emerged on Simon's face. "She's what, twenty-three at the most?"

"Twenty-four."

"And a recognized scholar in her field? Doubtful."

"She has an uncanny understanding of both art and furniture design. I'm almost hesitant to get the portrait appraised now."

Simon's brow creased as he stared at his brother. "Appraised? Didn't you just have it restored?"

"I'm using it as collateral for a loan to fund a project with the Ripon Women's Group. It's the only thing of value I own outside the family trust." He hated discussing his inheritance with Simon. Henry had inherited everything from their father, mostly through the family trust established to preserve wealth for future generations. Simon, being the bastard son, had received nothing.

Rising out of his chair, Simon turned to look out the window. "Maybe you should wait."

"No time. The group is getting kicked out of their place in a few months. I need to start the renovations at the castle as soon as practical so they have a place to move." Grabbing his billfold and the keys to his car from the dresser, Henry headed to the door.

Simon followed. "If a switch happened, which I doubt, when do you think it occurred?"

"A year ago. The only time it was out of my sight was during the restoration, but instead of restoring it, maybe they replaced it. I'd noticed a change from the original when it returned, but I thought the sharper color was the restoration and not new paint. Perhaps I was wrong."

They entered the garage, and Henry slid into the worn leather seat of his black vintage 1968 Jaguar. Simon followed. The wood dashboard was beginning to show its age, but Henry didn't have the funds to restore the car.

"If it was stolen, the odds are against you finding it again." Simon spoke with his trademark nonchalance.

The purr of the engine increased to a mild roar as Henry pulled into the roadway.

"My odds will increase if you can help me."

"Me?"

Henry nodded. "I've never asked for anything from you, despite your abuse of my name to gain access to the most obnoxious parties in England."

Simon grimaced. "I'm not sure what I can do for you."

Henry steered the car past the city limits and picked up speed on the highway toward London. The lights illuminating the road flashed through the windows. It did nothing to calm his nerves.

"I need access to events where stolen paintings are sold." He glanced at Simon to see his reaction.

Simon rubbed his bottom lip and stared straight ahead. "I don't think it's as social an endeavor as you'd think. You'll need to visit private galleries. Since you've never taken an interest in collecting stolen art in the past, I'm not sure anyone would trust your intentions."

"Provide me with a few introductions. I can do the rest. I'll even create an alias."

"You couldn't be anyone but yourself, and I say that with the highest respect for you and your benign pursuits. After five years of being a civilian, your life is more books than bullets. Keep it that way."

No one would regard Henry's exploits in the Royal Navy as tame. He'd held one of the highest security clearances. He had far more experience in the world than Simon gave him credit for.

"I need the painting or my plans will fall apart. Think of the women you'll be hurting if you say no."

Simon glared at him with a seriousness that bordered on a threat. "That's low, even for you." Despite Simon's tough exterior, he had a soft moral center Henry had exploited since they'd found each other years earlier.

"No one has a gun to your head." He downshifted, but still cut into a curve too fast.

Simon reached out to brace against the dashboard before looking back to Henry. "What if Gabe's wrong?" His brow furrowed. "I have a hard time believing a girl who hides from the police and dyes her hair the color of an Easter egg."

"I know it's odd, but I think she's telling the truth." He trusted in her ability to spot a fake. Something about her confident explanation and the details she knew on the tour of the house Her arrival was nothing short of destiny. She could help him find the painting, and he could protect her from the person Henry wanted to punch in the face for harming her.

He shifted gears again, and the car shot forward.

"You're bloody batty as hell," Simon huffed. "You trust the person who tried to smash up your house?"

"She didn't mean to break the statue. In fact, I think she was partially asleep. It would be nice, however, to know more of her background."

"I looked in her backpack before you took it to the hospital. Five hundred pounds, about twenty euros, a few clothes and toiletries, a Bluetooth speaker, and a pay-as-you-go mobile phone with no saved numbers and the history deleted. No identification, either."

"Doesn't that tell you something is wrong? Too much cash, no identification. I hope she's safe. She seemed vulnerable."

"As long as she stays in the house, she'll be fine."

***

As soon as Alex heard the last roars of Henry's car driving off, she made her move. She'd spoken too freely to a man she barely knew. And though she wanted to trust Henry, what did she know about him? An anthropology professor, probably just out of grad school, with a few million dollars' worth of art, running a battered women's shelter, and living with a guy who looked like a body-guard, knew his way around a kitchen, and acted more like a fraternity brother than an employee. Sure they seemed trustwor-thy, but so did successful criminals.

Instead of following her lousy instincts, she'd do the opposite. Don't trust Henry. Run from him, as she should have done with Luc. Then perhaps her life could start moving toward a comfort-able future.

She entered the bathroom, took out her color contacts, and found a pair of scissors. A blunt cut at the shoulders would be easiest to manage. Pink hair fell to the sink in chunks. She refused to give herself bangs, preferring to hide her face. The back would look pretty uneven, but she didn't have time to worry about perfection. As she snipped away inches of hair, she gained hope. Saying a quick good-bye to her grunge persona, she flushed the strands down the toilet and coated the remaining hair in the black dye she'd saved for just this purpose.

A short time later, dressed in a bright blue floral sundress and a heavy wool cardigan as her only protection against the chilly March air, a black-haired woman with brown eyes, short pink nails, and red running sneakers departed from Henry's house, never looking back.

She took an old bike from his garage and flipped her backpack over her shoulders. The bike needed a tune-up, but she managed to pedal it through rows of old stone buildings and traffic circles. A slow drizzle of rain slowed her pace. She'd changed the bandage on her hand before she left, but now it was soaked and made her fingers ache. When she arrived at the train station, she'd have to remove it.

Reaching the city limits, she coasted past fields and the dark silhouettes of farmhouses and stone walls. And then the sky opened up and released a torrential wall of rain that only a woman with nothing left to lose would try to navigate. Her tears blended with the rain, and the tension in her body stiffened as the cold leeched through to her skin.

One quick phone call and she'd be seated in the first-class section of the next plane to Boston and home, but that call would also bind her family to her nightmare. She wouldn't risk their safety. She'd never been the best daughter or sister, but she refused to be the worst.

She headed south of Oxford toward Abingdon. She could catch a train at the smaller station, and no one would follow her. Hopefully. The drama of the past two days combined with the downpour made the strenuous pedaling even more difficult. Darkness and rain hid the imperfections of the road, and she struggled to keep the bike upright. She tried to ignore the tingling in her hands, but focusing on physical pain made all that emotional crap disappear.

One lucky break, was that so much to ask for?

The road continued on forever, but her legs had found their rhythm. The faint lights of Abingdon appeared on the horizon, beckoning her forward. She picked up speed, not noticing the broken curbing until her front tire buckled and she fell to the ground.

CHAPTER 6

Simon and Henry arrived at Club Napa in Covent Garden in time for cocktail hour. Located in an old gymnasium, the club catered to the young, the famous, and the well connected. Victorian woodwork, large oak floors, and crystal chandeliers provided the place with an old-world feel. A smattering of the people here mattered, the rest were all looking for someone to invest in their brand or new business venture. The more unimportant guests included a drunken actor, a singer high on heroin, and a newly minted reality star flashing her breasts through sheer fabric.

"Drink?" Simon asked.

"The usual."

"I'll be back." He disappeared, leaving Henry alone between several groups of people discussing impressive things to make themselves seem more impressive.

A too-familiar heavyset gentleman garnished with a large graying mustache covering both his upper and lower lips lumbered toward him. As always, Uncle George wore his black tuxedo jacket open, unable to button it over his rounded stomach.

"Henry. Lovely to see you here." He clapped Henry's shoulder.

"You look well, Uncle."

"As well as can be expected, I suppose. You've likely heard my bill to create a tax-free zone in the shipyards stalled in committee. Three years of work in the loo. Disappointing."

"I would imagine." Henry scanned the room for Simon. No luck. He turned back to his uncle.

Uncle George's election to the House of Commons allowed him to bore his companions with a one-way stream of drivel. It also provided him enough ammunition to belittle every one of Henry's life decisions. Although he wasn't following his family into government service, Henry would be leaving his mark on the world. *If* he could get the original painting back.

"How is Aunt Mary?" he asked.

"She stays busy with her charity outreach. How's your little charity thing going? Homeless women, isn't it?"

"Battered women. I need more financing and a few corporate backers, but otherwise, it's moving along." Henry looked over his uncle's shoulder and across the crowd.

Where the hell was Simon?

"Come by the house this Wednesday night. We're having a small dinner party. There might be a potential wife there for you." George laughed at his own joke and hit Henry on the shoulder again.

The parade of potential wives Uncle George thought of as suitable was pathetic. Not one of them cared about Henry as a person. They only wanted his title and estate. What would his uncle think of Gabe? Henry smiled at the thought of her transformation overnight from a mysterious Goth girl to art aficionado. She'd be a nice change from the constant barrage of eligible, picture perfect bachelorettes flung in his face at dinner parties.

"I've already found my potential wife, Uncle." The words slipped out without a moment's hesitation.

The statement perked his uncle up instantly. He glanced around the room for Henry's mystery date. "Is she here?"

"No. I'm hiding her in my house until the pink dye wears off.

She's the girl for me, however. I've decided if she doesn't want me, I'll die a lonely old bachelor." A harsh laugh followed his inane statement. Gabe was no more duchess material than the socialites his uncle introduced him to at every event they attended. Although she would be a perfect dinner companion with her quick wit, intelligence, and subtle beauty. Pink hair and all.

He shook his head at the direction of his thoughts. Gabe had invaded his house and upended his plans, and yet he wanted to have dinner with her. She had her own very real issues to deal with.

Uncle George opened his mouth to add more twaddle to an already-dull conversation, but Henry cut him off.

"Give Aunt Mary my best. I see Stan Duckett by the bar, and I need to ask him if he can help with my little charity thing. Really nice speaking with you." Henry shook his hand and disappeared into the crowd.

Simon showed up at his side a minute too late, but he carried two drinks, making all forgiven.

"Is Uncle George doing well?" He handed Henry the scotch.

"As head-splitting as ever. What took you so long?"

"Ran into a friend." Simon took a sip of what looked like straight vodka. His subsequent silence told Henry everything.

Part of Simon's job was to keep tabs on many players in the European jet-set, but he didn't have the credentials to gain access to the more exclusive parties. Henry did. Several years back, they formed a partnership where Henry provided Simon the use of his house and entry to his upscale social circles. In exchange, Simon acted as a personal assistant to Henry. An even trade-off, considering Simon's cooking skills. Over the years, they'd built an amicable relationship.

They made a quick circuit around the party and split up while Simon went to work his magic with potential investors in a scheme Henry didn't have the clearance to learn about. An hour later, they regrouped as they were being seated for dinner.

"I wonder how Gabe is doing?" Henry followed Simon to table twenty.

"I'm not sure, but I can't wait for breakfast with her." Simon smirked, and Henry's gut sent him a silent alarm.

"Why?"

"Her reputed knowledge about art could prove useful."

Henry glared up at his brother and lowered his voice. "What does art have to do with arms trafficking?"

"Organized crime is a spiderweb. It reaches out in all directions trying to diversify, minimize risk, and maximize profit. Stolen art, like drugs, funds many of these transactions." An embedded agent for the foreign intelligence service, Simon took every aspect of his job seriously. Outside of work, he took little seriously. "If, as you say, Gabe has an unbelievable ability to appraise art, she's hardly the type to be employed by Christie's, Sotheby's, the British Museum, or the Tate. You tell me what her connection is to the art world."

"You think she's a thief?"

"I'm not sure what she is."

"Just because a person looks a certain way and has an unusual knowledge base doesn't mean she's a criminal."

"Says the anthropologist. Despite your eternal faith in everyone, I think it would be worthwhile to speak with her."

"She's in a vulnerable state right now. If she loses my trust, she could run back into a dangerous situation." He recalled his outburst in front of the portrait. Not his best behavior, but hopefully he hadn't scared her off.

Did he?

"Don't tell me you like her? She's no more a blueblood than I am. She's more like a middle class teenager with deviant tendencies."

To avoid drawing attention to their conversation, Henry tempered the anger threatening to take over his voice. "Her hand went through a window and she refused to take herself to the hospital, preferring to hide in my house instead. Did you even notice the scarring on her neck? According to the hospital, she also has a broken rib and bruises. Someone beat the hell out of her, and you want to add to her misery. Harassing a woman who needs help and using her for your own gain is low even for you."

Simon narrowed his eyebrows and turned into someone Henry had never seen before. Someone dangerous. "You have no idea how low I'll go for my job. Don't ever confuse me for someone with integrity. Your father beat that out of me years ago."

The reference to their father flushed ice through Henry's system. Simon was right. He didn't deserve Henry's judgment. He'd lived through hell and was now trying to make it right.

"I trust you, but I'm also obligated to protect Gabe." Even if that meant keeping Simon far away from her.

They split up to take their seats at the table.

The image of Gabe tired and afraid at the house left Henry unable to concentrate on the meal or dinner conversation. By the end of the soup course, guilt from leaving her alone pounded his head. He stood and said good-bye to the wife of an aging foot-baller to his left, who couldn't keep her hand in her own lap, and the elderly woman to his right who couldn't remember why she was at the dinner.

Interrupting Simon's conversation with a waif-like model, Henry whispered in his ear. "We need to go. I have a strange feeling about Gabe."

"I'm done anyway." Simon pushed back his chair and stood.

"You're leaving, Simon?" the doe-eyed blonde asked with a New York accent.

"Darinda, darling, meet Henry Elliott Chilton, Earl of Ripon. When he tells me I must go, regrettably, I must go."

Her eyes blinked as though she were telegraphing Henry a message. "An earl? Wow. What should I call you?"

"You shouldn't." Henry pulled on Simon's arm and walked away.

They returned at 1:00 a.m. in a downpour. Henry parked and

rushed into the house to see Gabe. The kitchen was empty. He called out to her, but no one answered. She wasn't in the study, either. He climbed two steps at a time to her bedroom. The door was open, the bed was made, and the room was empty of any trace of the woman except for her combat boots. He stared out the window.

Where the hell was she?

After circling through the other rooms in the house, Henry called out to Simon. "She's gone. You backtrack by foot. See if you can find her at a nearby pub. I'll take a drive."

Oxford wasn't even close to the size of London, but it wasn't a small village, either. She could disappear easily.

"I'll ask around at some of the local pubs about our pink-haired whiz kid. If I locate her, I promise not to interrogate her without her express permission." Simon pulled his black wool coat from a hook by the door.

"Permission freely given, not coerced."

"I promise. I have enough to do without creating work for myself. Besides, I intend on watching Chelsea take down Reading this afternoon. So find her or not, I'm calling it quits in time to grab a few hours of sleep." He gave Henry a salute and walked out the front door.

Henry drove around Oxford a few times. The pubs had closed and streams of people started bumbling home. Most of the women walked in groups after a night out drinking. Gabe would be alone.

He traveled to the train station, spoke with the ticket office, staked out the automatic ticket machines, and walked up and down the platforms, but she never appeared. Mozart's Arietta in G blasted out of his mobile.

"Did you find her?" he asked Simon while heading out of the train station toward his car.

"No, but when I returned to the house, I noticed your bike is missing from the garage."

Henry, finding his breath again, became encouraged. He

needed to locate this enigmatic creature who had invaded his life. "Brilliant. I think I'll take a scenic drive out of the city."

"Good luck." Simon had done his part and was probably headed to bed.

Two hours later, he was about to give up when he noticed a petite woman in a mud-splattered dress by the side of the road.

He pulled over and grabbed his umbrella. She didn't lift her head when he approached. Instead, she stayed crouched in a puddle examining a flat tire on a bike. Rain soaked her hair and her sweater, and pasted a thin blue dress to her lean, muscular legs.

"I'm all set, thank you. I'll be leaving in a minute," she called out to him without turning around.

The familiar voice eased the tension knotting the muscles in his neck. That bike, his bike, would be going nowhere. She needed a lift.

"Gabe, are you okay?"

Her head whipped around, and her mouth fell open. She struggled to get on the broken bike and ride away.

He reached her in three long strides and grasped the handle-bars. Her damp body shivered. She could warm up in the car. He didn't anticipate the backpack that smacked him in the head. The umbrella flew out of his hand as he tumbled into a puddle. The cold water leeched through his pants and shocked his system. He looked up to see her biking away. *Damn it.* He was trying to help her, not harm her.

The flat tire impeded her progress. He sprinted forward and caught the seat of the bike.

"Henry, why are you torturing me? Let me go." Her voice strained. She swung around, her newly black hair stuck to her cheeks, and glared at him with angry *brown* eyes. He caught the bag when she swung it toward him again, yanking it out of her hand.

"Get in the bloody car. Now. It's almost four in the morning, and I'm not in the mood to discuss your daft excursion across the countryside on *my* bike." His head hurt. Instead of mud-wrestling with a woman on the side of the road, he just wanted a shower and some coffee.

Gabe's feet, however, remained firmly planted on each side of the bike. Rain drenched the hair that had been lopped off at the shoulders in a most unflattering way. She must have done it herself. To hide from her abuser or from him? Her eyes glanced beyond him toward Abingdon.

He slung a strap of the pack over his shoulder before gripping her arm to keep her from running again.

"I have to leave. Please," she pleaded.

Her cheeks glowed red and puffy from exposure to the cold rain. She tried to pull herself free, but he wouldn't let her go. She was standing drenched to her knickers to evade discovery of some unknown malevolence, all because he'd lost his temper in the art gallery and probably scared the hell out of her. "I'm sorry if I scared you earlier. I was upset about the painting, not you. I mean it. I would never harm you. Ever."

He wrapped his arms tight around her waist and lifted her from the broken bike. As soon as her feet hit the ground she pushed away, but he was ready and held on. She sighed, almost admitting defeat. After a few seconds, her forehead fell into his chest. She needed him. He could feel it in the way the muscles in her back softened in his arms.

He kissed the top of her head. Her body shivered as her arms circled his waist, and she hugged him close. He could feel her body relax in his arms. She needed a guardian angel, and he'd just appointed himself to the task.

"It's late, and you look exhausted. I can help you. Trust me."

The beautiful enigma, who had crashed his party and his life, lowered her voice to a faint whisper. "I don't need Margaret Mead, Henry. I need an intrepid warrior with an underground lair."

He escorted her to his car. "Does the lair have to be underground?"

CHAPTER 7

Alex clenched her teeth, trying to ignore Henry humming along to Bach's Violin Concerto in D major. Cold, wet, clammy, and covered in goose bumps, her body felt as uncomfortable as her ears. Henry, still dressed in his tuxedo, struggled to place his old bike in the car. He finally managed to fit it in, but the entire backseat was now covered in mud to match Alex's clothes.

He'd provided her with a blue wool blanket before driving back toward the house. Her body warmed, and the exhaustion from her failed escape weighed her down. The loud music allowed her to avoid speaking to him.

She didn't want anything to do with him. His presence, however, relaxed her. She stared out the window through the darkness at fields and an occasional farmhouse, her eyelids becoming heavier, until a blue highway sign caught her attention and sent a rush of panic through her body.

"Henry?"

"Yes." He stared ahead at the road.

She tried to keep her voice calm. "Where are we going?"

"To my house."

"We're north of Oxford. Are we taking the long route?"

Still looking ahead, he responded, "Not that house. My house in Ripon."

"Ripon?"

"It's north of York. Remember the women's shelter I told you about?"

He still wanted to help her, even after she'd stolen his bike and messed up his evening? The thought lingered for a second and then evaporated. Everyone had motivations for their actions. She needed to learn Henry's. Even if he was helping her for purely altruistic reasons, she couldn't risk his safety or the safety of the other women at the shelter. Luc's brand of evil made Satan seem like a Tibetan monk.

Her eyes closed again, and she allowed herself the luxury of a light sleep.

When she awoke, the sun was trying to burst through the thick gray clouds. Henry turned the car off the main highway and onto a smaller rural lane. Fog covered the ground and cast a gloomy undercurrent across this otherwise peaceful location. She imagined flocks of sheep and herds of cows grazing in pastures around them, and perhaps a traitor to the queen strung up and left for the buzzards as a warning to the rest of the local village.

Henry continued to look straight ahead. Was he taking her directly to the shelter? The idea that he had more power over her life than she did made her uncomfortable. She needed to get her head together and plan her next move. They sat in silence for a few more minutes as she pondered her next step. She could hop a train for the Lake District and disappear. It would cost less from Ripon than from Oxford.

"I think I can manage on my own now. If you'll drop me off at the nearest train station***"

Henry yawned. His hair had curled after its soaking in the rain and fell over his temples in darker waves, giving him the appearance of a wealthy playboy after a night on the town. She felt like she'd fallen into an Armani ad.

He glanced toward her with a grin. "Too late. We're home. You might as well enjoy a warm meal and have some rest in a real bed."

Another person in control of her destiny. Not if she could help it. She couldn't hand the reins over to him, no matter how much she desired assistance. Matt had died because of her. Hiding from Luc needed to be an individual sport.

A stone wall came into view in front of them. Henry drove under the huge stone archway in the center of the wall and continued over a drawbridge. Alex, who was never shocked, was shocked. She sat up, returning her feet to the floor. An entire medieval castle appeared in the steaming earth in front of them. Not the largest one Alex had ever seen, but not the smallest, either. She counted four turrets visible in the light and small glass windows in each of them. The condition of the building was extraordinary, as if they'd driven the Jaguar back seven hundred years into the past. He drove into the back and turned into the garage.

"Home?" she asked. "You live in a castle?"

"I like to think of this as home. Yes." He hopped out, remarkably agile for a person who had driven over three hours nonstop, and came around to open her door. His bow tie still sat perfectly straight at his neck. Alex, with her hair sticking to her scalp and her outfit wrinkled and damp, pulled her sneakers back on and wrapped the blanket around her shoulders.

He started toward the castle's side door, but stopped and looked back to where she had planted herself. "Coming?"

"I need my backpack. Feminine stuff. I could go into detail, but I don't want to bore you about the storage and use of tampons."

Henry, grinning as though this kind of talk amused him, returned to her side. "You'd be surprised at what interests me and Margaret Mead." He opened the trunk, hefted the bag in his hand for a few seconds, and then tossed it to her. "That's a lot of tampons. Expecting a shortage?"

"A girl should always be prepared." She hitched it over her shoulder and followed him into the house.

Okay, he's charming and handsome and loves art and lives in a castle. And I'm not interested. Not at all.

They turned a few times through several passageways and arrived in a massive foyer with a gray stone staircase that could accommodate three large horses shoulder to shoulder. Vivid tapestries in blues, greens, and a pale yellow hung down the high walls. They were made within the past fifty years, but the workmanship and detail revealed a talented artisan.

She turned her attention back to Henry. A castle? Old money? That would explain his choice of profession. He could afford to muck about in Oxford. Summers off. Long holidays. It made sense.

Henry climbed the stairs. Halfway up, he turned around and looked down at her. "Let me take you to bed."

Why was he looking all seductive and adorable? Paranoia warred with her gut feeling that he was one of the good guys. Her stomach tightened. Luc had ruined intimacy for her. He'd taken her virginity by force and twisted sex into a four-letter word.

"I can crash anywhere. An oversize couch or maybe a bathroom floor." Still wrapped in the blanket, she slowed her steps. The bag hung by her side.

Henry walked back down the stairs, but stopped a step above her. He extended his hand until she took it. His grip was warm, but not overwhelming. "Relax. I'm bringing you to your own room. My room is in another wing."

So much for his seduction of her. Embarrassment coiled in her chest. "I didn't mean to be rude. I just don't want to be a bother."

"You're never a bother, Sunshine."

Henry showed her to a bedroom on the third floor, second floor to the English. She glanced around at the simple furnishings, more appropriate for a youth hostel than a medieval castle.

She threw her only piece of luggage on top of a red duvet. Red also dominated the art in the room. Mostly framed posters. A field of poppies. The Eiffel Tower in black and white accented by a woman in a red dress. Some sort of red surreal paint blob. What did she expect? A silk screen by Andy Warhol?

Locking the door, she scouted around for cameras as she always did, but since there wasn't much of anything in the room, there weren't many places to hide one. Comfortable with her security, she unzipped the backpack, dumping her few clothes on the bed. She removed her old iPod Shuffle, hooked it up to a small set of speakers she traveled with, and turned on her favorite Sting album. Sultry, rhythmic, and loud enough to mask her movements.

The cardboard liner in her bag was glued to a thinner piece of cardboard on three sides, creating a perfect hidden pocket for her two passports. The first passport, now expired, was embossed with the seal of the United States. The owner was born in Boston, Massachusetts, twenty-eight years ago, with long dark brown hair and bored, flippant brown eyes. A much younger Alexandra Cushing Northrop had overstayed her visa and let the passport expire rather than allow her father drag her home. The depressing part of her youthful rebellion was his failure to ever come looking for her. Her only contact with her family involved sporadic emails with her mother and sisters telling them she was happy.

It was for the best. Luc had no idea her family existed, and that kept them all safe.

Someday, someone might call her Alex again, but her best hope to get out of the country right now was taking on the identity of Luc's sister Danielle, a twenty-four-year-old woman with short brown hair and hazel eyes.

She'd taken Danielle's French passport just in case. Danielle wouldn't need it anymore, not since Pascal or another thug linked to Luc murdered her and her boyfriend. That would have been Alex's fate if she hadn't left when she did. Luc wouldn't report them missing in order to avoid being implicated in their deaths. She hoped to use Danielle's identity to board a plane out of

Europe. If Luc realized she had it in her possession, however, the passport could be used as a beacon guiding him straight to her.

She pulled the bottom drawer out of the poor-quality dresser and tossed it onto the bed. At the bottom of her backpack, she located a roll of duct tape, a fugitive's best friend. The stuff easily secured a plastic bag with her passports and a few hundred pounds on the back side of the drawer. No one should find it. Henry seemed smart, but not street-smart.

The dark shadows from the rainy morning hung over the window, making her drowsy. She stripped to nothing and crawled between the sheets. After staring into space, at the ceiling, and toward the window, she disappeared into her dreams.

Someone banging and banging on the door jolted her out of her hazy fog and roused her completely. She stretched her arms over her head and then rolled away from the noise.

"Get up, Sunshine. Time to start the day." His voice was cheerfully annoying.

She pulled the duvet over her head. "Go away, Henry. I'm sleeping in."

"You've slept for almost five hours. We have plans. Get up."

The banging continued. It wouldn't stop. Henry didn't seem the type to stop until he got what he wanted. And he wanted her out of bed. She could have withstood his attack for another few minutes, but her stomach growled. Food trumped sleep.

She jumped up and threw on her jeans, a black T-shirt, and a hoodie. She'd left the combat boots in Oxford, so she put on the red sneakers. They felt slimy on her bare feet, but they wouldn't be dry for another day.

She unlocked the door and glared.

Henry stood in front of her with a stupid grin on his face, wearing a pair of tan khakis and a camouflage jacket. His darn smile spread to her lips, like a contagious disease.

"Off to the hunt?" she asked.

"Not today. We're off to breakfast, or brunch to be more exact, since it's almost noon."

He stood in the door waiting for her to exit and then strolled next to her. "Did you have a good sleep?"

"I did, actually." As they turned from her wing into what looked like the main section of the house, she noticed the change in furnishings. A change for the better. "Do you house traveling youth in my section of the castle?"

He slowed. "I'm in the process of renovating that area, but I'm a bit short of funds right now."

Fantastic. Insult the host. Her past few months dressed as a kid with an attitude must have ingrained itself into her personality more than she would have liked.

"I didn't mean***"

"It's fine. I should have given you one of the Edwardian bedrooms next to me, but I figured you'd prefer having some space between us."

"I appreciate it. Everything, actually."

He continued down the hall a few steps ahead of her and then descended a secondary staircase toward the back of the house. At the bottom, they arrived in a large modern kitchen graced with a huge stone fireplace and plaster walls.

An attractive, middle-aged woman in a navy skirt and a yellow knit sweater was at the stove cooking. She wore her long auburn hair in a loose bun with several strands fallen out around her face. "Morning, sir. How was your drive?" Her smile revealed a warm affection for Henry.

"Uneventful." He strolled through the kitchen with his hands behind his back, stopping to sniff the morning meal. "That smells wonderful."

Alex inhaled the delectable aromas. Her stomach grumbled in response.

"Martha, I'd like to introduce my colleague, Ms. Gabrielle West."

"Nice to meet you." She nodded toward Alex and then continued with the meal preparation.

Henry led Alex into a dining room with large oak beams

across the ceiling and a medieval iron chandelier, likely created around the year 1300 and retrofitted with electric light fixtures. Several framed landscapes by John Robert Cozens decorated the dark wood paneling. In the center of the room, someone, probably Martha, had set a beautifully preserved William IV rosewood table for two. Alex examined the four rosewood side chairs with red silk cushions. Exquisite detailing.

"Please have a seat." He pulled out her chair, and then sat next to her.

"Thanks." Alex glanced at the Wedgwood china. Not too rare a pattern, but rare enough to impress. The familiarity of the fine china brought her back to her life before Luc. A life working with beautiful things. She took a deep breath and enjoyed the atmosphere.

Martha followed them into the room with a coffeepot and cream. When she left, Alex filled a teacup to the rim with coffee.

"Would you like some, sir?" She lifted the pot toward him.

"Yes, please." He leaned back in his seat, as though someone had always taken care of him. And called him sir.

The cook returned a few minutes later with their eggs and toast, then departed again.

"Is Martha a servant like Simon, a prisoner like me, or something more intimate?" The final thought depressed her for some reason.

"She helps run the house with her partner, Frank, and their two children, Irene and Penelope."

"Oh."

"And you're not a prisoner, Gabe." He paused. His eyes drifted over her now-black hair and grubby clothes. "You're a guest."

He added cream and some sugar to his coffee, and then stirred it several times. How could such a simple act as clinking the spoon against a cup send her straight back to the breakfast room in her parents' house? She blinked back the tears threatening to spill. The irritating sound reminded her of her mother's inability to stir her tea once and be done with it. She missed her.

She took a sip of her own coffee and tried to shift her focus from the past to the immediate future and her need to leave. She had her things. All she needed to do was slip out the door that night.

After a few sips, never a gulp, Henry focused his attention on her. "As much as I enjoy calling you Sunshine, Sunshine. It may be less awkward if you provided me with your real name."

"We've done this already. Gabe West. Gabrielle to my mother."

"Why don't I believe that Gabe is your legal name?"

"Your inability to trust is a mystery, which might be the reason you forced me into your car."

"You came willingly and happily. In fact, I think you like me more than you care to admit."

She did, but he was right, she wouldn't admit it. Instead, she changed the subject away from her name and her feelings. "This place suits you. Lord of the manor. You even have a moat to keep the barbarians from attacking and stealing the Wedgwood. Very practical."

"I like it." His eyes circled the room in satisfaction. His pride in the house showed through his mannerisms, from how he treated the staff to his careful gaze at the drawings on the walls.

"Have you owned this castle long?"

He nodded. "It's been in my family for four generations."

"Only four?" The family might not have been to the manor born. "Did you snatch it up from the king after he kicked out the previous owners? They must have been traitors to the Crown."

Henry laughed. "No. My ancestors purchased it from the prior owners in what was considered a fair deal at the time."

"Impressive. Any titles come with the property?"

"No, but my great-grandfather's service to the king earned him a title." Henry grinned and took a sip of coffee.

"Shut up. You're royalty? A duke. Say you're a duke. My mother would be tickled if she learned I hung out with a duke.

Kidnapped by one even. Oh, the stories she could tell her grand-children."

"Sorry to burst your mother's dream, but I'm merely an earl."

She stared at him. He sounded apologetic. Embarrassed. She frowned and patted his hand. "Don't worry, Henry. I've heard dukes and even marquesses have some pretty serious inbreeding issues. Not as many royals as there used to be. The problem occurs less with earls, because who would marry their cousin just to become a countess? You should consider yourself lucky." Her hand felt comfortable sitting on top of Henry's, so she left it there. "You seem to have survived your destiny without too much dim-wittedness. You did graduate from college, after all. Not with a useful degree, but not everyone can be a doctor, lawyer, or engi-neer. I'm sure this country needs anthropologists to maintain the empire. You're doing the best you can considering your less-than-desirable circumstances."

Henry's seductive chuckle warmed parts of her she'd thought had died after her nightmare with Luc. "I've never been pitied for my title before. Thank you."

"So." She pulled back her hand, placed it on her lap, and tried not to sigh over the heat remaining on her palm. "What should I call you? Hmmmm. I can't call you Earl, because I'd be reminded of a cousin from South Carolina, Earl Harper Jr. He never did finish third grade, but he can do his sums real well now that he works at the Laundromat. And being an American, I'd feel awkward calling you my lord or sir. It feels less aristocratic and more BDSM."

More crinkles appeared in his eyes with more laughter. "You'd best stick with Henry then."

"Henry it is." She liked his name. Reassuring and trustworthy.

In his presence, the strain of the past few days began to dissi-pate. Why run away from a comfortable house with warm food and a smiling companion? Perhaps she could stay a day or two.

He stood and led her through the great hall. Overstuffed couches and brown leather chairs filled each nook. It had been converted to a family room with three large sitting areas. One in front of a fireplace, one in front of a large-screen television, and one overlooking the most exquisite formal gardens and miles of hillside.

The enormous window framing the scene must have been installed in the past fifty years, allowing light to pour into what would otherwise be a dark space. She was ready to grab some popcorn and flop down on one of the couches for a movie night.

"My favorite place to relax." Henry surveyed the room corner to corner while he crossed to the back door.

"I see why. It's a wonder you ever return to the university."

"That's the brilliant thing about my academic position. I'm close enough to escape here on weekends. And I'm away enough to revel in returning."

"Sounds like a perfect life."

"Almost. It'll be better when the children arrive."

Children?

CHAPTER 8

enry led Gabe into the formal gardens. They stayed on the pea-gravel walkway to avoid the mud that always arrived when winter faded into spring. Usually the tulips popped up in time for spring recess, but this year, the cold had pushed them off a few weeks.

Gabe looked different with her shorter black hair and brown eyes. The hair color didn't suit her, but neither did that pink disaster. The brown eyes, however, had to be part of the original. The color evoked his favorite brandy dropped into melted dark chocolate. Real. Honest. Decadent.

She walked lightly over the path, almost skipping. Her eyes took in every corner of the yard. "Beautiful. Do you have a grounds staff?"

"I hired a gardener to maintain the formal gardens. A few people from town come and assist on a volunteer basis. In exchange, I open the property to hikers."

"What a perfect spot for an afternoon stroll." She stalled out near the end of the rose garden and pointed toward the large hedge maze. A rare and beautiful smile graced her pixie face. "I've always wanted one of those, but my mother never saw the point." She clapped her hands together, and her toes bounced under her until it seemed as if she'd levitated off the ground. "Race you to the center. Winner gets a prize."

She charged into the maze with the enthusiasm of a young schoolgirl at recess.

Henry watched her run off. He entered the maze and breathed in the smell of the hawthorn hedges. Pungent and earthy. His feet sank into the moist ground. Standing still for a moment, he paused to listen for the most exasperating but enchanting woman alive. Her giggles floated over a few rows of bushes. He made three turns and sat on the stone bench in the center waiting for her.

Gabe turned into the center circle and frowned. "You beat me."

Her cheeks glowed a healthy pink. She jogged over to the bench, stood a few seconds to catch her breath, and then sat next to him. The sheer joy in her eyes replaced the strain he'd observed when she'd left his house in Oxford.

"After hundreds of forays into the maze, if I didn't win, I'd have to blame it on the inbreeding."

"Touché."

They sat in companionable silence. A subtle Mona Lisa smile graced Gabe's face. Her top teeth peeked out between two lush lips. He wanted to lean in and***she kissed him. Soft, simple, and sweeter than his favorite peppermints shipped in from Greenwich.

When they separated, Gabe stared at him, wide-eyed and lips slightly open. "I'm so sorry. You seemed like you were about to kiss me and I wanted to kiss you too and words are never as clear as actions. So anyway," she tried to change the subject, but the blush on her cheeks and the way she bit her bottom lip kept the memory of their kiss dangling in front of them. "I guess that was your prize."

"My prize?"

"Getting to the center of the maze first."

He laughed and pecked her on the cheek. "As the winner, haven't I earned the right to choose the prize I want."

Her entire body tensed. Was she waiting for him to take advantage of her? The knobhead in her past who had shredded her trust in people needed a huge arse-kicking.

"What do you desire, Henry?" The hesitancy in her voice nearly killed him.

"Merely the answer to a simple question." He tried to reassure her with one hand placed over hers and a shift on the bench a centimeter away from her.

"That's fair." Her breathing slowed and her expression softened.

"How can I locate the original Lady Elizabeth?"

Sighing, she looked up over the hedges toward the sky. "That's not an easy question to answer. The reality is you may never recover it."

"I don't believe in impossibilities. There has to be a means of finding it." He gazed into her brandy eyes.

The corners of her mouth fell. "It could take months to track the location of an unknown portrait."

He didn't have months. "I could backtrack to find the restoration expert. I could search in some private galleries known to deal in stolen art. Simon knows people who can provide me access." He sounded desperate. He was desperate.

"If Simon knows people in those circles, then use his connections." Her jaw visibly tightened at the mention of stolen art or Simon or both. She stood and circled the area, brushing her hand over the tiny leaves of the hedge as she moved. "Why don't you call the police, fill out a report, and let the authorities handle it?"

"They have too many dangerous criminals to catch, and no time to invest in tracking a painting. I'd lose it forever."

She continued pacing around the bench. "I think it's already lost forever."

"It can't be. In three weeks, an appraiser is coming to see it."

"Why?" She stopped and turned toward him. "Are you going to sell it?"

"I was hoping to use it as collateral for a loan." He raised up his hands. "Hard to appraise a reproduction."

Somehow, this news seemed to recharge her energy levels. "*If you found the painting, it would be valued high.* Not priceless masterpiece high, but higher than the average portrait by Sir Thomas Lawrence because of the size and the subject matter."

She resumed her pacing at an increased speed. Her mouth quirked to the right as her mind went into action. At least he hoped it did.

"We're not talking a bidding war, are we?" he asked.

"I'm afraid not. Lawrence made many portraits, and Lady Elizabeth is not exactly a well-known member of the aristocracy. I can provide you with the names of several appraisers who can give a better estimate than the one the finance company will send out, provided you don't mention the source of the referral."

"Fair enough. I'm hoping to receive enough financing to begin the renovation of the wing you're staying in."

"Why don't you use the castle as collateral, or the Oxford house?"

"I can't. The Oxford house is mortgaged to the hilt, and Ripon Manor's value is tied up in a family trust that has every loophole sewn shut and sealed. My solicitor has already examined every possibility."

"Wouldn't a trustee want to fund a renovation of its main property?"

"Upkeep, yes, but I'm planning to alter the character and purpose of the wing. The trustee claims these modifications wouldn't benefit the heir."

She sat next to him. Her thighs brushed against his, creating a burning sensation inappropriately directed toward his groin. His heat-seeking hormones destroyed his concentration, and he struggled to stay in the conversation. She tempted him more than anyone ever had. Leave it to his quirky libido to fall for a woman who offered more questions than answers.

Focus, damn it.

The women's group needed him. His adolescent urges had to be contained.

"Who's the heir? Ask him or her if you can renovate." She wandered away from him without leaving the center space.

"That would be my uncle. He's not too keen on children taking over the property."

Her eyes widened. "What children?"

"The Ripon Women's Club helps victims of domestic violence and their families. Right now, we have an after-school program and a small house in Ripon proper that houses only three families. In fact, there's no room for you to stay right now, but you can remain here in the manor until you have a plan to move on. Ultimately, I'd like to use the ten bedrooms in the east wing to create a temporary place for the most needy women to raise their children in a safe and pleasant location."

"Battered women and their children?" she repeated.

"Exactly."

The fear he'd seen reflected in her eyes since the moment he saw her at his party shifted to something almost carefree.

"It's a wonderful idea. Imagine how a child who wears hand-me-down clothes year after year will feel being served in that gorgeous dining room and running through the hedge maze." She glowed with a radiance that drew him like a moth to a bug zapper. "You'll need a zip line."

"A zip line?"

"Absolutely. And a climbing wall. Maybe some horses. That's the kind of home I'd have wanted to be raised in."

A hint into her past? Raised by a single mother or maybe in a foster family? Whatever her past circumstances, she'd obtained a top-notch education. Despite her penchant for tattoos and unnatural hair color, she carried herself well.

Henry frowned. "Back to the original problem. It stays a dream unless I find the painting."

Her expression darkened. "Henry, you have no idea what

you're getting into. You could end up losing your life. No painting is worth that."

"I'll never find it if I don't try. I'd give everything I own to help these families."

"If people find out what you're doing, they'll kill you."

He thought about her comment for a minute. "What if I stay in disguise? I'll be an art buyer looking for a large portrait." It was brilliant. He could remain safe and help the Ripon Women's Group.

"*You?*" She seemed indignant.

Obviously, she didn't understand the depth of his learning. "I'm not a novice. I've studied art history and have purchased antiques for both houses." Rising to his full height, a good foot above her, he looked down at the pint-sized genius with his most imposing stare.

"Here's a simple question, then. What is the main difference between two of the most popular artists from the Impressionist period, Manet and Monet?" She crossed her arms and held his gaze without a flicker of nerves.

"Simple. Monet painted mostly landscapes, while Manet created many war scenes."

She shook her head. "Monet painted primarily outdoors and the lighting in his work reflects this, while most of Manet's paintings were created in a studio."

"Who the bloody hell will be asking me that sort of thing?"

"Someone like me."

They enjoyed the rest of the afternoon together strolling through the garden and exploring the hillside. When they returned to the house, Henry removed himself to his study, and Gabe ventured off to explore more of the gardens. Before he had a chance to sit at his desk, Simon called looking for more information on her. Henry refused to interrogate her. She was beginning to trust him, and he'd already assured her she'd be safe with him.

After putting off Simon, he pulled up a spreadsheet on his laptop, showing the finances of the Ripon Women's Group. They needed him, and he needed the painting. The painting, through some strange yet miraculous maneuvering by his mother's solicitor, belonged to him and not the family trust. The rest of his assets were tied up for the benefit of future Chiltons.

A multimillionaire on paper only, he couldn't fix a broken water heater at the castle without begging Mr. Martin Baum, the trustee of the Chilton Family Trust, for the funds. Even then, Martin took sadistic pleasure in dangling the carrot just out of reach ever since Henry's refusal to marry Martin's vexatious sister Hazel. With the family trust money more fiercely guarded than the Crown Jewels, Henry had limited options. His salary from Oxford barely supported the house there.

The insurance on the painting was currently worthless, since an insurance claim for a huge loss filed at the moment he needed money would be processed with greater scrutiny. The company could even bring him up on charges of insurance fraud. Not the public relations exposure the Ripon Women's Group needed to move forward and help more families. No, he wouldn't be reporting the theft just yet.

And thanks to Mr. Baum's tightwad attitude, Henry had never supported any of the many causes his friends championed, minus the occasional benefit dinner and such, so they'd never responded to his requests for assistance.

His only hope for funds resided in the painting. Later, when people learned of the women and children benefiting from the charity, they'd want to assist in making it more successful. Only then could he build an adequate endowment.

He rubbed his temples and turned toward a footstep behind him. Gabe's tousled black strands created an edgy appearance and the black eye makeup had returned. Even in jeans, worn red trainers, and a sweatshirt, the woman impressed him.

"Am I disturbing you?" she asked.

"Yes, but I appreciate your brand of disturbance."

She smiled and entered the room. In that moment, he would do anything to keep that ephemeral smile from disappearing. He looked at his watch. They had enough time to eat and run into town.

"Don't get comfortable. We need to have a quick dinner."

"Why?"

"You'll see." He stood and escorted her to the dining room. After escaping from hell, she needed to do something enjoyable, and Henry wanted to see her relax, if only for a moment.

Two hours later, at a quarter of nine, he stood with Gabe in front of the city hall of Ripon. A tour bus pulled into town, and a crowd formed around the city center. Then the official town horn blower arrived in full regalia, a black tricorne hat, beige coat with red embellishments, and an elaborately decorated horn. He sounded a low tune on each of the four corners of the obelisk, and then reported to the mayor, declaring, "The watch is set."

Henry loved how day after day, year after year, century after century, the tradition continued. He glanced at Gabe, who stood mesmerized by the simple ceremony. "What do you think?"

"I enjoyed it. Does he do this every Sunday night?"

"He does this every night. Rain, snow, bitter cold." He took off his jacket and placed it over Gabe's shoulders.

"Thanks."

"Let's go for a pint." Henry slipped his arm under his jacket and around her waist. Even through the sweatshirt, he could feel the chill in her body. They headed toward the Hornblower Tavern.

Once inside, Gabe rubbed her hands together and scanned the pub from the bar to the tables. "Can we take one of the round booths? They look warmer."

"Absolutely." He sat next to her on a curved cushioned bench, and then waved the waitress over. "Kate, two pints of your winter draft and some chips."

The waitress, wearing black trousers and a too-tight T-shirt, winked at him. "Sure thing, Henry."

"Sure thing, *Henry*," Gabe repeated.

Henry couldn't suppress his grin. "It's my hometown. I bet if I go to your hometown, wherever that is, everyone would know you, too."

"Not really." She wouldn't add anything else. Instead, she flipped through the menu and observed the crowd.

Kate returned with the pints and bent close to Henry, offering him a view of those assets she'd barely covered in the T-shirt. He shifted his attention to the more subtle beauty of the woman seated next to him. Gabe, eyebrows raised and lips pursed, remained focused on their server.

"Thank you. Can you please check on the chips?" She ordered her away and then faced Henry. "The staff seems friendly here. *Very* friendly."

"Are you jealous, Miss Sunshine?"

"In your dreams. You'd have to be a lot more"—she waved her hand in front of his chest—"everything to get me interested." Her body, however, had been moving closer to his each time the waitress came near.

Kate returned with the order of chips. Gabe sent her away again with a request for ketchup. She'd have the poor woman running all night in her current mood.

He rested his arm behind her back and slid toward her until she could rest her head on his shoulder. She shifted on the bench. Her hip touched his, and her head fell back into his embrace, as though they'd been together for years. He didn't want to like it so much, but he did. Having her in his arms felt right.

"Your women's group must love your enthusiasm toward their cause and all the assistance you provide," she said.

"I can't assist as many families as I'd like. The painting would have really expanded the program."

"It's that important?"

"Yes. Unless you know someone willing to write a check for thousands of dollars, the painting is the only way to access the funds."

"Could I help?" she asked, hesitation running through her words.

She wanted to help? Gabe surprised him again.

He lowered his voice, "I thought you were hiding from someone."

She shrugged. "We can do this. You could cover more ground with me, because I'd know the questions to ask."

"Thanks for the offer, but I don't want you placing yourself in danger." His arm tightened on her shoulder. Desire for the funds warred with his obligation to protect her. "I'll think of something."

She drank down her beer like it was water.

"Slow down, Sunshine. The beer will you hit you hard if you don't pace yourself."

"I'm fine."

He could see the gears in that sharp mind of hers considering her options. Her fingers tapped the table, and she swallowed the rest of the pint in time to order another from Kate.

With a heavy sigh, she turned toward him. "If a child has to live under the same roof as an abusive parent for one extra day because I didn't help, I'd never be able to forgive myself. You have to let me do this."

The sincerity of her words and the pleading in her eyes fogged over his brain. So against his better judgment, he agreed to let her help.

CHAPTER 9

———————— ❧ ————————

Alex stretched her arms over her head. She breathed in the smell of clean sheets and felt the sun tempting her eyes to open and face the day. Her leg straightened, and her bare foot brushed up against another foot—a bigger bare foot. Three shots of espresso with a Coke chaser wouldn't have awakened her faster.

She turned to her right and saw Henry, pants on, shirt off, lying next to her on the bed in the red room. The twisted sheet covered half of his legs. She grabbed at the sheets and pulled, but they refused to budge from under his leg.

Wham! She pounded on Henry's arm and then slapped his face, ripping him from sleep.

He rolled over to face her and gently grabbed her wrist. "Bloody hell. I don't care if you are a woman. If you hit me again, I'm heading to the bathroom for some ice water. And you'll be wearing it, not drinking it."

She pulled away and noticed his shirt on her body. There were many questions about how she ended up dressed in his clothes, but also relief that she hadn't woken up naked.

Her last sexual partner took everything from her and gave nothing, except a broken rib and a bruised neck. With Henry's body pressed up to hers, however, she hungered for something she'd never had. Intimacy. She tried to relax, but tears threatened to break free and ruin everything.

"Steady, Sunshine. It's okay." He backed away from her and sat on an armchair across the room.

"Why were we in bed together?" She blinked several times. The tears stayed away, but her expression must have given her fear away.

"You insisted I stay with you." His voice was soothing.

She remembered drinking and singing a few songs and dancing on the table and then on the bar while Henry tried to get her to put her shoes back on. Then the memory ended. "I don't remember coming back here."

"While you were calling out the bartender for letting the patrons put their mugs directly on top of the oak bar without a coaster, I phoned a cab and brought you home. You then insisted on stripping down to nothing and tried to strip me down as well. I left you in your room, but you came flying by my study in nothing but your birthday suit."

That sounded like something she'd do if hampered with alcohol, which was why she so rarely drank more than one glass of anything stronger than coffee. "Did anyone else see me?"

"No. I covered you up and stayed with you until you fell asleep. Regrettably, I fell asleep too.

"I'm so sorry. I'm mortified."

What a stupid mistake. I can't afford to lose control, ever.

"I've already forgotten it, although my cheek may remind me for the next hour or so." He rubbed his hand through his hair and sighed. "You'll always be safe with me. I promise. If you tell me what you're running from, I can even help you take down your enemies."

"We've been through this before. I'm hiding from something evil, and helpful is no match for evil."

In the dawn's early light without a button-down shirt hiding his amazing pecs, Henry could be described as masculine, rugged, and definitely beddable, but not tough enough to take on Luc.

"Maybe assisting me in finding the painting isn't such a good idea."

"Of course it is," Alex insisted. "I'll keep my identity undercover the whole time. It should be relatively easy. Besides, it's only for three weeks, until the appraisal."

Part of her wanted to help the children, and part of her wanted to stay with Henry a little longer. Deep down in the furthest recesses of her fear, she also craved the opportunity to find Luc again. Eliminating him would free her family from the threat he posed.

Henry stationed himself across the room. He wasn't leaving, but he wasn't encroaching on her space, either.

His easygoing nature beckoned her and scared the hell out of her. Why hadn't she met someone like him before Luc had beaten the ability to live in the moment out of her? Luc had used sex as a weapon. The effect of that violence still punched into her soul.

"Are you sure you want to help?"

"I said I would."

I just hope I don't regret my decision.

"Thank you." Henry smiled and stood to leave. "You're not tied into this, you know. If you want out, just say so."

"I know."

She closed her eyes and took a deep breath before hopping up to gather her clothes. She wanted to curl up with Henry on the bed, but a quick retreat would probably be for the best. The knots in her stomach told her she wasn't ready. The stolen kiss in the maze had been enough of an effort. Perhaps someday, sex would feel more like an act of love and not torture.

He turned to leave. She felt a tightening in her chest as she watched him go. And the thought of this moment, this chance disappearing, kicked her bravado into overdrive.

"Henry?"

He paused and then slowly turned around. His eyes fixed on

her face; her gaze dropped to his abs. Muscle, definition, solid. The professor was hot. Maybe sex didn't need love, maybe she just needed to lust after her bed partner. She walked toward him as though on autopilot. She could do this. She could seduce this man and feel strong. She sashayed over to him, hoping she looked confident.

"Like what you see?"

"I love what I see, partner. What's the L.P. stand for?" He pointed to the opening in the shirt that revealed the tattoo just north of her right breast forced on her one really ugly night.

"Love and Peace." She refused to back away as the fighter in her woke up, craving a man who seemed trustworthy and noble. She pulled him over to the bed, all hips and attitude, and made him sit on the edge. He no longer towered over her. In fact, his head was level with her shoulder.

She leaned over him and gave him a soft kiss on his lips. "Or maybe it means 'Lusty and Provocative.'"

"That describes you perfectly."

She kissed again, and this time he kissed her back. Her anxiety floated away as her body responded to the sensual connection with electrifying intensity. He pulled back.

"Are you with me?" He stared into her eyes, calm, poised, waiting. "We don't have to do anything except have some breakfast."

"I want this."

Yes, I want all of you. Your messy hair, your bedroom eyes, and that seductive grin.

His arms wrapped around her, and his lips touched her neck. They felt amazing on her skin. His tongue made a strong case for her to let go and allow him to eliminate the horrid memories of being branded Luc's latest whore. He moaned as her fingers pressed over his shoulders and across his neck.

One of his hands roamed down her thigh, too close to a place that had known only violence. She recoiled at his touch. The memories too fresh, too painful.

A hand over her throat, an order to stay perfectly still, rough, brutal sex.

Luc had marked her forever with a tattoo on her skin and one embedded into her soul. How could she release such a past and move on? Pulling away, she grabbed her clothes and held them in front of her.

"What's wrong?" His tone lowered into a soothing sound, without harboring an ounce of annoyance or frustration. He stood up, but didn't approach her.

Holding back tears, she turned toward the bathroom. "I forgot my number one rule. I can't sleep with anyone I work with. Ever."

***

Henry took the coldest shower of his life and remained under the icy drops for thirty minutes. He understood she'd been hurt in the past, but she had to know he'd never harm her. He would, however, hurt the bugger who had made this amazing woman cower in fear over physical intimacy.

Perhaps this was for the best. He had to focus on finding the painting. He'd be wise to treat Gabe as an assistant, or a work-mate. He shook his head. *Impossible.* His skin heated up just thinking about her.

He found her in the great hall stretched across one of the couches facing the window. Strong and vulnerable. She didn't seem the type to want pity, so he decided to give her a bit of tough love instead.

"You need a haircut. Get up." His tone came out more brusque than he'd wanted, but he had her attention.

She raised her eyebrows. He strode up to her and pointed at her foot propped on the armrest. Frowning at him, she moved it off the couch in slow motion. He then proceeded to do the same with her other foot. She sat up, not happy about his interruption.

"If this is to work, you need to play the part of a wealthy

heiress in search of some amusement in your otherwise humdrum life."

Gabe rolled her eyes and snorted. "Humdrum life? Is that how heiresses live?" She slid back into a prone position. "I think I'd enjoy a humdrum life."

Okay, that didn't work. Perhaps a bribe would motivate her out the door. "We'll find you some appropriate clothes as well. You must have been dressed better than this when you were working in the art world."

She smiled. "The art world is a forgiving place, Henry. If I do my job better than anyone else, I get to dress any way I wish. Besides, I'm more of a backroom kind of girl. Are you funding my miraculous transformation today?"

"Yes. But don't expect to be treated like royalty. I'm limited to an academic's salary." He helped her to her feet.

She started for the door and tilted her head in his direction. "I can make do with anything."

Their first stop was Shear Pleasure, a local beauty salon. Lynn, an old friend of Henry's mother, looked Gabe over and agreed that her hair needed work.

"Blonde? Your hair's been overprocessed and completely stressed, dear. If you must, I'll need to do a deep conditioning and slowly strip the color and then put back something softer. How short are you willing to go in length?" She picked at the ends of Gabe's hair like she was touching burlap.

"The hair in front needs to remain at least chin-length. Otherwise, cut away. Something with an attitude."

Henry interrupted, "Not too much of an attitude. She needs to appear classy."

"I've never seen you take so much interest in a girlfriend before." Lynn beamed at him as though he had met someone worthy of marriage after his numerous short-term relationships.

He didn't feel like explaining his private life to anyone, so he wished Gabe luck and strolled around the town square thinking about Lynn's comment. She'd known what an arse his father had been. In fact, most of Ripon knew of the earl's female conquests. They didn't, however, know of the abuse.

The image of his father, a man who went through women like tea bags, stabbed at his memory. His father was the all-time most despicable prat who had ever lived. Someone Henry swore to never be like.

Yes, he'd dated a lot of women in the past, and, yes, the relationships rarely lasted longer than a few weeks. But he'd always treated the women in his life with the utmost respect. So what if he didn't feel compelled to marry? It wasn't like he needed a wife. Besides, he'd never met anyone he wanted to settle down with.

He smiled, remembering the comment to his uncle about being engaged to Gabe. Too bad his uncle hadn't seen the pink-haired version of her. Being a gentleman, though, Uncle George would never comment about her hair or any other quality of Gabe's, especially if she was joining the family. She'd require tons of protection and assistance if she were to hobnob with the European upper class. She'd admitted she preferred back rooms of art galleries to the more public spaces. She'd be a sitting duck among a group of swans and swan wannabes. Too bad she wasn't really his fiancée. In Henry's experience, fiancées gained immunity to the harsh comments and rude attitudes of others.

If she did, in fact, stay with him to help locate the painting, being his fiancée would offer her a layer of protection. Not a real engagement, of course, but one created out of necessity, for a specific length of time. Three weeks.

He drove home and picked up a piece of his inheritance. Although possession was restricted by the trust to the current countess only, there was no countess currently, so she wouldn't miss it. He'd return it to the family jewels after they retrieved the painting.

When he arrived back at the salon several hours later, he held a small box in his hand that would help protect Gabe from at least some of the obstacles in their path.

"Henry. I'd love to work with Gabe again whenever you two

are in town." Lynn glanced back at him as she cut another woman's hair. "She's a pleasure."

He smiled. He liked having Lynn's approval. And she was right—Gabe was indeed special.

"I'll tell her. Where is she?"

As he said the words, Gabe entered from the back area. His art specialist had turned into a cool dark blonde with silky hair falling over one brandy eye to her shoulder and then angled to just below her ear on the other side of her face. It was funky, but elegant. And extremely sexy.

He strolled up to her and hugged her. "Wow. Every time I see you, you're a completely different woman. Beautiful in all your forms."

"Thanks. Lynn is a miracle worker." She settled in his arms comfortably, as though she hadn't pushed him away hours ago.

"It's your bone structure," the miracle worker called out. "You could go bald and still be beautiful."

"I think I'll keep my hair this length for a while." She looked up at him and sighed. "You really like it?"

"I do." And then he leaned down and kissed her. Her taste drew him in like an opiate. He pulled back before he embarrassed himself. From the wide-eyed look on Gabe's face, she seemed more shocked by his show of affection than enamored with it.

He handed her the ring. "You forgot this on the dresser."

She glanced down and gasped.

"I know you didn't mean to forget it." He held up the ring. A hundred-year-old three-carat black diamond sat surrounded by a white diamond halo mounted in a gold band. Expensive enough to impress, without costing him a dollar. Lifting her left hand, he placed it on her ring finger.

"Henry, is this your countess?" Lynn left her client to lift Gabe's hand and examine the ring. "I remember this ring on your mother."

"When this charming lady fell into my lap, Lynn, I knew she was destined for Ripon."

Gabe was speechless until she was outside the salon. She stopped in the middle of the sidewalk, clenched her hands into fists, and placed them on her hips. "Engaged? What are you thinking?"

"I'm thinking you're a beautiful woman I met at a social function. It would not stretch the bounds of reason to be engaged to you, darling."

She stepped back and made a noise like a growl. "Don't ever call me 'darling.' It's a term used by domineering assholes who pretend they care more than they do." Obviously, another part of her past rising up to ruin a nice moment.

"I hope you're not referring to me."

The tension in her face melted. She didn't smile, but the hostility had dissipated. "No. You're always a gentleman, even when I'm not such a lady. Where did you find this black sapphire? It's beautiful."

"It's a diamond."

She stared at the stone. "It's a corundum, not a carbonado. A sapphire."

Henry had no idea what she was talking about.

She sighed. "Forget it. You wouldn't understand."

"Do you like sapphires?"

"It's my birthstone. I suppose I have to like them." Sapphire? What month was that? September? "Well then, it's perfect for you."

"I can't accept it."

"Of course you can. Besides, it's sort of a loan, not a gift. We'll pretend to be engaged unless we're in active pursuit of the painting and using different identities."

She shook her head. "This isn't a good idea."

"What could go wrong?" He took a few steps down the sidewalk and spun around when he realized she wasn't following him.

"Everything could go wrong. What's the benefit of being

engaged to you?" Turning away before he could answer, she hurried down the street.

The idea had less merit than it did an hour ago. Henry sighed, his enthusiasm declining in as rapid a pace as her strides.

"A few reasons," he said, trying to catch up to her in order to eliminate the need to yell his answer. "No one would expect you, a person who dresses like a rock-star wannabe, to become engaged to an earl, so your identity remains protected. Second, I told my uncle I was engaged, because he really wants me to marry someone. Anyone, actually. Bringing you around should keep him at bay for a few months. And finally, and most important, my fiancée will have a certain amount of protection and insulation at functions."

She stopped again and whirled around to face him. With her hand fisted on her hip, her lips pinched together, and an expression that didn't welcome him into her arms, the feisty woman stood her ground. Feisty looked great on her. "Brilliant idea, Mr. Professor, but let me explain a few things. An engagement to your kind is the sort of thing that lands in newspapers. There will be pictures. People seem to know you here and will be interested to learn about your bride-to-be, and I'll be outed. I wish you hadn't given me the ring in public without speaking to me first. You are the biggest moron in the world. And trust me, I know some huge morons. I wanted to help you, not marry you."

"The engagement is only temporary. At the end of three weeks, we each go our own way. And the rags have more interest in the players on Manchester United than they do in me." She feared his popularity for nothing. The press never followed him. He wasn't that important outside of his hometown. And he preferred it that way. "At least try to make do. We can't break it off now. Most of Ripon will know in a few hours about the engagement."

"I can't believe you've exposed me like this." She marched away from him again, hitting her palms against each other. "Fine. Have it your way," Gabe called back to him. She veered off into a small boutique. "I suppose if I'm to dress to your standards, I'd better rectify my wardrobe right now."

She strode over to a familiar-looking saleswoman.

Terrific.

"Hi, I'm interested in buying your most expensive, classiest clothes." Gabe pointed to him and smiled. "My fiancé is paying."

"Fiancé? Henry, is this true?" his former babysitter asked.

"Miracles happen, Eloise. If you'll excuse us." He looped his arm around Gabe's waist and circled her right back to the sidewalk. "We can't shop there."

"Why not?"

"I honestly can't afford it at the moment."

"You really are broke?"

"Not broke so much as limited in my access to cash. I told you the trustee won't help fund anything to do with the women's group, and I can't imagine him approving a new wardrobe for you to help in my quest to board broken families in the east wing."

"Even if I'm your fiancée?"

"Especially. He wanted me to marry his sister and seems quite bitter about my refusal."

The anger faded from her eyes, replaced by amusement at his dilemma. "Fine. I have an idea. Where's the nearest consignment shop?"

Three hours later, Gabe, the pretend soon-to-be countess, looked every bit the part, from the sapphire on her hand to the tan leather bag on her shoulder. If he had half the ability to locate quality items the way Gabe could, he'd have the renovations on the castle completed at a fraction of the cost. She foraged for the best designs in the thrift store and at a small consignment shop located a few kilometers away. With her elegant almost-new wardrobe, even her attitude transformed. He could picture her surrounded by wealth and privilege. There's no way she'd be recognized as the pink-haired student who had rolled into his life a few days before.

When they were served dinner back at the house, Martha expressed shock at Gabe's transformation. "Miss West, you look beautiful."

"Thank you." Gabe's smile was genuine and radiant.

Martha remained a few seconds longer, arms crossed in front of her, staring at the ring and waiting for an announcement. No doubt the local gossips had already texted all of Ripon and the surrounding towns. He didn't want Gabe to become mad again, so he'd speak to Martha privately after dinner about the engagement.

Henry cleared his throat. "Thank you, Martha, that will be all for now."

She departed after a noticeable huff, turning back twice to glance at Gabe before reaching the kitchen.

"Pack your things tonight, countess. We leave in the morning."

"We do?"

"There's a dinner tomorrow night we should attend near London, and the Oxford house is closer. If you move quickly, we should be gone from here before the hundreds of photographers you fear track us down."

She grimaced, and he felt like the biggest cad in England. "One picture is all it takes, Henry."

CHAPTER 10

———————— ✐ ————————

After enduring a four-hour drive with Henry that included lunch at the Grey Pig Pub somewhere between nowhere and Oxford, Alex returned to his other home.

The few days in Ripon had been bliss. She didn't have to look over her shoulder for Luc and his thugs. In another life, she and Henry would have met at some house party to which her mother had sent her. They would have been attracted to each other before the third course of their first meal together. Two geeky intellectuals who loved children. In this life, however, they were thrown together to chase down stolen paintings and evil demons.

When they walked into the kitchen, Simon greeted her with an appreciative whistle. She reciprocated.

"And who is this beauty?" he asked. His smile was ever present, but it now seemed insincere for some reason. Perhaps he distrusted her because she'd run away.

Henry moved next to him. "The future Countess of Ripon. Show him the ring, Sunshine."

She displayed the ring in an elegant pose that also showed off her tall black Stuart Weitzman boots, black Dior skirt, and matching black vest over a white silk blouse. She'd never be tall enough to be a model, but for now, she could pretend to be a countess.

Simon raised his eyebrows. "A black diamond. Unconventional, as is the bride."

"It's a sapphire," she sighed. She should just agree with everyone to avoid a lengthy explanation each time she showed the ring.

"Aren't sapphires blue?" Simon held her hand toward the light to examine the stone.

She pulled her hand back. "Depends on the composition of the stone."

Simon glanced toward Henry. "Don't even attempt to convince me you know the difference."

Henry shrugged. He grabbed a soda from the refrigerator, offered it to her, and then took one for himself. "Tonight, I'm taking Gabe to meet the aunt and uncle. It should be a small dinner party and will be good practice for her before we go to any bigger social functions."

He hugged her close with one arm and kissed the top of her head. An intimate gesture that caused a million butterflies to take flight in her stomach.

"Gabe, why don't you go up and get ready for dinner? I need to speak with Simon." He kissed her again, this time on the cheek, before letting her go.

She climbed the stairs and shut her bedroom door, but remained in the hall. After taking off her shoes, she tiptoed back downstairs and hid behind the kitchen door. The men were sitting at the island, discussing her.

Simon swigged her neglected can of soda. "Engaged?" He sounded disgusted. "That creates more of a mess than you're in right now. You have no idea of her actual identity, and yet you've decided to marry her?"

"It's merely a facade, but hides her identity from whomever is pursuing her. Besides, I think she feels safer with me than being alone, and she's agreed to help me find the painting. With your help, too, of course."

"What's to stop her from taking that ring and pawning it off for travel funds?" Simon's tone full of suspicion.

"She gave me her word she'd help me, and I trust her."

"You're going to beggar yourself on some con artist," Simon said.

Henry's voice darkened. "You're wrong. She's not what she seems. I don't know who or what she is, but there's more integrity and grit there than meets the eye."

She smiled at the compliment. Perhaps she'd found a champion.

***

Henry explained the background of his aunt and uncle during their drive to Mayfair. When he told her some of the basic table manners expected at a dinner party with this circle of people, Gabe shut her eyes. Hopefully, she was still listening, so she wouldn't feel out of place. His aunt's pedigree rivaled the queen's, and she entertained in a similar manner.

He pulled up in front of his uncle's place on Upper Grosvenor. A valet helped Gabe to the sidewalk.

Henry looked her over once more. He liked what he saw. Her makeup was soft and pretty. One eye peeked out from her new sleek hairstyle, and her posture could not have been more perfect on a debutante. She wore a fitted pale pink dress embellished with a ruffle over one shoulder. Crystal stilettos displayed perfect feet and pink toenails. Her tempting legs were exposed to two inches above her knee. Classy, yet sexy as hell.

Uncle George greeted them at the door to his town house. "Henry, so glad you could come." He let his gaze swing to Gabe and held her hand with both of his. "You must be the lucky girl. Henry has told me about your engagement. Congratulations."

"Thank you. He's told me so much about you. Your work as a member of Parliament is admirable." Gabe spoke with an almost aristocratic affectation similar to the Kennedys of Boston.

Uncle George beamed.

During the walk from the foyer to the living room, his uncle introduced a poised and polished Gabe to several couples connected to his uncle through Parliament, two Russian socialites new in town, and a few single men to mingle with the single women. Gabe navigated the minefield of aristocrats with practiced grace. She spoke without hesitation, yet without a need to overpower anyone else. She never contradicted or argued with anyone and made no comments on the authenticity of the paintings hanging on the walls.

Uncle George pulled him aside while Gabe discussed the wedding with Aunt Mary. "I like her." He slapped Henry on the shoulder.

She'd passed the first test.

"As you should. I told you I'd found the perfect woman. She happens to be American, but that seems to be her only flaw."

He laughed. "She's pretty, soft-spoken, and a real angel. She'll make you some beautiful children. Perhaps you can hand the reins of your little charity thing to her, although I doubt she'll approve of housing all those dysfunctional families in the castle."

A small hand slid over his arm, and a warm feeling flooded his heart. *Gabe.* He turned to see her gazing at him with feigned admiration. What an actress.

She focused on his uncle. "May I call you Uncle George since we'll be family soon?"

"Absolutely."

"Thank you." She beamed warmth mingled with something indefinable, yet hypnotizing. "I overheard you speaking of the Ripon Women's Group. Henry's work with them is inspiring. With the changes he proposes, he'll improve the lives of many wonderful women and children whose only crime was picking a lousy boyfriend or husband." She squeezed his arm. "Knowing these families can benefit from the generosity of the Chilton family compels me to assist him in the renovation of that section of the castle. What a legacy Henry will leave to future generations.

I'm so proud of his efforts." She turned those lovely eyes back toward him and made him wish for a moment that their engagement wasn't fictitious.

Aunt Mary called everyone to dinner.

After Uncle George left to help her, Henry linked his arm in hers, and they strolled into the dining room together. "Enjoying yourself?"

"Your family seems nice. Your aunt adores you." She smiled up at him.

"By the end of the evening, I'm sure you'll become her favorite." He stopped a moment to kiss her. He'd never been so addicted to a woman. Suddenly, the party was overcrowded and boring. He wanted to take Gabe home.

The dining room could sit twenty people in comfort. Rose-tinted curtains framed amazing views of Hyde Park. The table covered in white damask glimmered with crystal glasses and silverware. A huge bouquet of white roses and lilies, his aunt's favorite flowers, decorated the center of the table and guaranteed that no one on the far ends of the table would see the other side.

Gabe sat between a Russian model and Frank Stevens, a thirty-year-old viscount and the founder of a biotech firm near Greenwich. Henry tried to hear their conversation, but caught mere snippets, something about Frank's need for capital and Gabe's suggestion of angel investors. From Henry's vantage point, Frank appeared mesmerized by her, completely caught up in their conversation. She acted as though Frank was the only person in the room. Her sweetness came across as seductive. At least to Henry it did. And he wanted that seductive look all to himself. Jealousy burned in his chest, but she wasn't his. And never would be.

CHAPTER 11

I f Alex had to speak to Frank for one more minute about the potential for a biotechnology boom in developing countries, she'd be forced to cut out his throat with her fish knife. Instead, she raised her eyebrows, fixed her mouth a shade lower than a smile, and nodded in agreement with whatever he said.

Regretfully, Frank took that as encouragement to continue speaking. "Our major competition is a US company, Oak Industries. They hold most of the patents in the field and the CEO, Peter Northrop, works nonstop to keep the company on the cutting edge of vaccine development and HIV treatments. It works, because no one beats Oak in biotechnology right now."

Crap. Of all the people in London, to be paired with someone who knows Dad. God must be having a huge cosmic laugh over this seating plan.

Had Frank ever met her father? If he had, he may also have met her mother. Alex didn't inherit her mother's abilities as a socialite, but she did inherit most of her facial features, especially her petite nose and light brown eyes.

At the mention of Oak Industries, she rubbed her thumb over the bandage covering her acorn tattoo. She didn't want to talk about anything related to her family. The topic soured her stomach and thoroughly depressed her, especially since Frank had spoken the truth. Peter had never been the best father, but was always the best in business.

Frank took a sip of wine and stared at her. "You look remarkably familiar."

"I do?" she asked, flipping part of her hair in front of one of her eyes.

"Yes, but I can't place your face. Have you been to any parties in Silicon Valley recently?"

"No. My work keeps me in Europe."

"Give me time. I never forget a face."

Their conversation needed to move away from the biotechnology field. Pretending to drink more than she had, she expounded on the wonderful bouquet in the Chianti complementing the savory beef dish. It worked. Frank followed her into a discussion of vineyards in Italy. She sat through the rest of the meal smiling and providing innocuous answers to probing questions.

One of the Russian beauties whispered to her friend in their native tongue. They probably assumed they were either being quiet enough not to be overheard or no one had the intelligence to learn such a random foreign language. A stupid practice, by stupid people.

The lanky brunette told the fake redhead that the blonde sitting next to her was going to marry the earl. The redhead glanced at Alex and smiled. She then raised her eyebrows in condescension and giggled. Even if Alex didn't know Russian, it would be hard to miss the slight.

"What was he thinking?" Red asked in Russian.

Her thin counterpart whipped her hair back and smirked. "He wanted a pretty little thing that wouldn't cause him any trouble. It won't last. She has nothing going for her. She's flat-chested, short, and has a boring personality. He'll be sick of her before the honeymoon is over."

They continued to rattle on about their own prospects for

marriage and then switched back into English in an attempt to convince the men around them to go clubbing after dinner.

Alex picked at her food and ignored her wine, except for the occasional toast. Her manners were impeccable. When dinner had finished, everyone mingled together until a uniformed butler served tea and dessert in the living room. Frank followed her to the dessert table. So much for an escape.

He hovered over her as she picked up a chocolate-covered strawberry. "You should come out to the Funky Goat with us."

"Funky Goat?"

"It's a club in King's Cross. We're leaving in a few minutes if you need a ride?"

Henry approached them, and the stress of Frank's pursuit dissipated.

"That's so kind, but I'm pretty tired and want some time alone with Henry."

"That's right. I hear congratulations are order."

Henry moved in and wrapped his arm around her waist. Perfect timing. "Thanks, Stevens. I'm lucky she said yes. Will you be in London long?"

Frank's gaze turned from Henry back to Alex. "Regrettably, no. I must be getting back to our office in San Jose."

"Call me when you're in the area again. We can catch up," Henry said, his lips caressing the top of her ear.

The intimacy caused Frank to mumble something in reply and slip away to speak to someone more available.

"How was dinner?" Henry turned to Alex.

"Perfect. I haven't had foie gras terrine with caramelized apples in forever."

His support felt good. She rested her head on his shoulder.

"I'm glad you liked it. Do you mind if we take off early? I think we've accomplished what we'd set out to do."

They'd proven everything important. They could appear as an actual couple, Alex could behave well enough to be acceptable in the right circles, and she wouldn't pass gas at a dinner table. What a proud moment.

It wasn't difficult. She'd pretended to be her mother for the evening. Gabrielle would have been thrilled to see her embracing her birthright for once. "I'm ready to go. And my feet are ready, too. I haven't worn heels since my last formal dinner party."

"And how long ago was that?"

"A long time."

They bid good-night to his aunt and uncle, before Henry left to retrieve their overcoats.

She approached Red and Bony in the foyer and whispered to them in Russian. "Henry didn't choose a woman like either of you because it's cheaper to pay your type by the hour than commit for life."

She walked away to join Henry without bothering to wait for their reactions.

***

Henry glanced at Gabe during the drive to Oxford. Her head tilted toward him, eyes closed, and body relaxed. She'd been the most sought-after guest at the party. Her intelligence bubbled up in everything she'd said. Frank had been captivated. His eyes had remained transfixed on her all evening. Who could blame him? She was a beautiful dinner companion who listened thoughtfully and offered intelligent commentary on subjects ranging from economics to the new director of the Bolshoi Ballet.

After pulling the car into the garage, Henry tried to rouse her. "Wake up, sleeping beauty."

"Ten more minutes," she whispered.

"If you don't walk by yourself, I'll be forced to carry you."

"Go ahead. My feet are swollen from the high heels." Her eyes remained closed, but her back arched in a cat stretch.

He bit saying something, opened her door, and picked her up. She weighed nothing. Wrapping her arms around his neck, she tucked her face into his shoulder. Her breath sent shivers all the way through him.

He entered through the front door and climbed the main staircase. Without thinking, he headed toward his room and placed her on his bed. The light from the hall illuminated her blond hair as though an angel had landed in his presence. How long had it been since a beautiful woman's hair fanned out across his pillow? Too long.

The guest room would have been a better location for her, but his body placed the woman who made his blood boil where it wanted her. His brain, however, kicked in and ordered him to remove her from his bed. His brain lost the argument. He'd leave her alone after one quick kiss good- night. A kiss would be an appropriate finish to an evening spent acting as an engaged couple. In fact, it would make them more comfortable with each other in public. She yawned and then licked her lips. Just one kiss.

One simple good-night kiss on the lips, however, turned into much more when she feathered her fingers over his cheek and returned the kiss.

"Taking advantage of someone sleeping, Sir Henry? Desperation becomes you." Her breathing became heavy, and her expression turned sensual and welcoming. She stretched her arms over her head. The movement shifted her dress above her thighs.

"It's Lord Henry to you." He lifted her chin and deepened the kiss. She tasted of chocolate, the chocolate- covered strawberries served at the end of the party. God, he was hungry for chocolate. Starved.

"Good night, Lord Henry." Her eyes closed, but a slight smile lingered on those pretty lips.

No chocolate for him tonight. He wanted to stay with her, but it had been a long day for both of them. She needed to rest, and he had to leave before he messed up their business relationship.

He made his way to the den. A wood-paneled room created for watching television and unwinding within close proximity to a fully stocked bar. Simon was lounging in his favorite leather recliner, nursing a beer.

"Did you see Nicola tonight?" Henry headed over to pour himself some scotch.

"I did. She told me to say hi to you in between screams of ecstasy."

His hunger for Gabe unsatisfied, Henry was in no mood for Simon's bragging. He made himself a double. They both drank in silence. Despite his current mood, Henry liked living with Simon. The house was too big to live in alone. They rarely bothered each other, rarely became involved in each other's lives. It worked.

Simon stared at the fireplace. "Where's your fiancée?"

"Sleeping. She had a few glasses of wine. If she's not asleep by now, she will be any moment."

"How did she perform?"

"Like a thoroughbred. My aunt is already prepping invitations for the wedding. Several of the male guests followed her from room to room panting after her. She spoke to several influential MPs and managed to converse with intelligence on a diverse amount of subjects. I'd love to know her background."

"Me too." Simon nodded. "Something's not right about her. Think about it. She's hiding from someone. She has an impressive knowledge of art she couldn't have picked up in school alone. My guess is she's a well-educated American who ran with the wrong crowd. She's pissed someone off and her only way to stay alive is to live in hiding."

Henry took a sip of scotch and placed the glass on the table next to him. "Interesting theory. How are you going to test it?"

Simon leaned his head back on the chair. He brought his fingertips together in front of his chin. "Keep watching her. She'll screw up. Give it time, and then we'll get to see the real Gabe West."

CHAPTER 12

Alex sat on the stairs and absorbed Henry's and Simon's words. Simon had better instincts than Henry. Henry saw what he wanted to see. A woman who had a good head on her shoulders, yet never applied herself to anything. Simon seemed to look through her disguise and hit closer to the heart of her being.

That scared her, especially since she didn't know anything about Simon except that he baked killer cinnamon rolls.

What if he found out her identity? She couldn't have Simon messing up her plans.

Without making a creak in the stairs, she slunk back up to Henry's bedroom.

The next morning, a cloudy day greeted her. Typical for this part of England. She made her way toward the kitchen deep in thought.

Bacon. She strutted into the kitchen and straight to the man at the stove. Simon's only redeeming quality had to be his breakfasts. A pile of crispy bacon sat on a plate next to him. She helped herself to three long and greasy pieces.

He appeared too interested in her, but she saw through the act. He wanted to interrogate her, not sleep with her. Perhaps she could use his interest to gather information from him instead. Not that she was even the least bit seductive, at least not according to Luc.

She took a deep breath and slid into his arms, but his touch felt wrong, and her heart wrenched at her attempt to seduce. To keep herself from running back upstairs, she focused on Matt, murdered while protecting her at the pub. Simon pulled her closer, as though testing her. She tamped down her skittish side and placed her free hand on his chest. *Careful.* She was playing a dangerous game with a dangerous guy.

"Did you grow up with Henry?" she asked.

"Nearby."

"It must be annoying to have to serve your old friend."

His head dropped down, and he rubbed his cheek through her hair. "Doesn't bother me in the least."

"I would ask you to refrain from manhandling Gabe until the engagement is officially over, and you've broken it off with your longtime girlfriend." Henry's voice boomed into the kitchen from the doorway. So much for information-gathering.

"I thought this engagement was pretend, Henry." Simon spoke so close to her lips, Gabe could taste the coffee on his breath. He smirked, and returned to cooking.

Her stomach soured at the false intimacy. She backed away from Simon, moving closer to Henry. The heat in his eyes sent a threat toward Simon. His competition chuckled. This could only get worse if she stayed in the room, so she grabbed some coffee and headed to the door.

Henry snapped at Simon. "Stay away from her."

"Yes, sir." Simon winked at her as she passed him. He was enjoying pissing Henry off.

Halfway up the stairs, she overheard Henry ordering him to "keep your fucking hands off her or find a new place to live."

The afternoon dragged on. Simon disappeared, and Henry went to complete some work in his study. He didn't speak to her all afternoon. Perhaps it was for the best. She needed to stay focused on self-preservation. With nothing better to do, Alex located an interesting book titled *Saints, Scholars, and Schizophrenics: Mental Illness in Rural Ireland* on the bookcase in his bedroom and sat near him in his study to read. Twice, she descended the stairs to locate a snack or a drink and rummage through some closets and drawers. A few times, she took a bathroom break to search the medicine cabinets. She also fell asleep for an hour.

"Want more tea, Henry?" She needed another break from staring over the rim of the book at his intense expression. His silent brooding gave her a stomachache, most likely because she had caused his sour mood.

"No, thanks. Feel free to watch the telly downstairs if you're bored."

"Okay. I'll be back."

She headed down the stairs, but stopped on the second floor. Her need to know about Simon lured her to his bedroom door. Was he really Henry's employee? Doubtful.

She opened the door and slid inside. His bedroom had none of the expensive furnishings with which Henry surrounded himself. Every piece of furniture seemed forged of steel and black lacquer. Piles of newspapers covered a glass coffee table, and clothes covered everything else. He was a pig. Each dresser drawer she opened contained unfolded shirts, socks, underwear, and nothing of interest.

His closet smelled of dirty gym socks and a strong men's cologne. He only had three suits and a tux. The rest of his wardrobe consisted of jeans and sweaters. In the back of the closet, she spotted his laptop. Bingo.

She sat near his bed and tried to turn it on, but it required a password. She tried Nicola's name, "Ripon," "I hate Henry." Nothing worked. She wished she'd taken computer science more seriously. A hacker's knowledge would come in handy. Frustrated, she placed it back in his closet.

Her heart pounded, and her nerves made her efforts more frantic. Searching the pockets from each of his coats, she found several parking receipts, a pair of tickets to a play in London, and a credit card that said Simon Dunn. She took the card in case she needed to make a quick break for it. She could repay him when she regained access to her funds in Paris.

She had a few more places to search. Reaching behind his headboard, she found a small hidden drawer. Sure enough, he owned a handgun. She pulled it out. It was loaded. Handguns being mostly illegal in the UK, he was either in law enforcement or doing something against the law. From the cavalier way he went through life, she guessed the latter.

She wanted to tuck the gun in her waistband. Perhaps she could kill Luc with it, but her intuition told her Simon would miss it. Instead, she emptied out all fifteen rounds of 9mm bullets into her front jeans pocket. Disarming the gun made her feel safer.

She put the gun back and searched around his mattress. The hallway floorboards creaked under the weight of a heavy tread. Pulling the duvet back in place, she dived under the bed. The sound of thumping in her chest muffled the noise in the hall. She tried to calm herself, hoping no one could hear her telltale heart.

The door opened and from the hefty footsteps that entered, she assumed it was Simon. She tried to relax, but her fear made that impossible.

The duvet lifted up, and Simon's hand reached forward, like the bucket of an excavator, and dragged her body until she was kneeling at his feet.

"Well. Well. Well. Can't stay away from me? I don't blame you. Henry is sort of a dry sot at times." Simon sat on the bed in front of her.

Shit.

"Hmmm?" She yawned. "Simon, please leave my room."

"This room is mine, as you damn well know. What are you up to? Napping under my bed? Even I don't think you're that barmy." He was holding his phone and glanced between it and Alex's guilty face.

"Maybe I'm crazy about big stupid men with huge muscles." She reached for him, but he backed away.

Mr. Happy actually glowered at her. "Stupid?"

He was definitely not stupid. If only he was.

"No real job. Can't afford your own place. Relying on Henry to finance your life. And then you go and try to sleep with his fiancée. Nice friend. "

"So you think Henry would take your word over mine?"

"We are getting married, after all."

The door opened and Henry stepped in. "Blood is thicker than water, Sunshine."

"Blood?" What did blood have to do with this?

Henry nodded. "Simon's my brother."

Henry's brother? That didn't make sense. "He's a spare?"

Simon smiled again, making the world almost right itself. "No. The bastard son of his father. And he's my baby brother. I'm nobody's spare."

That made sense.

"Are you done searching his room?" Henry asked.

"Why would you think I searched his room?"

Simon stood and handed her his phone. "The cameras."

His screen displayed a great color video of her rummaging through his drawers.

She scanned the room and couldn't locate one camera. She hadn't seen any security around Henry's rare and expensive works of art, but they used cameras in Simon's disaster of a bedroom. It didn't make sense, but she wasn't going to argue the point.

Henry became a bit more agitated as Simon cooled down. "You went through his drawers, under his bed, into his closet, sat on the floor playing with his computer, and then found his hand-gun." They never mentioned his credit card. No camera in the closet?

Simon took out the gun, checked it, and reached into her

pocket for the bullets. Luckily, the jeans had a loose fit. His hand wouldn't have fit into them otherwise.

"Do you have a license to carry that?" Alex asked.

Simon took hold of her chin. "Do not *ever* touch my gun. Is that clear?" He slipped it into the back of his pants. "I'll be downstairs. Next time you snoop through my things, pick the clothes up as you go, so I benefit as well." He left Alex alone with a constipated-looking Henry.

"I think I'll go take a shower." She tried to walk by him, but he blocked her path.

Henry shook his head. "I need to trust you, Gabe. You obviously don't trust us, which considering your need to run and hide from a mystery man, I sort of understand. But I need to trust you. Otherwise, I'd rather go it alone."

"Simon doesn't trust me. He never did."

"You smashed things in my house, live under an alias, stole a bike, made a pass at him in front of his brother, and rummaged through his belongings. Why should he trust you?"

"He probably shouldn't."

Henry stepped closer and brushed a blond wisp away from the front of her eye. "I believe in you, although you're seriously pushing my limits. I find you intelligent, classy, full of life, and a breath of fresh air. You're even in possession of a family heirloom I can't afford to lose. And yet I don't know how to gain *your* trust."

"Every time I trust someone, they either let me down or die."

He wrapped his arms around her. They felt safe. "I'd never hurt you, and I promise to avoid death at all costs. By the way, you looked ridiculously uncomfortable trying to seduce Simon, so I'm assuming you still like me, but you're trying to push me away. Don't." Henry pulled her into a deep kiss, powerful enough to knock her off her axis.

"You're not mad at me?" she whispered as they came up for air. He should be. She tried to steal a firearm.

His chin rested on her head, and his arms tightened around

her shoulders. "Disappointed you went through Simon's things. Jealous as hell when you rubbed your body against his. But never mad at you."

She stepped back from him and looked toward his face. "I'm scared. I don't generally inspire lots of faith from people."

"I trust you. Just stop driving me crazy. Dinner's in an hour." After another kiss on her lips, he turned and left her alone in the room.

The taste of the kiss lingered on her lips. Three weeks? She could make it to the end, but would her heart?

CHAPTER 13

H enry could kiss Gabe forever. Yet he didn't have her forever. A chill spread over him. He wanted more time. Three weeks could never satisfy his growing attachment to her. She filled him with a sense of warmth he'd never felt before. Yet she was still an enigma. Snooping in Simon's room? What was she doing? Did she think Simon was the enemy? He trusted Simon with his life.

When Henry had learned of the existence of his older half brother, he searched him out. What he'd found had disgusted him. His father had provided every material advantage to his future heir. The other son had received nothing. Simon's mother had worked as a housekeeper for some of the well-to-do in town. He'd excelled despite his hardships and earned himself a spot on a club football team and a university education.

He and Simon had spent long days together as teenagers. From what Simon had told him, the earl enjoyed beating his mistress as much as he'd enjoyed beating his countess. They'd banded together to protect their respective mothers. A bond was forged even stronger than the half blood they shared.

He found Simon in the kitchen slicing up chicken. After pouring himself some cabernet sauvignon, he sat at the table.

"Sorry about our houseguest." She was a walking contradiction and the most frustrating female on earth.

Simon never lifted his eyes from his cutting board. "She's smart. Really smart. She located the gun in the first pass around the room. Given ten more minutes, who knows what she would have found. She doesn't trust me, and she shouldn't. Yet she tried to use that body of hers to try to find out more about me. You overreacted a bit, but puppy love can make a boy do silly things."

"I don't—"

"You certainly do. You're an open book. Gabe, however, is a pretty good actress. She's also overflowing with street-smarts on top of her crazy art knowledge. She'd be an asset to MI6, if she weren't American. *If* she's American."

Henry wouldn't give her up to Simon's work. Granted, he had no controlling interest in her, but he did have his three-week engagement, at least, to keep her around. "I need her more than you do right now."

"I understand." Simon slid the chicken into the skillet. The sizzle released an amazing aroma of olive oil and rosemary. "I scrounged up an invite to an underground exhibition in Edinburgh."

Twelve stone lifted off Henry's shoulders with the news. Maybe he did have a shot at rescuing the painting. For all of his father's faults, and there were many, Simon was his greatest gift to Henry.

"Can you get us in?"

Simon grimaced. "I can take Gabe, but you're a bit too posh for this type of event."

"Why?" he asked. Gabe couldn't attend the event without him. He wouldn't allow it.

Simon looked up from the skillet. "She'll easily pass for my latest piece of ass. You, however, are a total swot."

"I'm going." He sounded like a spoiled brat, but damn it, it was his painting.

"Then we'll have to give you a makeover, because someone

will slit your throat if they think you're searching for art someone stole from you."

"I made over Gabe, and she looks fantastic."

Simon laughed. "You had a lot to work with when transforming Gabe. Making you over won't be as easy."

"I can do it." Gabe, sexy despite being dressed in her jeans and a black T-shirt, crossed the kitchen, opened the refrigerator, and took out the orange juice. "I can make him into an art dealer with anonymous wealthy clients. I'll even be his arm candy."

"No. You have to be my companion." Simon shook his head, but didn't smile. He'd stopped playing games with Gabe, thankfully. "If Henry is there on business for his clients, he needs to be alone. I'm always accompanied by some female, usually Nicola. It would seem odd if I went solo. You can stay by my side for a little while until I leave you with Henry so he doesn't put his foot in his mouth."

She sat on one of the stools and picked at the black olives. Black olives and orange juice? And they doubted his ability to blend in?

"Fine." She continued to steal from Simon's dinner prep.

"Fine?" They were crazy. Henry needed her with him. He'd look like a fraud if he was left alone, despite his earlier claims to the contrary.

Simon smacked Gabe's hand with his spatula before she could finish off the olives. "We'll keep Gabe as close to you as possible without her appearing like your date. If she stays next to you all night and whispers in your ear every time you're asked a question, people will suspect you're a copper."

"I'm sure Henry can pass himself off as someone important if he tries really hard." Gabe's smile told him she was enjoying this turn of events.

"We have one problem. Gabe has no identification." Simon turned to her, and Gabe's hand froze before a slice of tomato entered her mouth. "Do you?"

"Identification? Not with me."

Simon's fist clenched and then released as though he wanted to throttle her. "Can you get some?"

"I'd rather not use my own ID right now. Do you have a good source who could make me one?"

Henry waited for his answer, but Simon placed his hands on the countertop, inhaled, and turned back to the food preparation without answering. He did have the ability to obtain her a fake identification. His employer could make her into anyone.

The chicken looked done, and Simon placed it on a serving platter. "We don't have time. You can't fly without identification, so we'll have to drive."

Gabe's shoulders relaxed, and then a glint of humor sparkled in her eye. "Road trip? I call shotgun."

***

The sophisticated and trendy crew of three spent seven miserable hours traveling to Edinburgh. Henry wanted to escape both Gabe and Simon by the end of the day. He insisted they stop for lunch and appropriate breaks. Simon, however, wanted to arrive before a football match began, and Gabe wanted to tour the Old Town before it became too dark. Their lunch at a charming inn near Manchester had been marred by rude comments and the incessant tapping of Gabe's fingers. After lunch, Simon and Gabe, who had appropriated the front seat of Simon's Range Rover, refused to speak to him for messing with their plans. He ignored them as well and tried to catch up on some of his reading.

Gabe insisted that Colin Fisher, Henry's new identity and a man she seemed to prefer over plain Henry, wear designer jeans, the black leather boots she'd demanded he buy on their shopping spree, and a white linen shirt open at the neck. Since he rarely ventured out as the Earl of Ripon, except to the occasional benefit, he shouldn't worry about being recognized. Just in case, however, Gabe slicked his hair behind his ears. The gel caused his scalp to itch. She wouldn't let him pack more comfortable clothes for the ride home, saying he had to stay in character the entire journey. It would be a miserable weekend. And the prospect of locating one stolen painting among thousands was slim.

Henry did find a light at the end of the tunnel through hell. The Balmoral Hotel. Opulent, elegant, expensive. Simon paid, or maybe his employer did. His brother wouldn't say.

When they entered the suite, Simon locked himself in one of the bedrooms, leaving Gabe and Henry to fend for themselves. Gabe immediately raced to the other bedroom, but Henry arrived first and claimed the space.

"Henry, you better share that bed with me. I refuse to sleep on the couch."

"You claimed shotgun in the car; I claim the bedroom." The prospect of sharing the room with her looked good. Better than good. Even if he slept on the outer edge of the bed, he'd be within arm's reach of her.

"Fine. I'll go ask Simon if he'll share." She sauntered across the reception area.

Henry caught up with her halfway to Simon's room. "I get the right side of the bed. We both stay fully clothed."

Gabe smiled like the Cheshire cat. "Deal."

She turned and walked back to their bedroom. He remained on the large recliner in the living room for an hour to give Gabe time to fall asleep, although she never did what was expected.

Trying to enter the room quietly, Henry maneuvered toward the bed, but Gabe had shut the lights off. He couldn't see a bloody thing. He tripped over her suitcase and fell with a thud.

"Henry, I'm trying to sleep. Be quiet."

He struggled to stand up, then limped over to the bedside table and turned the light on.

Gabe was sprawled in the middle of the bed. She was wearing *his* T-shirt. She'd better have something on underneath. He only had a limited amount of restraint, and she'd already taxed most of it. She hadn't pursued a more intimate relationship with him since Ripon. He wouldn't pressure her, but damn, he wanted her.

Sexual frustration would not help his performance at the art show.

When he finished dressing in his boxers and a clean under-shirt, he slid beneath the covers careful not to touch her. He failed.

"Can you move over a foot?" he asked.

She didn't answer. Her eyes were closed, her breathing was heavy, and her body was weighed down like a petrified tree. It was like someone had snapped their fingers and knocked her out. He tried to get comfortable, but unless he wrapped his arm around her, half his body would be off the bed.

Giving up, he rolled toward his tormentor and rested on the edge of her pillow. Her scent smelled of his shampoo and her own particular brand of aphrodisiac. She yawned and shifted her head onto his shoulder. He remained uncomfortably aware of her for most of the night, staring at the wall and wishing he wasn't a gentleman.

After what seemed like a five-minute nap, he sensed someone watching him. Cracking open an eye revealed Simon standing next to the bed, fully dressed and ready to start the day.

"I heard from Roman, tonight's host. He wants to meet you. Now."

Gabe's arm stretched across Henry's chest. Simon raised his eyebrows and grinned.

"Me?" Henry asked.

Gabe slowly came to life, but continued to rest her head on Henry. Her subtle movements woke up parts of Henry's body better left sleeping.

"He doesn't trust you're legitimate, and he'll barricade the exhibition before he allows an undercover officer entry." Simon started toward the door.

"I'm up." Henry stretched, but Gabe's position restricted his movement. "What about Gabe?"

Simon shrugged. "He doesn't need to see my current lover. She's unimportant to him."

Henry's stomach dropped. Without her, he'd have to rely on

the knowledge gained in the two art history classes he took years ago to prove he was a legitimate buyer.

She wrapped her arm around Henry's waist and gazed up at him from the pillow. "Morning. Sleep well?" She kissed his cheek. "I slept like a baby."

At least one of them did. Moving Gabe away from his shoulder, Henry swung his legs off the bed and sat up. "I didn't sleep at all because this sexy blonde wearing a T-shirt and probably nothing else planted herself on my chest and cut off the circulation in my arm. I may be unable to shake anyone's hand today." He shook out his arm. It was numb, but functional.

"Have fun at your meeting. Can you order me an American breakfast from room service? Double the bacon, double the coffee. No cream." She pulled the covers over her shoulders and placed Henry's pillow on top of her head.

Henry ignored her and headed to the shower. He needed to get his game on.

CHAPTER 14

A lex glanced in the mirror and didn't like what she saw. The minuscule length of the black skirt left her feeling skanky, the pewter blouse opened too much, revealing her lack of a bra, and the four-inch heels would cripple her by noon. On the other hand, it should be hard to recognize the real Alex without her brown hair and the conservative clothes she'd always worn with Luc.

In the lobby, she shimmied her way from the elevator to the restaurant. After a deep breath, she wandered in. Simon sat with his back to the wall, facing her. He'd exchanged his typical jeans and tight T-shirt for an Armani suit and an open-collar shirt. The transformation took him from bouncer to billionaire.

Henry sat next to him. He wore black from head to toe, and he rocked it. Maybe it was the slicked-back hair with natural blond highlights that contrasted with the midnight shades. Whatever it was, her split personality not only ached for the nerdy guy in the castle surrounded by a gang of children, but the delicious bad boy who looked decadent in designer clothes and kissed her senseless.

A heavyset dark-haired man sat with them. She couldn't make out his face from the way he was positioned in his seat. The men spoke in low voices regarding something she probably knew more about than all three of them combined.

Simon, Henry, and the other man stood when she approached.

Alex tried to keep her accent generic American. Not too difficult after being gone for so long. "Baby, there you are. I was getting nervous in the suite all by myself." She ran her hands over Simon's shoulders and nuzzled his neck. She refused to glance at Henry, because the guilt would show in her eyes, her attraction would change her body language, and they wouldn't stand a chance at convincing this guy she was with Simon.

Simon's arm curved possessively around her waist. "Belinda. You met Colin Fisher last night. This is Roman Ledovskoy. He's hosting the party tonight." Simon called the waiter over and ordered her some coffee and a fruit plate.

She ignored Henry and observed Roman. His age fell somewhere between forty and fifty. Expensive clothes, platinum Rolex with a mother-of-pearl face. She put out her hand, and he grasped it, not releasing her until she lowered her eyes in deference to him.

"Nice to meet you."

Roman scanned her body, perhaps considering her as potential conquest. "Simon, you have impeccable taste in women."

In a breathy whisper, she replied, "You're too sweet. Will there be dancing tonight? I love dancing."

"Regrettably, no." He zoned in on her legs. "It is more of a cocktail party. A time to view some beautiful art."

Alex sighed. "I'm sure it will be fun anyway."

The waiter returned with her coffee. She added cream and three packets of sugar, and then took a tentative sip. Disgusting, but Alex was known to drink only black coffee. "It's never sweet enough." She reached for more sugar.

Simon placed his hand on her knee and squeezed hard to shut her up. She'd have a bruise there if he did it again. Staying silent, she retracted her hand from the sugar bowl and took another sip of the coffee. Tilting her body slightly toward Simon's gave her a better view of Roman. He was not one to be trifled with. A lot like Luc in attitude, but not even a close second to him in appearance.

Roman turned his attention to Henry. "As I was saying, the drawings will be the highlight, but I'm sure you'll be satisfied with many of the oils."

Henry acted bored and spoke as though this meeting was a waste of time. "I'm interested in romantic and neoclassical portraits and still lifes. There are few drawings in which my clients have ever shown an interest."

"I am fairly certain we will have several pieces to your liking. If not, there will be similar exhibitions of new pieces in some other cities this year." Roman stood. "It was nice meeting all of you." He lifted Alex's hand and kissed it. "Until tonight."

After Roman disappeared, Henry called for the check. "I need to go back to the room and review my notes."

Simon nodded to him. "You did great. If Belinda curbs her sweet tooth, we might pull this off."

They all stood.

Alex leaned on Simon's shoulder. "Honey, if you had ordered me room service, I wouldn't be suffering from hypoglycemia."

"You can order something when we get upstairs. Simon's buying. He loves to spoil his girlfriends," Henry said before walking away.

"My employer's an earl. He pays extremely well." Simon laughed and placed his arm around Alex's shoulders to escort her up to the suite.

When they arrived, he locked himself in his bedroom. She still didn't trust him entirely, but like Henry, he gave out a confusing amount of good vibes to offset his cloud of secrets.

Alex called room service and ordered four fried eggs, a pile of bacon, three slices of toast, and two pots of coffee, no cream. "Do you want anything, Henry?"

"I don't think they'll have anything left after your order."

She spoke into the phone. "Nothing else. Thank you."

Henry paced in front of a large window overlooking Edinburgh Castle as though preparing for a dissertation in art. She could picture him lecturing to a class full of college women enamored with the hunky professor.

Ambling up behind him, Alex tapped his arm to grab his attention. "Do you need help, Colin? I know something about drawings. Are they charcoal, drafts, shaded?"

"All of the above. I think they carry an amalgamation of any type of art they can sell for a boatload of money without it being traced back to them."

Simon walked in. "You need to buy something tonight, Henry. I've narrowed it to one of two pieces, if Lady Elizabeth isn't present."

"I can't afford my own painting. How am I going to buy one that's not mine?" Henry ran his fingers through his hair and then made a face indicating he'd forgotten about the hair gel.

"Stolen art at these events is heavily discounted. Besides, I'll give you the cash. It's a show of good faith. You need to pay to stay in this game."

Simon seemed to know the game too well.

***

Henry and Simon, both dressed in black tuxedos, waited for Gabe to finish getting ready in the bedroom. It was nine o'clock, and Simon needed to escort her to the event. Henry would take a taxi and arrive a half hour later.

"Make sure you don't leer at Gabe," Simon advised. "People think I know and respect you. They also know I'd kill you if you took my girlfriend, or even attempted to."

"I'm not tempted." He was certainly tempted, but he'd curb his desires for the good of the mission.

Simon snorted. "In addition, don't get ticked off if others place their hands on her. She's tough and will handle it fine. I need to be her protector tonight. Not you."

"I think you're overestimating my attraction to her."

The door to the bedroom opened, and Henry's face froze. She was magnificent. Wearing a red silk gown that floated over her skin from the top of her breasts into a pool of fabric on the floor, Gabe drifted toward them. Her expression remained aloof. Her golden hair draped over one eye. Full round lips, covered in red, begged to be kissed.

Simple pearls decorated her neck and ears. She stood sensual and seductive, yet submissive. His image of her shattered. She was indefinable. A marked contrast with the woman he had met only a week ago.

"The expression you're wearing right now is the one you can't wear for the rest of the evening." Simon punched his shoulder and then walked up to Gabe. "Belinda, you look ravishing."

"Thanks," she whispered as though his compliment caught her off guard.

"I only see one problem with your outfit." Simon handed her a blue velvet box. "I cannot have a woman of mine wearing such common jewelry."

Henry watched as she lifted out two teardrop diamond earrings and a heavy gold chain with a large teardrop diamond pendant. She gazed up at Simon and thanked him.

"They're on loan, so be careful."

"I will." The gratitude in her eyes beamed toward Simon and provided Henry a stiff punch in the gut. He wanted her to look at him with those brandy-colored eyes.

Simon went back to his room for his car keys.

After she secured the earrings, she handed the necklace to Henry. "Do you mind helping me with this?" Her voice was halting. Was she nervous?

He placed the necklace around her neck, his face a mere breath away from hers. The scent of her expensive perfume intoxicated him. Forgetting all of Simon's instructions, he moved his mouth to the base of her throat and kissed her. She let out a sharp breath of air and clutched his arms. He continued kissing her neck and bit her ear with enough force to cause her to gasp, but her grip pulled him closer.

"Enjoy the next few hours with Simon," he said and then took one more bite. "When we return to this room, you're mine."

Her hands clung to his arms, her breath heavy. She stood silent and still, staring at his eyes until she released him and stepped back. She appeared to struggle to regain her composure. Thank God he didn't have to ride with them. He needed a drink.

Simon returned to the room, took Gabe's arm, and escorted her to the door. After they departed, the bar beckoned to Henry.

He'd composed himself by the time he arrived at the estate several miles from the city. A huge stone manor house illuminated by hundreds of twinkling lights and doormen dressed in full Scottish regalia reminded him of Ripon Manor.

Handing the doorman his invitation, he entered the main foyer and admired the beautiful tartan accents draped over the windows and the wool tapestries covering the walls. What had Gabe thought of the decor?

After procuring some eighteen-year McClelland's, a better-than-decent scotch, he wandered around looking over the forty or so people in the main room until Roman approached him. "Mr. Fisher. Welcome to my home. Once you are comfortable, I can show you the gallery."

"Lead on."

They climbed a flight of stairs, and Henry followed Roman down a long hall into a modern section of the house and a large room sectioned off like a museum. The configuration of the walls allowed each piece of art to stand on its own.

Henry glanced around the room for Lady Elizabeth. So far, he saw no sign of her. As they turned a corner, he caught sight of Gabe speaking to several men. Simon stood behind her focused on another group of men. From where he stood, she appeared shy and reticent, holding back her vibrant personality so no one recognized her.

He continued strolling through the gallery looking for his

painting. As he made his way into the final exhibition area, Simon approached him carrying his trademark vodka.

"Find it?" Simon asked.

"No." He held his frustration back.

"There are other locations."

"I understand. How's Belinda?" Henry tried to sound nonchalant.

"None of your business." Simon's voice told him to shut up about her.

Henry pulled himself back into his role as art buyer and shifted his eyes from the people in the room to the walls and the millions of dollars displayed. "I'd like to find a painting, but I'm unsure which. Any suggestions?"

"Let's take a stroll, and I'll point out my favorites." Simon led him back through the maze and suggested several charcoal drawings and sketches that Henry could purchase for his fictitious clients. "This one is part of a sketchbook stolen a few years back."

They studied the drawing. It seemed familiar. "Who's the artist?"

"Picasso."

"My budget is fifty thousand."

"Negotiate. Otherwise, go with the Dürer in the corner. It's less well known, but in good shape. If you'll excuse me, I need to find Belinda."

Simon would look after Gabe, so Henry turned his focus to his task. He stared at the drawing and wondered why anyone would go through the trouble of stealing a painting worth a million-plus pounds, only to recover a mere fraction of the value.

Several gentlemen arrived in front of the Picasso and debated the merits of it. Not wishing to be caught lacking in art intelligence, Henry wandered away to find the Dürer.

CHAPTER 15

⟋⟍

The exhibit offered too many distractions. How could Alex act like an empty vessel when the hosts were exhibiting *Luxembourg Gardens* by Henri Matisse? Was this the first time it had been seen since it was stolen in 2006? When she walked out of the building tonight, she might never see it again. The thought depressed her. She wanted to stare at it to absorb the colors and the emotion, but she'd risk giving herself away and placing Simon and Henry in danger if someone discovered her identity. What would her mother do in this situation? She paused at her stupid question. Her mother would never be in this situation.

After Simon abandoned her to a group of buyers from Bahrain, every man in her vicinity tried to proposition her. The name Simon Dunn carried weight in these circles, because they backed off immediately upon realizing she was his, at least for the night.

She spoke softly with whomever she met and tried to merge into the background. Her champagne glass had been refilled as soon as it dropped to one-third full. She'd be passed out on the floor if she drank all the champagne offered to her. Roman and his cronies seemed to like their women impaired and would be offering champagne throughout the evening. Alex placed her now-full drink on a decorative table with other glasses to speak to whomever was within her vicinity. When the conversation waned, she lifted up a nearly empty glass next to hers and wandered away. Within two minutes, she was holding a full glass again.

The echoes inside the room enhanced the volume, rhythm, and cadence of the guests' accents. On a normal night, she'd listen in to pick up new phrases and practice her comprehension. Tonight, however, her eavesdropping had to focus on things related to Henry's painting.

A familiar French tenor voice carried over the wall and straight into her gut. Brian Fouchet, one of Luc's art dealers. She ambled away, but kept tabs on his whereabouts. If Luc was in the building as well, her entire plan could end without beginning.

Sipping more champagne, she glanced up at a Picasso drawing. She knew the one. It was one of thirty-three from his sketchbook stolen in 2009.The paper had been manhandled and the charcoal had faded in places, but it was otherwise in decent condition. She heard someone approach and turned to see Henry standing next to her, mouthwatering in a Dior tuxedo. He wore wealth well.

"Mr. Fisher. Are you enjoying yourself?" She faced Henry, away from the opening to the room where Brian stood.

Henry acted disinterested in her. She was glad. Her heart bounding with excitement over his appearance would not help her monitor Brian's movements.

"I'm disappointed in the lack of quality portraits in the gallery." He brushed an arm across the scooped opening in the back of her dress, but didn't linger.

"Portraits must be a popular form of art." She held her voice steady through the bloom of shivers he'd caused. "I had my portrait done in high school. It sits over the fireplace in the den of my parents' main house. Standing for hours was dreadful."

"I would imagine." He was drinking scotch. Hopefully, not too much. He needed to be clearheaded. "What do you think of this drawing?"

Her eyes lifted to the painting, while her ears listened for Brian, still standing on the other side of the partition. "I like it. It's a Renoir, if I'm not mistaken?"

"It's a Picasso, but I understand the confusion. It's hard to tell all the artists apart."

"Are you going to buy it?" She couldn't hear Brian anymore. A surge of panic prepped her legs to run, but common sense forced her to remain in place.

Henry continued talking, unaware of the threat within his arm span. "I'm debating between this and the Dürer."

Fluffing the long side of her hair over half her face, she leaned in to whisper to Henry. "Do you want my opinion?" She rolled her finger over the rim of her champagne flute, trying to ignore the tension gripping her heart and freezing her muscles.

"I'd love your opinion." Henry sounded fascinated.

Brian moved behind her as she spoke to Henry. He was speaking French to one of the Russians. Something about creative financing options.

When he passed her, she took a deep breath. Her shoulders relaxed as the beat of Brian's footsteps faded away. "I would take the Picasso."

"You would?" He smiled with laughter sparkling in his eyes, pretending her opinion didn't matter. Despite his actions, he'd listen to her.

She swirled the champagne in the flute. "Absolutely. I mean, he's super famous. I've never heard of Durber before."

"I think you mean Dürer." Roman strolled up to her, encircled her waist, and pulled her close as though he'd purchased her for the night. Simon had warned her that Roman, as host, could and often did take advantage of his position to get closer to the wives and girlfriends of his guests. He wasn't as tall as her two companions, but he had five armed guards who provided him with all the strength he needed.

"That's exactly who I meant." She tried to act impressed with his wealth, power, and grandeur, but it may have come across as too welcoming of his advances. He began rubbing her arm with his thumb.

"Are you buying?" Roman asked Henry.

"I'm interested in the Picasso. Any other buyers?"

Roman nodded. "Two. Make me your best offer."

Henry stared at the sketch. His brow furrowed for a moment as though he needed to think about what to say next. "Forty, cash at the door."

"Too low."

"I'm only authorized to bid up to fifty."

"Sold." Roman fondled Alex's arm, but otherwise ignored her. "I'm glad you came tonight. You should attend the auction in Atlanta next week. I hear they have a few portraits in the time period your client is interested in, and you can walk with good provenance on any item you buy."

Atlanta? Would Henry want to search overseas? That would require using Danielle's passport and possibly surviving another hair appointment. She'd be bald by the end of this adventure.

"I'll consider it." Henry sipped his scotch and moved the discussion to the history of the house.

Roman's hold on her tightened, forcing her to lean into him to maintain her balance on the darn stilettos. His hand migrated south. Henry noticed. His grip on the glass tightened enough to cause the veins on his knuckles to bulge. She smiled blankly at Henry to assure him she didn't care, but his eyes darkened and his Adam's apple throbbed.

Simon and his wonderful smile approached, one hand in his pocket and the other carrying a drink. He stepped to her side, and Roman immediately released her. She was thankful he'd come when he did, because Henry was about to make a monumentally bad call.

"I hope to see you in Atlanta, Mr. Fisher." Roman shook Henry's hand and turned to Simon. "You have a beautiful companion. Take care of her." He kissed her on the cheek and walked away to speak with another guest.

Simon began discussing the logistics of the sale with Henry. Standing a few steps behind them, she glanced at a small sketch from an unknown fourteenth-century artist while watching for Brian. A waitress handed her another glass of champagne. She held the glass, but didn't drink.

She moved to stand with the men, but froze in place as Brian stepped in front of Simon and Henry. She sucked in a sharp breath. Glancing down at the floor, she flipped her hair over her eyes so she could observe him.

"Simon, what a surprise. I didn't think you liked art, only more interesting deals." Brian clasped Simon's arm and greeted him like an old friend.

"I don't, but I promised Colin I'd help him acquire a few pieces for his clients. Brian Fouchet, meet Colin Fisher."

Brian sized up Colin and must have found him acceptable. They shook hands. Brian pointed to the lounge area. "Come. Let's all share a drink."

"I have some business to finish." Simon slapped Brian on the shoulder. "When I'm done, I'll meet you in the great hall."

Simon treated Alex, standing behind him, as though she didn't exist. She appreciated the gesture. Her legs barely held her in place while she waited for Luc's right-hand man to leave her vicinity.

Brian, after what felt like seven lifetimes, left to return to the exhibition area. His departure sent the air back into the room. Alex could breathe easier. She exhaled, fighting to keep herself from hyperventilating. She'd spent weeks evading Luc's men, and yet she'd almost walked into her enemy's grasp dressed as a party favor.

Simon and Henry meandered off to obtain the payment for the Picasso, while Alex hustled to the ladies' room to regain her composure. She'd meet them out front. A few minutes later, she headed to the main stairway. A large hand clasped her arm and spun her around. Roman? No. *Brian.* She tried to pull away, but he grabbed her chin. He was never the most handsome man in a room, or the most powerful, but he used those around him with the skill of a puppeteer.

"Alex? You look remarkably well for a dead woman," he said in French in a volume only she could hear. "Who or what brings you out of hiding?"

She couldn't let him connect her to Simon or Henry, so she stayed silent. Maybe he hadn't seen her with them. Maybe.

He stayed perfectly still, staring into her eyes with venom. He'd hold her until Luc was notified of her location unless***

She stepped back and pulled him with her. Her foot slipped on the stairs. She let out a loud screech and tried to brace herself for the fall. Brian backed away with wide eyes and a pinched mouth. Her free foot slipped over another step, and she dropped backward, hoping she didn't break anything as she flung herself down the stairs. She landed in two strong arms. Roman.

"Are you all right?" He carried her to the bottom of the stairs. A minor hero in her continuing tragedy.

She blamed the long folds of her gown and thanked Roman for his assistance with a hug and a gracious smile. Brian hadn't followed, but he would. The second Roman released her, she headed into the great hall and the crowds of people milling about after purchasing some art. She located Brian at the top of the stairs speaking with two other men. They spoke in angry hushed tones and then all of them bounded down the stairs two and three steps at a time.

She cut into one room and then circled around until she found a small back hallway. One glance back over her shoulder made her blind to the people in front of her. She slammed into someone taller and stronger than her. Henry. Her wrap and his coat draped over one of his arms.

"Ah. There you are. Ready to go?" His body blocked her escape, and she struggled to free herself of his embrace. He clasped her tighter the more she fought. "What's wrong?"

She reached out to drag him farther into the more private area of the house, but the man was an immovable object, unless he wanted to be moved.

"I've been spotted." She tried to act composed, but words rushed out in panicked whimpers. "We need to leave. Now."

Was Brian behind them?

"We need to go. Please," she begged.

Henry draped his long trench coat over her, shrouding the red gown in black. He then arranged her wrap over her shoulders and her hair, making her into a mere shadow of the vibrant blonde in the red gown.

"Shhh. I'm here. I'll take care of you."

He held her so tightly she couldn't increase her speed to anything faster than a stroll. The side door was the closest exit. Henry maneuvered her through the door and into the field-turned-parking lot, where millions of dollars' worth of automobiles stood in soggy grass and mud.

"Who is he?" he asked, his mouth touching her ear as though propositioning her for a night of sensual activities.

"I can't tell you."

His arm never left her waist, a guide, a protector. The easy manner with which he escorted her between cars tempered her urge to run as fast as she could away from Luc's malevolent employees.

"Where's Simon?" She relaxed a fraction of a shiver at the sight of Simon's Range Rover.

"He's meeting with a colleague. He'll find his own way back to the hotel."

Instead of opening the door, he spun her so her back leaned against the SUV, and then he kissed her. Deep, wet, hungry, and soul crushing. What the hell was he doing?

They needed to leave as quickly as possible. She tried to lift her head, but he murmured through volcanic kisses to relax. Relax? Her muscles didn't loosen a bit. She'd relax when they left Scotland and Luc's men behind. Hundreds of miles behind. Henry's hands brushed through her hair, and his mouth lingered over hers, refusing to let anything separate them. It almost seemed as though he was swallowing her entire being, covering her physically and emotionally so his body and his infectious cool dominated the scene.

Footsteps passed behind them, and his intentions became clear. He was shielding her from everyone's view. If anyone walked by, they would see a couple unrushed and intimate. Since Alex had never made her sex life a public spectacle, no one would assume she'd be making out with a man in the parking lot. They'd be correct in believing she wanted to jump in her car and race away, tires skidding and dirt flying. That wouldn't happen with Henry around. Everything slowed around them, and she began to trust his instincts. She kissed him back. The beating of her heart still stammered with intensity, but this new intensity had more to do with Henry than Brian.

She could hear people leaving the exhibition and driving away. He continued to kiss her lips which at any other moment would melt all her defenses. Her body sagged forward into Henry's strong arms. She left her hands by her sides, and allowed him to engulf her presence until she disappeared into him and became a person no one would notice except the man overwhelming her.

After what felt like an hour or two of this sustained concealment, his lips stopped moving, but he remained touching her, his breath coming in and out in heavy waves.

"Shhh. Stay quiet for another moment." He rested his forehead against the top of her head. His body stilled until his breathing became normal. Almost undetectable. "Ready to go?'

She couldn't speak, so she just nodded her head and then slid into the SUV.

They didn't speak on the way to the hotel. What could she say to him? *Thanks for hiding me from Brian and, by the way, your kisses have me wanting you in every possible way.* Instead, she rested her hand on his thigh. He glanced over at her, but wasn't smiling. There was nothing amorous in his expression at all.

Terrific. Not only had Brian recognized her, and a stolen Picasso was sitting in the back of their Range Rover, but the man she now craved beyond rational logic stared ahead at the road, not speaking to her. She'd escaped a relationship with Luc to avoid being involved with stolen art, and here she was wanting a relationship with the handsome buyer of a missing masterpiece.

When Henry threw the keys to the hotel valet and escorted her inside, he walked a respectful distance from her in case they had an audience. Still covered up by his coat and her scarf, she plastered her face with bored resignation and avoided any contact with him as well.

As soon as the door to the suite closed, Henry grasped her by the shoulders and his boredom switched to anger. "Who was following you?"

She struggled out of his grasp. She didn't want to speak about her past. "It was most likely a misunderstanding. A man who thought I was someone else."

"Bullshit. Something happened to change you from a relaxed, sophisticated woman to a person whose hands could not stop shaking in the car."

"I've been poked, groped, manhandled, propositioned, and leered at tonight. I'm sorry I'm not more enthusiastic about being treated with less respect than an Italian sports car." She allowed the coat and scarf to drift to the floor, leaving her vulnerable in an evening gown that left no doubt she wore nothing underneath. Henry's glances earlier in the evening made her feel wanted; now he seemed immune to her appearance.

"Tell me what happened." Henry remained face-to-face with her. He didn't seem to be buying her explanation.

If she told him the truth, he'd try to locate Luc and end up like Matt. She wouldn't risk his safety. "I can't."

He clenched his fists, but backed off, as she expected he would. As a gentleman, he'd respect her wishes, but he needed to release his tension, and huffing about seemed to work for him.

She didn't want to argue. She wanted a warm bath and a

pillow. "I'm helping you find your painting. You don't need to know more about me."

His voice deepened, and he spoke with a formidable tone. "I would never force you to reveal anything you didn't want to, but I'm confused. You act as though you trust me, but then you keep me in the dark when something evil encroaches. You won't tell me your name or where you're from. Someone's looking for you, but I don't know whether it's the police or the leader of a drug cartel."

He took off his jacket and threw it on the back of a chair. The bow tie came off next, and then the cufflinks. By the time Henry had finished taking off his rich man's uniform, he'd rolled up his shirtsleeves, unbuttoned the neck of his shirt, and tossed his shoes to the foyer.

Alex could feel his frustration and wanted to make him understand. She found a decent merlot in the bar and poured herself a glass. Henry moved to the window. His eyes faced the illuminated city on the hill behind them.

"Tell me everything," Henry insisted, still staring out into the night.

"I can't."

He bristled and returned his focus from the view to Alex. "Then tell me what you can. Our partnership won't work otherwise. I need to know if someone's going to break down my door and take you away."

Since that possibility had increased threefold since running into Brian, Henry should know something about her past. Without a baseline of knowledge, he wouldn't stand a chance against Luc.

"Where do I begin?" she asked more to herself than to Henry.

He responded anyway. "As close to your identity as you can, because I'm not in the mood for either Gabe or Belinda right now."

Perhaps she could share a blurred vision of her past. Enough to appease him without giving him the ability to hunt Luc down and get hurt. She closed her eyes for a moment and tried to frame her next set of words with precision. "My father wasn't an easy man to live with. He demanded perfect grades, appropriate activities, and conservative dress. I failed at all three. He didn't think I would amount to anything if I didn't refocus my life on my schoolwork. I disagreed. He threatened to disown me when I didn't fall in line."

The years of fighting with her father destroyed her sense of self. Even now, she couldn't quite forgive him for the humiliating lectures in front of her peers and being sent to a new school when she didn't fall in with the right sort of people.

Henry stepped closer, but Alex raised her hand to prevent him from interrupting. She needed to finish. "I disowned him before he could disown me. Europe had all the treasures a girl like me would want, so I booked a flight to Rome and disappeared. I even changed my name so no matter what I did in life, he couldn't take the credit. I'm not proud of running away, but I was young and rebellious. And it worked out great for a while. I found my calling and lived a happy and comfortable life."

Her voice caught, and she cleared her throat to continue. "I started in a position as a nobody at an auction house. I moved up fast, because I was good. I could see flaws no one else noticed. They paid me in cash, and I stayed in the background."

Henry kept his eyes focused on her. "Don't take this the wrong way, but why would an auction house trust you to make their appraisals without even a college degree?" The tone of his voice softened, and his anger seemed to be dissipating.

She took a sip of the wine, holding the glass with a trembling hand. "Instead of classes, I spent my time in high school at galleries and museums. Once I learn something, I almost never forget. With my ability to see flaws in paint and other details, I caught mistakes by some of the more established experts. They came to rely on me to inspect works before they bought or sold them."

"Sounds like a nice life. What happened?" Henry stood over her now, every bit the English earl.

She savored her wine, easing the tension in her stomach, while deciding how much Henry should know. "I met a man I'd thought was the love of my life while doing an appraisal. I gave up everything for him. No one else had ever wanted me around. When he asked me to stay with him, I said yes. Who doesn't say yes to her soul mate? I never told him my real identity. I would have, but things turned nasty so quickly." She stretched her legs across the glass table. The red silk draped over the edge and rested on the floor.

Henry knelt by her side. He clasped her hands in his, a pained expression creasing his eyes. "Are you married?"

"No." Her voice cracked as she tried to laugh at his question. "We didn't last that long. After he discovered my desire to live more inside the law than out, he decided I was a liability. Suffice to say, he wants me eliminated, and I'm trying hard to avoid that fate."

"Can I know your name?"

"No. My tormentor doesn't play fair. I need to keep him away from my family and anyone else I care about. He's already killed one man who tried to protect me. I'd rather take my own life than watch him kill the most important people to me." Her face flushed red, and the tears came down, but she ignored them and continued to drink.

He sat next to her and removed the wineglass from her hand. Wrapping his arms around her, he embraced her misery. Her body shuddered, and sobs broke loose from the wall she'd erected around her past. Why did she tell Henry anything? He'd try to play the hero, and he'd be hurt. Somehow the thought made her tears flow faster.

Henry lifted her chin and stared at her face in the way she analyzed a painting. "Don't ever think about taking your own life. Do you hear me? *Ever.*" His grip loosened, but he gritted his teeth as if holding back a harsher set of words.

She countered his anger by cradling his cheek in her hand and kissing him. His lips tasted like scotch, smoky and sweet. He kissed her back, yet left her in control. She indulged in his attention, pulling away when her body began to urge her forward to a place she still feared after Luc's assaults. Her head rested comfortably on his shoulder, and she allowed his strong arms to support her. They remained locked together for what seemed like hours. For the first time in forever, Alex felt safe.

He brushed his lips over her ear. "I can protect you if you let me."

"No offense, Henry, but you're not super qualified to be rescuing me from anyone."

The overconfident professor actually grinned. "Did I ever tell you about my stint in the Royal Navy?"

"Simon mentioned you were a medic and a potato peeler? Not too much action in those jobs." Luc and a gun versus Henry and a frying pan.

Laughter erupted from him.

She pulled her head back and glared. "It's not funny. I actually care about you."

His laughter slowed, yet his eyes glinted with humor. "You care?"

"Yes. I care about you. A lot."

He pulled her closer and kissed her again. "I care about you a lot, too. And don't worry about me, I failed at food service and was reassigned. Let's just say I'm more capable of watching your back than being a line cook."

The door slammed open, and Simon rushed inside the suite. He was speaking on his cell phone and gave only a cursory glance to Alex and Henry. "I'll be there by lunch. Bye."

He yanked off his coat and jogged toward his bedroom. The phone went back to his ear, and he disappeared.

Henry and Alex huddled together on the couch. She didn't want to leave his side, so she tucked her legs up and snuggled as close to him as possible without sitting on his lap.

Ten minutes later, Simon emerged from his room with his suitcase. He wore jeans and a white cable-knit sweater, whistling as he approached. "I have to go see Nicola. Henry, you can take the car home. I'm transporting your purchase with me for safe-keeping and to keep your hands clean. I hate to strip you of your riches, Belinda, but the Cinderella jewels must be returned."

Simon helped to remove the necklace. She handed over the earrings and thanked Simon for the loan. He disappeared out the door as quickly as he'd arrived.

"There go the glass slippers."

Henry squeezed Alex's shoulder. "Cinderella never needed the glass slippers, Sunshine. They were just an extravagant prop on an otherwise perfect woman."

CHAPTER 16

imon flew from Edinburgh to Gatwick and stopped at SIS headquarters in Vauxhall to drop off the painting. The government would use it to fund the export of illegal weapons to groups allied with Britain, and eventually funnel it through several legitimate dealers to clear title so it could be transferred back to the rightful owner.

Around lunchtime, he went to visit Nicola at her flat in Chelsea. He'd rather be drinking a pint at the Rusty Dog Pub near Henry's house, but she was expecting him. He strolled down the third-floor hallway and waved to an older couple who lived in the flat next to hers. Mr. and Mrs. Dempsey out for their afternoon stroll.

Leaning on Nicola's doorframe, he rapped three times. She opened the door, her long brunette hair cascading over one shoulder. He scanned her top with the V-neck cut low enough for her silicone breasts to escape if they felt so inclined. Jeans tight enough to be skin accentuated legs that went on forever. She must dress like that to drive him crazy.

She stepped forward and placed a hand on his hip. "Hey, gorgeous."

"Hey." He wrapped his arms around her and pulled her into him so tight, he instantly became aroused. Her body fit Simon's perfectly. He dipped his head to taste her decadent lips. She opened her mouth slightly. The tease. He took everything she offered and then drove his tongue inside her mouth for more. She moaned and allowed him to continue to possess her. Her hands brushed over his head. Those long, slender fingers then moved down his back, caressing every vertebra. The two lovers moaned erotic sounds, making sure their neighbors could hear the foreplay.

He grasped her ass with both hands and lifted her off the ground. Her legs wrapped around him, shooting Simon's core temperature up thirty degrees. Their mouths never parted as he carried her into her foyer. He kicked the door closed and loosened his grip so she could slide down his body back to earth. Once her feet hit the ground, they separated.

"If you're going to shove your tongue down my throat, you need to brush your teeth. And use mouthwash." Nicola, breathing hard, straightened her clothes. The shirt had lifted up and her tight abs peeked out over her painted-on denim.

"If you're going to be a bitch, get another partner." He headed to the kitchen to grab a soda and cool down.

"Trust me, I've tried. No one else in the agency wants you." She followed him.

He grinned and took out two Cokes, handing one to her. "I guess you're stuck then."

"Guess so."

They moved from the kitchen into one of the back bedrooms. Two desks stood side by side covered with files, a large computer, and two laptops. Surrounded by beige carpet, white walls, and wooden desks, the only color in the room came from small multi-colored pins placed on a large map of the world. An old pizza box and several discarded coffee cups from Starbucks decorated the floor.

Nicola sat at the left desk and brought up her email screen.

"I'm glad you came over. Teodor contacted us. He said he'd take the Matisse until the artifacts arrive."

Simon scanned the message. Sure enough, an email from "paulsmith" at some weed killer website counteroffered Simon's suggestion of a money drop.

"Where's the Matisse now?" He couldn't afford to lose the painting.

"The back closet in the vault."

"Fine. Set it up. Tell him that in addition to the three crates of Glocks, I want fifty Colt Pythons."

"Ambitious."

"Always."

The art funded international arms deals he and Nicola organized. Simon acted as a middleman bringing buyers and sellers together. None of the parties, except his partner Nicola, knew of Simon's affiliation with MI6.

Nicola pushed her hair behind her shoulders, exposing her long neck. Man, she turned him on. If she wasn't such a stickler for following rules and regulations, Simon would have tried to change their relationship from business to personal a long time ago. He'd prefer a diversion with a kindred spirit to a meaningless one-night stand with a waitress he'd never see again.

She studied the screen and brought up her calendar.

"I'll be in Paris for the next two weeks working with our art supplier, Luc. He's handling the artifacts from Afghanistan."

"Careful around him. He's known as much for murder as he is for art deals. Want me to come? I could be your hunky boyfriend. Brainless, but great in bed." He sauntered over to her.

In her amazing way of making him feel emasculated, she laughed and smacked his ass. "Not this time. I may have an inside track to his supplier. I hear Luc lost his girlfriend a few months ago and may be on the lookout to replace her, so a big, hunky boyfriend would be a liability. As of right now, you and I have broken up. You cheated on me, you bastard."

Simon laughed. "If you put out more, I wouldn't need to sow my oats with lesser females. And yes, I am a bastard."

She'd willingly enter the bed of an enemy in order to gain every advantage possible. Although he hated Nicola placing herself in the middle of a dangerous situation, they both chose to live their lives undercover, always at risk of being exposed. Still, he felt protective of her. "Call me if you need backup. I'll take the train over."

She waved him away, never one to ask for assistance. "You'll be calling *me* for backup, pansy boy."

Simon walked to the small window overlooking Battersea Park on the other side of the Thames and savored a few sips of his drink. *Should he ask her? Probably.* If a man couldn't trust his partner, he might as well shoot himself in the head to accelerate the inevitable.

He leaned on Nicola's desk. "A dinner guest of Henry's claimed the Lawrence in his gallery was a fake."

Nicola stopped typing on the computer and whirled her chair in his direction. "Did anyone else hear him?"

"No. *She* was some pretend college student who I still can't identify."

Her brow creased. "How did she know?"

"Something about the eyes in the portrait. Not being an expert on paint, I have no idea what she was talking about, but Henry believes her. She mentioned she was hiding from someone. I want to know more about her. She might be useful. Henry thinks so. He's decided to use her to find his painting. They helped me acquire the Picasso in Edinburgh and are going to Atlanta in a week for an auction. If they can buy it there, then everything can continue without too much involvement by us."

"And if they can't locate it?"

"Then we'll take control. Locate it and then offer enough money to the seller to take it off the market."

Nicola shook her head. "That could take a few months. And neither of us can leave until you've met with Teodor."

Simon's heart raced at the thought of Henry being hurt. Regret and guilt soured the Coke in his stomach. Taking his brother's painting had been a monumental mistake. "Last night, Roman hinted that he'd sold the painting a week ago to Quinn. We missed the damn thing by a few days. Where is it now?"

Nicola pulled up a satellite tracking program and typed in a unique identifier. A light popped up on the screen in the United States.

"Zoom in," he ordered.

The screen zoomed in on Georgia.

"Atlanta. Must be the Carleton gallery."

"Good. If it hasn't been sold already, Henry can bid on it for a fraction of the value, and we'll keep the insurance companies and our contacts in the dark. I'll reimburse him somehow without letting him know how it ended up on another continent."

Nicola shook her head. "We went through a lot of work to put it out there just to retire it."

"I didn't think he'd ever learn about the switch. What were the chances of some punk girl identifying a chemical in a blue pigment?"

"Punk?" A disparaging look appeared on Nicola's face. She was horribly intolerant of anyone who didn't fit her version of normal.

"Sort of. She had pink hair when she showed up in Oxford, dressed like a drug addict in need of a fix, although now she dresses more like an American heiress." Simon pulled out his mobile and sent Gabe's picture to Nicola.

"Did she have a name?"

"Gabrielle West."

"Do you happen to have a picture?"

"Check your email."

Nicola turned back to her screen. "I love your efficiency."

"Efficiency with a smile, baby."

She brought up a photo of Gabe riffling through Simon's dresser. Her eyes narrowed, and her mouth formed into a frown.

"The picture's at a funny angle, so I may not be able to use the facial recognition program, but I'll try. I'll also search for missing art experts and thieves and see what I can find."

Nicola had a cold, calculating, and relentless mind wrapped up in the body of a supermodel. She'd track down the identity of Henry's bride-to-be. Yet he needed to protect Henry as well. "For now, I want this investigation to remain outside the Office."

Nicola typed on the keyboard again, looking up Gabe's alias. "For now."

***

Henry woke up intertwined with Gabe on the couch, fully clothed and aching from their contorted positions. Not wanting to run into anyone from the party, they packed their bags and fled the hotel before the sun crested the horizon. When they arrived at Ripon Manor, they both escaped to their own rooms. Henry contacted the university to arrange for someone to take his classes for the week after recess and then fell asleep. When he awoke, he was starving in so many ways. A few eggs would at least ease his stomach. He searched out Gabe, but Martha told him she'd gone for a walk. It was dark when she'd returned.

Had her abuser been at the gallery? Someone had been there, and damn her that she refused to divulge the person's name. Chasing the painting was becoming less important than protecting Gabe. The trip to Atlanta seemed more and more perilous.

At dinner, Gabe, dressed in tailored blue trousers and a pewter silk blouse, appeared listless, as though a balloon had deflated a portion of her essence. Her expression, the sullen eyes and taut lips, seemed like a remnant of their conversation the night before. He blamed himself for her mood. Probing into her past did not endear him to her.

Martha served a dinner of fresh rosemary chicken sautéed vegetables and steaming bread that filled the air with a sweet and savory scent. She left the basket of bread on the table before returning to the kitchen. Henry followed her.

"Martha, would you mind terribly if I served the rest of the meal myself? Go home and have some time with your family."

"I'm in your way, am I? Good to know you value the companionship of your fiancée." A soft smile graced Martha's face. "I left a strawberry trifle in the refrigerator for dessert. I'll see you in the morning."

"Thanks. You're a treasure."

When Henry strolled back into the dining room, Gabe was standing by the china cabinet absorbed in the wood carvings that decorated the edges.

"Do you approve?" he asked.

"Very much. The men and women who took care of the house for the past two hundred years did a marvelous job protecting the wood. Not even a chip in the corners."

Henry moved behind her. She smelled of coconut shampoo infused with red wine. Different and unique, like her. Despite his hunger, he refused to touch her. She needed to make the next move in their relationship or let things simmer where they were. The simmering, however, was boiling his blood.

His breath caressed her ear, but he left a barrier between them. His body's response to her was instant and hard and weakening his resolve. He fought to calm the urge to pull her into his arms and carry her to a place where secrets didn't matter, only physical need. Her reflection in the glass of the cabinet showed her waiting for him to do something. He glanced over her shoulder at the dishes on display. "Do you recognize the pattern on the Wedgwood?"

She turned her head, and her lips came dangerously close to his. After a quick inhalation of breath and a lick of her delectable lips, she turned her gaze back to the china. "Can I take it out?"

"Go ahead."

She opened the cabinet and removed a teacup. A green vine bordered the rim with red floral accents. His mother's favorite serving pieces. Gabe pointed to a signature on the bottom of the cup. "This is a handwritten mark for Wedgwood and Bentley. I'd probably date the set in the 1770s."

Her admiration of the workmanship was evident in the way she held the cup and examined the markings. Replacing the piece in the cabinet, Gabe ran her hand lightly across the wood and then returned to her chair at the table. Too sensual, too tempting.

Henry sat next to her and tapped his fingers next to his fork, an activity that didn't involve an embarrassing tent in his pants. "Do you have identification for the airplane? I need to purchase the tickets."

She bit her lip, holding back more of her true self, and then nodded. "I'll write out the information in the morning, but please, don't share it with Simon. Not yet."

He took in a calming breath. By tomorrow, he'd have a name and an address. Henry needed to learn her true identity, craving the information like an adopted child searching for a hint of his past. He'd have to share it with his brother. Simon could locate her tormentor quicker and without exposing them all to unnecessary danger. The knowledge would also enable Henry to better protect her.

He rose from his chair and placed his hands on her shoulders. "I'll understand if you can't, but I'm asking you to trust me tonight. All night."

Storm clouds appeared in her eyes. She was battling so many demons. Part of him wanted to hug her and eliminate all her fears, yet the other part, the part with knowledge about rape victims, reminded him that she couldn't be pressured.

Her eyes focused on him, her look intense. Would she come? No. He saw the moment he lost her; she dropped her gaze to her dish, and her shoulders drooped down in defeat. "Thanks for the offer, but I can't. Not yet."

He kissed her on the cheek, and then strode off to find some scotch.

CHAPTER 17

———————— ✑ ————————

A lex's gut assured her that Henry would never hurt her. His actions told her the same thing. He'd helped her hide from Luc in Oxford and helped her to escape from Brian in Edinburgh. He'd slept in her bed and never crossed the line. He'd never lied to her. Alex paused to allow the last piece of ice chilling her heart to melt away. She trusted him. Yes, she really trusted him. And she'd let him walk away.

She lifted the plates and shuttled them into the kitchen, leaving the bottle of wine in the dining room. The old Alex would have finished off the bottle of merlot and the open bottle of chardonnay she'd found in the refrigerator. That wouldn't solve her dilemma.

Not wanting to leave the dishes for Martha on her night off, Alex washed a dish, rinsed a dish, and then placed it on the drying rack. The warm, soapy water and the sound of the water flowing into the sink and the feel of the heat between her fingers soothed her. By the time everything was neatly stacked on the counter, she'd decided to embrace life, not hide away from it, even if she risked being hurt again.

She climbed to her bedroom, brushed her teeth, and undressed. Button by button, she removed her blouse and then shimmied out of her pants. When she had stripped down to only a black bra and matching silk thong, she glanced around the room at the dime-store art. Regrettably, Henry's reproduction would have a similar value. How awful to lose not only a valuable piece of art, but a precious family heirloom.

Poor Henry. He was trying to do the right thing by protecting battered women and their children. He was a good man. It had been a long time since she'd met one of those. She should have gone with him when he'd asked. Not because she owed him, but because she wanted him more than she'd ever wanted anything in her life. Perhaps it wasn't too late.

Still dressed only in her underwear, she wandered down one hall and then another to find him. Opening a few doors in search of his room, she located her destination behind the fifth or sixth door. A large cave of a bedroom. With only the hall lights illuminating the interior, Alex crept into the room with caution. She bumped into a large dresser. Her hands rubbed over the intricate carvings and smooth marble top. The shadows in the room came into focus as her eyes adapted to the light. She looked down at the dresser she'd caressed only a moment before. This baby was a Louis XVI–style gilt-bronze-mounted marquetry inlaid piece. She wanted to examine it in the daylight. Her mind flashed to Jean-Henri Riesener, the probable designer. A giggle burst out of her. She'd come here to seduce a handsome and brave man and had been seduced by an elegant dresser instead.

She stepped with careful footing to the outline of the bed and the lump under the covers.

"Henry?" She shook the mattress.

No answer.

"Henry?" Was he mad at her? Her heart tumbled a bit. She could wake him, but that seemed rude and inhospitable. Perhaps this wasn't such a spectacular idea. She sat on the edge of his bed. He wouldn't care if she slept next to him. They'd slept in the same bed before. After sliding under the covers, she tried to sleep, but her side of the bed was too chilly. She moved closer to Henry and his body heat. The indent his weight created in the mattress helped her roll toward him. A large arm reached out and pulled her in further. Realizing that his arm brushed across her skimpy bra, she felt her cheeks heat into a blush. The rest of her burned with a strong sexual hunger that had been stored away behind icy walls. The ice, left over from Luc's physical and emotional assaults, had melted and now boiled.

His arm tugged her closer until they lay face-to-face. She inhaled the scent of his breath, a sexy Henry smell laced with scotch. He must have gone off for a drink after dinner, after her rejection. The faint glow from the hall provided enough light for her to see two sleepy eyes staring at her. His expression revealed both a desire for her in his bed and a hope that she leave. The ambivalence entranced her.

"Henry?"

"Hmmm?" His voice was low and reassuring.

"I want to thank you for helping me out last night. Not only did you sneak me out of the castle, but you remained a perfect gentleman all evening. I appreciate it."

"No problem," he whispered. He continued to stare at her.

He moved closer until their mouths touched. She reveled in the taste of him. His hand caressed her face, slanting her chin closer to him. Their kiss deepened until she was trembling in anticipation. She shifted her entire body toward his and froze.

"You have no clothes on," she whispered.

He kissed her again, traveling from her mouth to her neck to behind her ear. "I rarely do at night. Except that strange evening when you took off all of your clothes and my trousers remained firmly zipped. And in the hotel room."

"I appreciated that."

He tightened his grip. "I appreciate this visit more."

"I'm sorry I've been so unpleasant toward you."

"Already forgiven." He lifted his hand and caressed the side of her face. "Are you sharing my bed tonight to torture me or seduce me? If you want my opinion, I prefer the latter."

She did, too. "I don't know how to seduce you, but if you help me, I'm willing to try."

Her lips touched his. She felt awkward, but brave. Henry moaned and pulled back. "Are you sure?"

She kissed him again. "Absolutely sure. But I can't promise I won't freak out."

"We can go as far as you're comfortable."

She was starved for this type of intimacy with the well-built guy who had earned her trust and stole her heart. "I feel very comfortable with you tonight."

Her words seemed to energize him. His mouth covered hers. Connecting to him became her sole goal. She pressed closer. His hand roamed behind her and unclasped her bra. Alex moaned into his mouth. One tug and the bra was history. His head dropped to one of her breasts, the one Luc had branded. His hand continued its travels down her back, across her thigh, and reached between her legs. She froze as a split second of panic caused her to shudder. He started to retreat, but she clasped his hand to hold it in place. If he pulled away, she'd regret it forever. He took the hint and continued. Damn, he knew exactly what he was doing.

"As much as I love your choice of knickers, they're in the way." He pulled them down an inch, paused, and then continued until she felt the flimsy fabric drag across her legs and over her feet.

He returned his focus to her breasts, his scruff adding a unique sensation to the experience.

"That tickles," she cried out, and then dissolved into laughter.

He continued to overwhelm her nipple until she squealed. He lifted his head with a bemused grin. "Should I stop?"

When she didn't answer, he slipped a finger into the wetness between her thighs. Anxiety hovered in the background while her body appreciated the decadence of a man's attention on her most sensitive areas. Not for his benefit, but for hers. She thrust her hips toward him, trying to control the location of his fingers.

His long legs with the most amazing muscle definition

stretched out next to her. The pressure of such a solid man resting so close to her liquefied her insides, yet scared her as well. He continued to pleasure her breasts with his tongue and teeth.

He paused for a moment and reached over to his bedside table. Hearing the tear, she watched him sheath himself in latex. She stiffened briefly, preparing for Henry to thrust into her. The idea that he would dominate her body in the same way Luc had shot a tremor of panic through her. Her face grimaced in preparation for the pain.

Luc had preferred her under him, her legs spread and lying still, but Henry surprised her by rolling to his back and lifting her to the top position. The shift took away some of the fear. He'd left her in control. Empowered, she slid her body down his and angled him inside her. Each shimmy of her hips and drive forward was hers to decide, but she wanted even more. Pressure grew, and feelings of intense need overwhelmed her.

"Henry," she cried out.

He lifted his hips and pressed deeper. Her fears disappeared, and a dizzy, euphoric feeling brought her higher and higher.

"Come closer, Sunshine." He pulled her toward him and kissed her so deeply, a conquering and melding of souls. She rode him until blissful waves shook her entire body. The feelings intensified as he grasped her hips and rocked her further until everything burst open in color and light and intensity. And then he shuddered and trembled beneath her. Lips still connected, they slowed to a stillness except for the sound of heavy breathing and contented sighs. She rested her head on his shoulder, exhausted.

"Good night, Gabe," he murmured.

I'm not Gabe.

"Alex," she mumbled in reply and slid into a contented sleep.

***

Alex? Who the hell was Alex?

Henry spent a night that should have been heaven with the

most amazing woman he'd ever met in a cold panic. Did he just learn the name of *the love of her life* as she'd described her former boyfriend? If this guy had been her former lover, his technique with her had been despicable. It had been impossible to anticipate what would please her, because so many things had made her skittish. What sort of man would break a woman down and almost destroy her ability to make love? She couldn't love him still. How could a woman love an abusive man? The answer kicked him in the gut. His mother and Simon's mother both had loved their abuser.

She stirred in his arms. Half her body rested on top of him with one leg curved across his thigh. Blond hair covered most of her face. He smoothed it behind her ear and tucked her head under his chin. Her breathing created a soothing, rhythmic meditation to ease his frayed nerves.

She'd panicked as he was prepared to enter her. Her body had noticeably stiffened and her eyes had flinched. Henry had almost stopped everything in order to hold her and relax her nerves, but his mind told him Gabe would recoil at the idea of him comforting her. So he'd rotated her on top and allowed her to control everything. If she'd wished to stop, she'd be in a position to do so. Thank God, she hadn't, because being with her had been heaven. What they shared wasn't sex; it was better, more satisfying.

Which is why her saying this guy's name as she drifted off to sleep didn't make sense. Not only had it seemed like the guy had abused her sexually, but he'd also taken out his aggression on the rest of her body as well. She wore the scars to prove it. Reminded of his father's rages, Henry's stomach clenched like a fist. He wanted a few minutes alone with this idiot to explain the basic principles of chivalry.

He fell asleep hours later, waking when Gabe's hands began a detailed exploration of his body. She spent the next hour caressing every minute section of him. The attention drove him crazy, but he gave her the control. When it was his turn, she seemed a thousand times more relaxed than the night before. She allowed Henry to take the lead. Her body welcomed him without the slightest pause or hesitation. He savored the emotion rocketing through her eyes as she came apart under him.

"Good morning." She let her hand drift across his cheek and down his neck, her contented smile shining in his direction.

"Great morning." He kissed her, and then rested his head back on the pillow to look at her.

She wanted to be with him. No artifice, no duplicity. Nothing had ever felt so perfect, so right. He wanted her to stay in his bed forever, despite her unknowns.

As soon as they returned from Atlanta, he would request an end to all of her secrets. But for now, until he'd gained her trust completely, he'd be patient.

At breakfast, she placed a passport next to his plate. A French passport. Henry peered at the woman in the photo. *Danielle Perrault.* She was twenty-four with short brown hair and hazel eyes. She had a heart-shaped face similar to Gabe's, but her cheekbones didn't sit as high and her eyes seemed too close together. She was not blessed with Gabe's symmetry.

The adorable tilted position of Gabe's head and the annoyed twitch of the left side of her mouth made the differences between the two women even more noticeable. "As you can tell, it's not me."

It appeared authentic right down to the stamps on many of the pages. "Did you steal it?"

"The previous owner won't miss it." She shrugged and feigned a relaxed smile that didn't begin to express happiness. She grabbed the streaky bacon with her fingers and took a bite. Her eyes dropped to focus on her coffee cup. Her bad manners almost shifted the attention away from her apprehension. Henry could see through the facade. She was nervous, as she should be.

If caught with a fake passport, she could end up in jail. And what about the monster chasing her? He rubbed his temples to massage away some of the tension building inside him. "I know you want to help me, and I'm eternally grateful, but nothing, not even the Ripon Women's Group, is worth you being placed in danger."

She rested her hand over his. "It'll be fine. Please don't stop me. I need to focus on something other than my pathetic life. And if we succeed, think of the families we'll help."

Using his own words against him. He glanced down at the passport.

"She's younger than you." He tested a theory. "That could be a problem."

"Only by a couple of years." She pulled back her hand and huffed out a breath. "I'm twenty-six."

"Not twenty-four?"

She glared at him, but stayed silent. One more crack in the facade she'd created around herself.

"I hate to say this, but Miss Perrault has brown hair and greenish eyes." Henry glanced between the picture and Gabe. It was close, but not perfect.

Her shoulders lifted in a slight shrug. "Your choice. Either we forget chasing down your painting, or I need some hair color, makeup, and colored contacts. It may cost up to a hundred pounds."

He rubbed his temples again. "My hundred pounds?"

"Henry, whose painting are we searching for?"

CHAPTER 18

S imon hated the idea of French cafés. A quiet English pub had more privacy and better beer. He tucked himself into the farthest corner of the place and ordered a Coke. Only two other tables had patrons at them, located on the other side of the room. Simon kept his distance. He didn't trust anyone, the waitstaff included. He caught up on emails for almost an hour, then the energy around him shifted. She made it. Nicola strutted between the empty tables and chairs wearing a tight black skirt cut to reveal the maximum amount of leg and a loose white blouse without a bra. She radiated sexual satisfaction. Someone was getting some, and it wasn't him.

Glances of lust followed her from a table of men by the door. They'd better put their eyes back in their heads and focus on their own pathetic lives, because Simon required privacy for this conversation. The information Henry had given him about Gabe's fake passport linked her to Luc Perrault. That placed his brother in the middle of something deadly.

"Darling, nice to see you." Nicola kissed him on each cheek when he stood to greet her. Her face held zero emotion.

"Sit." He pulled out the chair next to him. "How's your holiday?"

They sat close enough to carry on a conversation safely. After Nicola ordered a café au lait, she leaned back in her seat away from Simon. They couldn't jeopardize her cover by appearing to like each other. Her new French lover had a jealous streak the width of the Pacific Ocean.

She rolled her eyes and appeared bored. "Luc told me that Danielle, his sister, is traveling around Thailand and won't be returning for several months. Seems odd when her passport is traveling to the States this afternoon."

Simon took a sip of his drink, slammed the glass down, and then clenched his fists. "I've contacted Interpol. They'll be monitoring Gabe's movements with Danielle's passport in and out of the US. I'll have them contact the Thai government to track down Ms. Perrault and her companion Travis Poole, some Yank from San Francisco."

"You're on the ball, as usual. As to the other name, Luc never mentioned an Alex, and I'm hesitant to ask. I did overhear him speaking about an ex-girlfriend who disappeared about two months ago. She's some sort of linguistic genius, knows around twenty languages." She shook her head and stood.

Simon grabbed her arm and pulled her closer. His expression flashed to emulate the anger of an ex-suitor. "This girlfriend could be Gabe. We need more information. If he's the one she's running from, and he finds her, she doesn't stand much of a chance. Luc doesn't mess around when he wants someone dead. Three of his associates have ended up in the morgue so far this year."

"You're not even positive she's the girlfriend."

"I'm not positive about anything with Gabe. Although she did mumble in French when she first appeared in Henry's house, I've never seen her act as though she understood anyone speaking a foreign language. She does, however, have Luc's sister's passport. To be safe, we should keep them apart. Stay close to Luc for the time being. If you sense things going south, get the hell out of there." He released her, and she stepped back.

"I know how to do my job. I'll stick to him like glue once he returns." She strode across the cafe.

Simon threw down a few euros and followed. "Returns?"

"He'll be back in two days. Don't worry." She sauntered toward the door, but he caught her arm again.

When they stepped outside, Nicola pulled away. She had to appear as though he wanted her back, but she preferred staying with Luc. Simon braced himself. She'd always staged these scenes with more emotion than necessary.

"Go to hell." She slapped his face hard. Pain shot through his jaw, and his eyes watered. She'd held nothing back, the pain in the ass. By the time he blinked away the stinging, she'd fled across the street.

"Already there." He turned and walked in the opposite direction.

***

Alex didn't feel safe in the United States until she and Henry were sitting in the rented red Mustang convertible and driving away from the airport. During the entire journey, she'd spoken fluent French and broken English. Aside from an uncomfortable double take by a Homeland Security agent, she breezed through airport security using Danielle's identity. Sneaking into her home country while posing as a foreign national caused conflicted feelings. She hadn't been home in eight years. If Luc wasn't pursuing her, she'd consider winding her way up the East Coast to her home in Concord. A year ago, she would have returned a success in her field. Her father would have been proud. Not so much now. Now she was a fugitive with no job and no future.

Henry pulled up to the valet at the W hotel in the middle of Atlanta and handed over the luggage, except for a computer bag containing the cash to purchase the portrait. A tour bus load of people crowded around the sleek registration desk. Harried employees dressed in black tried to ease everyone's nerves by offering free drinks in the bar. Alex took a coupon and kissed Henry on the cheek.

"I'll hang out in the bar while you check us in."

A moment's hesitation told her he didn't want her to leave. "I don't think that's a good idea." He clasped her hand as though she'd run if he let her out of his sight.

"I'm thirsty. I'll be right back. I made a promise to help you, and unless the dreaded zombie apocalypse occurs, I'll be by your side until you have the painting back in your possession. I have a gut feeling we'll be celebrating tomorrow night."

He kissed her, and an honest-to-God warm fuzzy feeling filled her insides. She'd never been cherished, not by her parents, her friends, or Luc. With Henry, however, she could imagine someone wanting a happily ever after with her, even if the "ever after" lasted for only three weeks.

"I'll meet you in a few minutes. Don't get into trouble."

"*Moi?* I'm the queen of coolheaded and rational decision making."

He frowned. "I'll try to speed things up."

Alex found her way to the crowded bar. No one had turned down the free drink, especially the people on the bus tour. She located a table in a quiet corner and ordered a Diet Coke.

A manicured guy in a well-made business suit came up to her table. His grin made him appear like a politician scoping out a new personal assistant. A very personal assistant. "Hey, beautiful. Mind if I sit down?"

She shook her head. "I'm waiting for my boyfriend."

He frowned, and moved to another single woman sitting at the bar. Alex watched him in action. Within three minutes, he had his hand on the woman's knee. And she wasn't complaining. An older, heavier-set guy at the far end of the bar glanced over at Alex. He rose and stepped toward her. Great.

This was not the easy free drink she'd anticipated. She rose to leave before he could annoy her and noticed a badass stud in faded jeans and a brown leather jacket at the entrance. A scowling badass. There wasn't an ounce of English anthropology professor in that guy. And as much as Alex adored the Earl of Ripon, she totally crushed on his alter ego.

He nodded his head toward the door, and Alex followed him out. How could she resist when he was acting all possessive and protective? It was a major turn-on. He led her out of the room and up the elevator. At the feel of his strong arms wrapped around her, her heart steadied from a heavy staccato rhythm to something pretty damn close to love.

Henry leaned against the wall of the elevator. The muscles in his shoulders lowered from pissed to more relaxed. "You were the center of attention."

She couldn't help but smile at her adorable champion. "I think they wanted to buy me a drink with their free drink coupon."

"This hotel is the closest one to the gallery. Did you notice anyone who will be at the gallery tomorrow?" He lifted his eyebrows and waited for her answer.

"They don't exactly announce their intentions to random strangers."

His took a deep breath and exhaled slowly. "Exactly. And yet you placed yourself in a situation where someone might recognize you. Since I don't know who's after you, I have to assume everyone wants you."

His worry now made sense.

When they closed the door of their hotel room, Henry turned toward her. "I don't know whether you attract trouble or trouble attracts you. How long did I leave you alone? Five minutes?"

"Trouble tends to locate me wherever I am." She snuggled into the smell of Henry and new leather. "Why would I look for trouble? I landed a bona fide earl, complete with a castle, and a reproduction of a portrait of a woman I've never heard of. Do you take me for a fool, Colin?"

"I'm Henry tonight. I wish I knew your real name. I don't tend to sleep with women until after I have their names."

"You can call me Gabe, Belinda, Danielle, or Sunshine. I'll even let you call me Baby for this night only."

"Come closer, Baby." His devilish smirk told her where they were headed for the next few hours. When she shimmied up next to him, he kissed her. She pushed his jacket off and removed his shirt. A dramatic swing of her arm sent the clothes soaring to a nearby chair. A sexy, bare-chested Henry reached behind her and unzipped her orange dress. He peeled the dress from her shoulders and pulled it down her body to the floor. Alex stood before Henry in a hot-pink bra, matching thong, and uncomfortable strappy sandals.

"Nice." He tugged her closer and removed the top half of her lingerie.

A knock on the door interrupted his hand's journey across her bare stomach.

"Ignore it. They'll go away," Alex said, licking his lips. He tasted of the peppermint he'd had in the car. She pressed her lips into his until he kissed back with a carnal intensity that urged her into actions she'd never craved before.

Another knock. He retreated and left her panting and frustrated.

"Hold that thought." He threw her his shirt to cover up. She slipped it on and scooted behind the door an instant before he opened it.

"A package for you, sir."

"A package?"

"It says it's from your brother, no name is given." Henry took the box from the bellhop and handed him a decent tip. Alex could hear the kid mumbling a thank-you as Henry shut the door behind him.

"A present from Simon?" she asked.

"Apparently." He ripped off the tape and opened the package. Inside, a handgun, complete with a box of ammunition, rested between large pieces of Styrofoam.

He pulled out the gun, checked the chambers, and sighted it

toward the window. Wearing the same smile as a little boy on Christmas morning, he tilted it back and forth, feeling the weight of it in his hand, and then opened the smaller box, took out several rounds, and loaded his new weapon. Guns and Henry didn't seem a likely partnership, except for the shotguns displayed at the manor for killing innocent ducks and pheasants. Yet he handled his present as though he and handguns were old friends.

Something seemed strange about the entire package. "How did Simon ship a weapon and bullets from the UK to the US?"

"I assume he used a source in the States. Quite thoughtful." He placed the gun in the bag with the money and unpacked his tuxedo for the auction.

She watched him move around the room. Those muscles should not be gracing the torso of a dorky anthropologist, but she appreciated them all the same.

"Henry, what is that tattoo on your shoulder?" A two-inch high sword with two wavy lines behind it decorated his right shoulder. She didn't recognize the symbols.

"From my days in the service."

"The mess hall or the medic division?"

"Special Boat Service." He continued unpacking and never looked toward her.

Her lack of knowledge about British military operations irked her. She hated not having information at her fingertips. "Boat maintenance?"

"Something like that." He smirked, and Lord help her, she wanted to bite that smirk right off those amazing lips.

"You're not going to tell me, are you? Give me access to your computer, just for a minute."

Holding his shaving kit in his hand, he stopped unpacking and stared at her. "Sorry, *Baby*. I'll let you use my laptop and tell you more about me when you spill a little more about yourself." He lifted her wrist up. "What's your coat of arms? An acorn?"

"No." She pulled her wrist out of his hand. "From my recollection, the Chilton coat of arms has a single red chevron across it. No dragons or crossed swords for you?"

"Nice deflection. Are you a student of heraldry?"

"I've memorized a lot of family crests. It comes in handy when evaluating paintings, but I learned yours because it sits over the fireplace in the great hall at the castle."

Henry placed his shaving kit in the bathroom. When he returned, he took hold of her wrist and kissed her tattoo. "And the acorn?"

She laughed. "An acorn is a baby oak. It's not my family's coat of arms, but should be. Instead, the family crest is green and white and isn't much more interesting than yours."

He kissed his way up her arm, stopping at her neck. "Does yours include a dragon?" he asked before returning to his seduction.

"No." She tried not to moan, but he was nipping at the edge of her ear, and she could hardly speak.

"A skull and crossbones?" He blew his warm breath over the damp body parts as he finished nibbling them.

A shiver ran down her back. She curved her body into his arms. "Fun, but no."

Henry yanked his shirt over her head. He tossed it onto the chair again.

"I'll wait for you to disclose your secrets at your pace, but I'm growing impatient." He stepped back, leaving her feeling very naked with only her thong covering a minimal amount of skin.

"Can I give you anything besides background information?"

He crossed his arms over his chest and those damn biceps flexed. "No. I have a Mustang convertible, a castle, and a gun. What more could a man want?"

"Come here and I'll show you." Alex dragged Henry by his belt loop toward the bed.

She undressed him, stopping with his zipper down and his jeans hanging off his hips.

"Are you going to finish?" he asked, choking out the words.

"I hope so, but you look so hot in those jeans. I'm hesitant to take them off."

Henry chuckled and stripped Alex of her one remaining clothing item, and then he sat on the bed waiting for her next move. She loved how he gave her control when she needed it. She felt stronger and less vulnerable with him than with anyone else.

When she finished removing his clothes, his erection demanded attention. She hesitated, and then knelt in front of him. From the heated look in his eyes, her gift was unexpected, but appreciated. She licked him from base to tip and then took his entire length in her mouth.

"You don't have to do this," he moaned.

Releasing him from her throat, she peered up at him. A slight smile curved her mouth. "Should I stop?"

His breathing was getting ragged. "I don't want you to, but if you're not comfortable—"

"I want to." After giving him a smile that told him not to argue, she returned to her exquisite form of torture.

Her hands slid up his legs, and she caressed him with feather-soft touches. Sex was amazing with the right person— empowering, comforting, exhilarating. And dominance could shift from one partner to the other at any time. His long aristocratic fingers wove through her hair and held her close. Not controlling, but comforting, encouraging. And she drew him in further and massaged him with her lips and her tongue from the base to the tip and back again. His low moan encouraged her to go deeper. He dropped his hands to her breasts, stroking her, motivating her, and leading her further into her own arousal and sexual satisfaction.

He pulled her up onto his lap and kissed her until she melted into a state of helpless surrender.

"I need you, Sunshine." His voice strained between heavy breaths and long kisses.

"I need you, too." And she did. She needed the strength, and his acceptance of her flaws and imperfections, and she needed him physically in her and near her and by her side.

They tumbled back onto the bed, and she rolled onto her back. He pushed off her and returned with a condom. He hesitated before sitting next to her and brushed his fingers through her hair.

"Nervous?" she asked.

"Terrified. You're tying my heart into knots. Be gentle with me." He kissed her on the lips with such sweet intentions, tears formed in her eyes.

"Relax, Lord Henry. I promise not to hurt you."

He grinned at her comment with the confidence of a man born to wealth and power. And yet he didn't scare her at all, not like Luc had. Henry somehow uncovered all of her weaknesses and twisted them into strengths. He gave her a quick kiss, and then they fumbled with the condom until any remaining awkwardness floated away with their laughter. His touch changed this once-brutal position into something tender and empowering. She felt both completely controlled and completely in control.

His lips grazed under her ear, and his moans reverberated into the deepest regions of her chest. The sensations shot lightning bolts of hot electricity through her system and sent her over the edge and into oblivion.

CHAPTER 19

—————————— ❧ ——————————

Henry had spent the entire afternoon intoxicated on Gabe's unique brand of sensuality. Her previous inhibitions created by a lowlife seemed to have evaporated. Playful, sexy, and adventurous in and out of bed, Gabe could satisfy a man for a lifetime. By the time they finally moved to the large bathtub to play some more and prepare for the auction, Henry's time with Gabe had permanently altered his heart. No one would take her place. Another woman could fill certain roles in his life, but this intelligent, gorgeous seductress had managed to wipe out the competition and make him unable to consider anyone else in her place.

Reluctant to separate, they forced themselves to prepare for the night's big event, finding Lady Elizabeth. Henry wore his tuxedo. The gun Simon sent to him was secure in a holster at his waist. He didn't want trouble, but he'd protect Gabe from any threats that came her way. No matter what.

Gabe donned a shimmering gold gown. Her short brown hair, which must be close to her natural color, fell over one of Danielle's beguiling green eyes. This woman didn't look anything like Simon's date in Edinburgh. He hoped. Despite Gabe's penchant for bacon and high-fat breakfasts, her body showed not the slightest bit of extra body fat. A lean warrior with the face of a fairy, she bewitched him.

She strode over to him and straightened his bow tie, which didn't need straightening. Henry had been wearing tuxedos all his life and would never create a crooked tie. Her proximity was a wonderful excuse to smooth down the lines of her dress, which didn't need smoothing. His hands glided over the silky material. He felt nothing underneath her dress from the bodice to the top of her thighs. Too bad they were late. He'd never get his fill of her.

They hired a car to drive them to the Mandarin Oriental exactly two blocks away from the W. The invitees to this soiree would never walk the streets to their destination.

A uniformed doorman helped Gabe out of the car. Henry tipped the driver and told him to return when he received a text. They may wish to depart in thirty minutes or be gone all night. Hopefully, the former.

"Ready?" Gabe wrapped her arm around his.

Henry clasped her elbow and gave her a reassuring squeeze. "Absolutely. The gallery is on the forty-fifth floor. This card will gain us entry." He showed her a business card that had one word on it, "Lakshmi."

"Hindu goddess of wealth. Very appropriate," Gabe stated.

"How did you know that?" He'd always believed himself to be highly intelligent, but Alex's depth of knowledge eclipsed everything he'd learned in a lifetime of university classes and reading books.

"Henry, information is readily available on the internet. I could have Googled it."

"If you had access to my computer, or you saw the card before this minute, I would believe you."

She sighed. "Doesn't everyone know deities?"

"Maybe Greek and Roman mythology, not necessarily Hindu."

She shrugged her shoulders as though it was no big deal that she'd amassed so much information in however long she'd been alive.

Another uniformed guard asked their destination.

"Floor forty-five." Henry handed the man the card and was led to a private lift.

Once inside, he pressed up against her and drank in her enthusiastic response. Their kiss lasted forty-four floors. Hopefully, they'd find the painting tonight, so he could channel all of his energy into keeping her by his side for longer than three weeks.

When the doors opened, they stepped out into a huge foyer decorated with large vases of orange, yellow, and red roses. Henry handed Gabe a champagne flute, and they meandered around the gallery looking at the art. She perused a few of the works for sale, keeping her expression neutral. The displayed, mostly stolen, pieces of art all had good provenance, ownership papers obtained by skirting the law, so legitimate buyers wandered the rooms with confidence in their potential purchases. Most of the buyers had no idea they were walking through the gray market for art. The more knowledgeable collectors understood that sculptures and paintings were never priced this low in the real world, but they didn't care about the art's origins. They looked at it as an investment. Not one work of art in this gallery had the cachet of the stolen masterpieces they'd viewed in Edinburgh, allowing buyers to display them without fear of prosecution.

"What do you think of this one?" Henry pointed to a painting called *Woman With a Pigeon*.

"I don't think your clients will like it. It's too dark." Which meant, she wouldn't buy it.

She took a tentative sip of the champagne and glanced around with a vapid expression directed at the people more than the art. Henry could sense her mind taking in information from the pretty boys showing off for their dates to the crowds forming around certain works of art and not others. Although Gabe had been sipping her champagne for thirty minutes, the liquid remained near the same level.

"Do you like it?" he asked about another painting.

"No. I'm more partial to romanticism. It sounds prettier." She giggled as though her whole purpose was to please the man in her life. As fascinating a prospect as that was, he loved standing beside a genius. He'd prefer to have a companion by his side who would challenge him, not just decorate him. Perhaps he'd have the opportunity to accompany Gabe to a museum after all of this subterfuge to listen to her unrestrained opinion of the art around her.

They continued to chat about the many paintings, icons, and statues that surrounded them. Her eyes revealed a nuanced understanding of every work of art in the room, but she divulged only a mere hint of her intelligence. Turning the corner into one of the many secondary spaces, Henry stalled in front of the other woman in his life, Lady Elizabeth Gillett. He bit back the grin threatening to emerge as the weight of losing her lifted up and left him practically hovering off the ground. Larger than most of the art offered for sale, she had a new gilded frame, but otherwise appeared exactly as she had been before being replaced by the new version.

"She's beautiful." The clouds in Gabe's eyes dissipated as the discerning art appraiser analyzed Henry's most precious asset. "The frame appears in good condition, but the other one is authentic, so I'd probably return it to the original." Her voice stayed low, beneath the hearing range of the others in the room.

"I agree," Henry whispered in her ear. He couldn't resist nuzzling her neck while he was there. He had the woman of his dreams next to him and Lady Elizabeth in front of him. Life was near perfect.

Alex stared up at the painting and then turned back to him. "The colors in her face and in the background are more suitable to the time period. Her eyes have a softer sheen and the entire picture encapsulates the movement of her balancing on the horse. In my opinion, this is one of Lawrence's finest pieces. If***no, *when* you buy it, leave it up in Ripon. She'll grace the halls of that old castle, displaying something amazing for the women and children to enjoy."

A few others gathered in front of the painting to view it. Gabe moved closer to his side, but Henry acted bored with his date and his painting. Being possessive of anything in this room could lead to trouble. He only had so much money to fend off competitors.

"There's nothing here worth buying. Can we find some food?" Gabe asked.

"Maybe there's something in the next room." Henry led her away from their potential competitors and perused several more items.

A gentleman in a very expensive suit strolled over to them. He held out his hand to Henry. "Richard Quinn."

Simon had mentioned that Mr. Quinn was a part owner of the gallery and might introduce himself.

"Colin Fisher."

"Nice to meet you." He turned his attention to Gabe. "Enjoying yourselves?"

"Yes. This is the best champagne I've had in forever." Gabe lifted her glass in a toast and took a sip.

Richard smiled at her, approving of her comment and her appearance. She had to be careful. She didn't realize the potent reaction her flirtations were causing with the men around her. For someone who didn't wish to be noticed, she created a stunning vision in gold.

Richard waved over a server to provide Gabe with another glass. "I'm glad you approve." He turned to Henry. "Mr. Fisher, have you found anything you wish to take home for your clients?"

Henry gave him a slow nod. "Perhaps. What time will the lot in room eight be auctioned?"

"We're planning on having those five paintings and the two statues moved to the main gallery in about half an hour. Are you interested in anything in particular?"

"The statue by Edvard Eriksen, the Emile Claus painting, and perhaps the portrait by Thomas Lawrence."

"Good choices. We look forward to seeing your bids." He nodded to them and walked away.

Henry placed an arm around Gabe's waist to protect her from the onslaught of admirers. The muscles in her arm stiffened. He glanced in the direction of her gaze. A group of unknown men stood by the bar discussing something serious.

"Colin, do you mind if I run to the restroom?" she whispered in his ear.

"By all means, go. I'll wait here."

Instead of turning away, the golden goddess embraced him. Her arms encircled his shoulders, floated down his arms, and rested on his waist. The woman was pure sexual energy. Her hand brushed over the gun, but he shifted her away from it. He didn't need her accidentally discharging it.

Nuzzling her lips against his neck, she molded her body into his. He tried not to physically react, but she raised his temperature just being in his line of sight. When she touched him, he became insane with the need to scoop her up and rush her back to the hotel.

Not yet.

First, they needed the painting. She brushed her lips over his mouth and then ended the kiss with a sigh. As she walked away, her hips swayed with an invitation to Henry for later.

***

Alex didn't want to run away, but what choice did she have? When her eyes locked onto Luc, standing in the corner of the gallery speaking to a bunch of men, including Brian Fouchet, she knew her fairy tale had ended. Henry didn't deserve to be caught in her nightmare. After everything he'd given to her including a piece of his heart, she needed to protect him as well as her family. And now that he'd found the painting, the Ripon Women's Group would thrive.

Luc stood out in a crowd of wannabes with his jet-black hair, dark eyes, and a scruffy elegance that women lusted after and men envied.

Did he see me?

Even if he hadn't, she needed to get out of there. She clasped her hands together to keep the tremors from being too evident and forced her legs to walk in a confident, quick step.

The ladies' restroom was near the elevator. She could hide in there for a few minutes and take the next available car down. Her only choice. Henry's gun had been her best means of killing Luc, but he'd pushed her hand away from it, probably thinking he was protecting her. But she was kidding herself; she didn't have had the guts to kill Luc in cold blood.

At least she'd left Henry behind. Her heart, however, deflated in her chest as she stepped through the crowd farther and farther away from the only person outside of her family she'd willingly die for. Wearing a plastic smile, she wandered between small groups of men and women and arrived in the foyer. Some of her tension lifted as the restroom came into view.

"Alexandra Northrop, as I live and breathe," the female voice rang out, sounding cloyingly familiar.

Alex ignored it and tried to continue forward. A woman's hand grasped her elbow. *Crap.* She gazed over her shoulder, trying to keep her face as covered as possible. "I think you have the wrong person."

"No, I don't. We went to the Winsor School together. Holly Knight. Remember? You were on academic probation eight times during one year. It was a school record."

Holly Knight was the bitchy daughter of an oil commodity brokerage firm executive. No surprise she'd buy stolen art at discount prices. The pieces would probably be donated to a museum for a juicy tax write-off. Dishonest to the end. Alex had hated watching Holly and her friends torment many of the less fortunate students. They stayed away from Alex because her father's power and her mother's social connections had few rivals.

Perhaps if she acknowledged Holly, she could get out quicker.

"Holly? What a surprise. What have you been up to all these years?" She kept her voice low and her actions subtle.

"I've done it all. In fact, I married one of Jeff Bezos's right hand men, Sam Porter. We have a beautiful son and an amazing property in Palm Beach. I have to introduce you to Sam. Are you married?"

"No. Not so lucky."

"You'll find someone. You're adorable. How are your parents? Still have that gorgeous house on Martha's Vineyard? You were the envy of everyone when the Kennedy boys decided to crash your sixteenth birthday. What a group of hunky guys. Remember?"

"Fun times. Are you staying for the auction? I'd love to catch up, but I need a minute in the ladies' room."

"Absolutely. I'll be with Sam by the blue boxy painting two rooms over."

"The one by Georges Braque?"

"Yes, that one." The style was cubism, not boxy. Holly may have inherited a trust fund, but she'd never acquired the brains to go along with her wealth.

"See you soon." Alex waved and started toward the bathroom.

Three steps away from Holly, she saw Luc coming toward her. Like a predator stalking his prey into a corner, all of his attention focused on her. He had to have heard her conversation. *Shit.*

He strode with a confidence that had once controlled Alex's thoughts and actions. His eyes penetrated her calm facade, and a tsunami of terror almost knocked her off her feet.

A crowd of thirty people separated her from him. He was closing the gap. The doorman would never let her pass now, especially if Luc told him to detain her. Pushing off panic, she searched for another way out.

One chance. That's all she had. Throngs of people crowded into the foyer waiting as the gallery staff brought two new groups of auction items into the next room. The chaos of the crowd and the servers and the men moving the art seemed like an accident waiting to happen. When she brushed against one of the waitresses carrying the trays of champagne, a plan formed in her mind.

She pivoted toward Luc and stared into his callous blue eyes. He sneered. She shot back her own brand of confidence. *Not today, Luc.* Volleying back a wink and a smirk, she pushed her stiletto into the toe of the closest waitress's foot and gave her a hip check; the girl yelped, drawing all the attention in their direction.

As the girl fell, Alex *attempted* to save the tray of champagne flutes but instead, she launched them toward Luc and another cocktail waitress carrying another tray. At least forty Baccarat crystal stems soared into the air in Luc's direction. Everyone scattered back, except Alex. The crash of the crystal on the tiled floor drew more people into the foyer. She ran straight past Luc, temporarily blinded by the champagne dripping from his eyes.

Slowing to a graceful pace, she moved from room to room searching for an exit and trying to avoid Luc, Brian, and Henry. A few of the waitstaff hurried out the kitchen door, probably to clean the mess. She darted inside.

The kitchen was deserted except for two college-age boys who were dressed in kitchen whites and arranging dessert trays. With a drunk wobble, a grab for the counter, and a display of her breasts, Alex caught the attention of the two young men.

"Hi guys, is there a bathroom here? The main bathroom has a line five women deep." She danced foot to foot and bit her lower lip.

"Down the hall, but it's kind of gross." The shorter of the two pointed toward the food pantries.

"Trust me, it will be grosser if I don't find a bathroom." She gave them a simpering laugh and waddled away.

Luc would be searching for her and blocking exits in a matter of minutes.

After closing the bathroom door, she glanced around at the cleaning supplies and the hooks with employee belongings displayed for her selection. Her chance of escape had just increased significantly.

Alex angled her arm behind her and tugged the zipper of the gown. The gown ripped from the force she used, but she'd never wear it again after tonight. She stuffed it and her heels behind a pile of cleaning supplies. With luck, no one would find it until the next day.

She rummaged around. A pair of jeans and a stained white T-shirt left in the corner of the room fit her needs perfectly. She wet her hair down, pushed it behind her ears, and placed a Braves cap on her head. The contents of her small purse fit easily into her pockets. She hid the purse with her dress. Her feet would have to stay bare in order to move as quickly as possible.

With a small prayer for Henry's safety, she bolted out the door and made her way to an illuminated exit sign. Stairs. An alarm system linked to the exit door could announce her location, but this was not the time for cowardice.

Pushing it open without pause, without hesitation, she hustled through and ran down the stairs. No alarm rang out in her ears, but that didn't mean a silent alarm hadn't been triggered in an office at another location. She spun down the stairs floor after floor. Forty-five floors needed to be covered as quickly as possible. Her chest hurt from running at top speed, and the dusty air of the stairwell dried her throat. Around floor twenty, she tripped. Her body fell five stairs to a landing. She remained on the ground as the energy that had motivated her down the stairwell evaporated. Standing, she dusted herself off to soothe her nerves and then continued. Her legs hurt from the exertion, but she didn't stop until she was one floor below the lobby.

Completely out of breath, she placed her hands on her knees, inhaling and exhaling until her legs stopped shaking and she could exit the stairwell. The door opened easily into a nonpublic area.

"Hello?" a voice called out from across the maintenance room.

Alex was silent for a moment, tucked behind a stack of

wooden crates. Her father repeated his philosophy of life so often, it had engraved itself into her psyche. *Success comes to people who don't panic in a crisis.* One lesson from him she took to heart.

Taking several deep breaths, she calmed her fears and gained a jolt of energy. A security guard passed her hiding spot on his way to the stairwell. She counted to three, then bolted.

A large loading dock stood as a beacon to her freedom. She blasted through the plastic barrier and hopped off the platform. Clenching her fists to get control of her fear, she slowed as she turned onto the main road and then strolled by the entrance to the building and into the night.

CHAPTER 20

Henry ran toward a loud explosion of crystal in the foyer. Everyone else had the same idea. Where was Gabe? He pushed his way through the crowds. Shattered glass hindered his path. Champagne coated the floor among the remnants of crystal flutes. Several individuals had cuts on their legs. The clumsy waitress sat on the ground weeping among shards of broken glass. No sign of Gabe.

A dark-haired man, screaming expletives in French, had the most damage to his outfit. The champagne had covered him from his head to his feet. God help that waitress who couldn't keep her balance.

"*Merde.*" He called to someone Henry recognized as the man Simon joined for a late-night drink in Edinburgh. "*Brian, trouves Alex rapidement.*"

Several new servers approached the guy to help him. He waved them all away, clearly upset he couldn't find this Alex fellow. *Alex?* It couldn't be a coincidence. His presence would explain Gabe's departure from his side almost ten minutes ago. Did she run from him or run away with him?

"Pardon me," Henry called out to a passing waitress. "Have you seen a woman in a gold evening gown?"

The petite blonde angled her head toward Henry. The look on her face told him to avoid mentioning his connection to her. "The bitch who tripped Candy? Everyone's searching for her."

That didn't bode well for Gabe's fate. Where the hell was she? He searched each section of the gallery and waited by the ladies' room several minutes. By the time the mess in the foyer had been cleaned up, his nerves sizzled, but panic wouldn't help him. Patience and a plan had been his best weapons in the military and would be now.

Although he hesitated to enter the lift, his instincts told him she'd left the building. Perhaps she'd returned to the hotel. As the doors closed to take him downstairs, the auctioneer announced the starting bid for the Sir Thomas Lawrence portrait, *Lady on a Horse*. Acid churned in his gut, and his throat constricted. The auction. He fought the urge to throw his hand between the closing doors and bolt into the auction room. The doors sealed shut and so did Henry's chances of securing the painting to fund the castle renovations.

The ride took forever. He wanted to pound the door in frustration, but the elderly couple next to him didn't need to see a lunatic unleashed. He held back his aggravation and rage by clenching his teeth and his hands. The painting might be lost to him forever, but he had bigger issues to deal with. He mourned for his legacy, he mourned for the Ripon Women's Group, but those feelings were diminished over the loss of Gabe. He'd give up everything he owned to return her safely to his side, no matter why she'd fled.

Stepping into the lobby, Henry reached into his pocket to retrieve his mobile to text the driver. Something hard rubbed against his fingers. He knew the instant his fingertips touched it. The black sapphire ring. She must have dropped the ring in his pocket when she hugged him. Alex didn't kidnap her. She'd either left willingly with him, or she'd escaped Alex and had given Henry a token to say good-bye.

He exited the building and walked toward his hotel as he dialed Simon.

Simon's voice sounded jovial. "Henry, do you have the portrait?"

"No." Henry didn't wait to be questioned by Simon, he needed answers quickly. "Did you find out who Danielle Perrault is? Or Alex?"

Simon paused, and his voice turned more serious, mirroring Henry's tone. "Sorry about the delay, we've been searching for more information. Danielle Perrault is the name of the sister of someone we're monitoring. He provides the fine art collateral for the gunrunners to use in their larger purchases. Luc Perrault."

"Luc?" *L.P. The initials over Gabe's breast. Shit. If Danielle was this guy's sister, was Luc Gabe's ex-boyfriend?*

"Yeah. We still haven't figured out who Alex is."

"What's he look like, this Luc fellow?" Henry picked up his pace toward the hotel.

"Longer dark hair, medium height, medium build. More Mediterranean than French."

Simon perfectly described the man covered in champagne. From the way he'd ordered everyone around, he had to be the biggest player in the room. "I think I saw him at the auction. Screaming at that French guy you introduced me to in Scotland."

"Brian Fouchet?"

"I guess." He paused for a red light at a busy intersection, his impatience growing.

"Give them space. They care less about art than they do about profit. Do you think Gabe is actually Danielle?"

"No. She appears too different from the passport photo. Gabe also has a tattoo on her chest. The initials 'L.P.'"

Simon swore. "That's a bloody significant thing to forget to tell me. Where's Gabe now?"

"I don't know. She disappeared. I'm heading back to the hotel to search for her."

The phone went silent for a few seconds. "Be careful. Luc is deadly. He's one of the biggest dealers in stolen antiquities from Afghanistan and Cambodia."

Luc had to be the man who had threatened her and forced her on the run. He had to be the man who had hurt her physically and emotionally. Panic rose in his gut. He'd led her right into his hands. "I'm going back to our hotel room now. I have to find her."

"Without the portrait?"

"Are you serious? I don't care about the damned portrait. I have to find Gabe."

"I understand, but she could go back to black hair and Goth clothes and disappear into the nearest university town."

She had five hundred pounds in addition to some euros and dollars. She could make a clean break.

"If she goes underground, we'll never find her." Henry jogged toward the hotel.

"We need more information. Anything else you can think of about her identity?"

"One more tattoo. An acorn on her wrist."

"I noticed that one. I'll call the analysts at the office to see if they can decipher all of this new information. Get back to the hotel and see if she made it."

"I'm on my way. How can we be sure she's linked to this Luc person?"

"This is going to sound funny, but have you noticed whether Gabe is fluent in any foreign languages?" Simon asked.

"She spoke fluent French on the plane over. Why?"

"The ex-girlfriend of Luc is some sort of linguistic genius. No one is sure how many languages she knows, but it's a lot."

***

Alex tucked all of her loose hair into the baseball cap as she walked. She bent over to alter her posture and cruised through the lobby in bare feet and stolen clothes with a firm destination in mind. Her hotel room.

The elevators, however, weren't cooperating. Alex monitored the front door for signs of Luc or Henry. The tapping of her foot, the only outward sign of her agitation, stopped as soon as she realized how impatient she appeared. When she heard the soft *ping* announcing the arrival of the elevator to the farthest left, she strolled over, allowed a heavyset businessman in a golf shirt to exit, and then slid in and rapidly pushed her floor button three times. As the doors closed, Alex prayed no one would throw a wayward foot between the doors to stall her escape. When the elevator finally lifted, Alex paced back and forth until she reached the eighth floor.

Sprinting down the hall, she entered the room, ripped open her suitcase, and took out her two passports. She changed into a plain black T-shirt and her own jeans and threw on the new Converse Henry had purchased for her.

Henry.

She couldn't think about him right now; she needed to protect her family, especially if Luc did learn her true identity. Besides, Henry would be better off without her. A life in the country raising a gaggle of children with a devoted spouse could be his future. Her future, on the other hand, had become tainted the moment she fell for Luc, and Henry didn't deserve to follow her into such a mess. She jogged to the door carrying her most practical possessions in a plastic laundry bag courtesy of the W. Her new suitcase was far too big to drag down the elevator. She paused at the front closet. Henry's new leather jacket reminded her of him. She threw it on and hustled out the door.

When the elevator hit the lobby, she headed to the valet and handed him the claim ticket.

"What type of car?" he asked.

"Mustang convertible. Red." She tried to sound breezy and carefree, but her heart thundered beneath Henry's jacket.

"Nice. I'll be right back."

The minute the man left for the garage, Alex spotted Henry entering the front door. She ducked behind the valet stand. His footsteps passed her hiding spot and traveled toward the bank of elevators. She remained hidden until his elevator arrived and departed. She had maybe three minutes to get the car.

Where was the valet? There was no one in front of her. She stood with her back pushed against the outside of the building. Each time an elevator door opened, she ducked down in case Henry returned. After the arrival of six different elevators, the valet drove up to the curb. Alex practically pulled him out of the driver's seat.

"Here, keep the change." She handed him one of the two hundred-dollar bills Henry had given her earlier. Most of her funds remained in euros and pounds, the equivalent of monopoly money outside of a major bank or exchange.

"Don't you need change?"

"All set. Thanks." She never looked back, just hit the gas and drove. The car traveled through Atlanta going straight and turning right on red to avoid stopping until she found the expressway. The champagne in her system would have a minimal effect on her driving, as she'd only had about ten sips the entire evening, but her body required food. The pangs from her empty stomach and her revved-up nerves interfered with her focus. Clear focus equaled escape. Clouded focus would result in total chaos for her and everyone she loved.

Outside the city limits, her heartbeat slowed down, and the queasiness in her stomach faded to just short of an ulcer. Cold air whipped over the top of the windshield and heat blew onto her feet and traveled up to warm her torso. She found a classical music station on the radio. The fugue by Bach soothed her nerves, but reminded her of Henry's love of classical music. A sharp pain in her chest replaced the hunger in her stomach. She allowed her tears to fall as she drove away from the one person who tolerated her obsession with art and her unique personality and seemed to enjoy them.

Henry would someday fade into a bittersweet memory, but Luc inhabited her current nightmare. He must have heard Holly screech out her real name. She needed to contact her family and warn them immediately. If only she wasn't such a coward, Luc would be dead, and her family would be safe. Protecting them took priority over everything, including her aversion to murder.

She pulled off the highway in a nowhere town and found a convenience store. A sign on the door indicated that no bills larger than twenty dollars would be accepted. Using her Belinda clueless personality, she convinced the clerk to accept a hundred-dollar bill in exchange for some gas, Slim Jims, a Coke, and a map of the area. The skinny kid with blond hair covering his eyes not only gave her change, but he offered to take her out for a drink when he got off work in an hour.

He seemed like a genuinely nice person who would make a girl ten years younger than Alex blush with his sincere compliments. Her hand brushed over his when she reached for the change. "I can't tonight, but why don't you give me your phone number, and I'll call you if I free up tomorrow?"

"Seriously? Cool." He grabbed an advertisement for a local strawberry festival and scribbled his name and number on it.

Alex graced him with her most genuine smile, the kind of smile that entranced young men and made teachers overlook missing homework assignments. "Thanks. Can I borrow your phone for a second?"

"Sure." He slid his cell phone to her.

She walked a few feet away and called her parents' house.

The number was no longer in service. Of course not. They often changed the unlisted number to prevent every Tom, Dick, and hustler from trying to contact her father about their newest innovation or her mother about a worthy cause that required the family foundation's support. Her parents protected their privacy for safety and sanity reasons. Only their longtime friends knew the number. Alex, however, had been AWOL for so long no one could have informed her of the change without an international manhunt. Her last email to her sister Julia had been too long ago. Calling her father's office wouldn't help. It was closed at this hour and their personal cell phone numbers were more difficult to obtain than the Permissive Action Link codes on the nation's nuclear arsenal.

Alex walked around the shop trying to devise a method for contacting her family. Cardboard Easter bunnies and eggs decorated the walls and the windows. The family always spent Easter weekend at their cottage in Martha's Vineyard. She recalled those periods as nirvana, marked by cool weather, deserted beaches, and time alone with her sisters, her mother, and occasionally, her father. Everyone should be there now. She dialed the cottage number. Disconnected.

Keeping a cheery disposition and trying to avoid plunging into a fit of despair, she acknowledged the store clerk with a wink and perky scrunch of her nose. She had one more chance at warning them: her sister Anna's cell phone. Anna often refused to follow the security demands made by their father. She'd jumped off the career path and out of the media's glare to raise two children with her loser husband, Jason; at least that was the intel from Julia when they'd last spoken.

A little girl answered. "Hi. You've reached Anna Northrop Dillard's phone. Please leave a message." What could Alex say? That she was being chased by a murderer and was warning the family before they became Luc's next victims? Yep. That's exactly what she needed to say.

"Anna, it's Alex. We may be in Code Delta. I'm on the way to the cottage." Her heart raced with the realization that she'd just warned her family of a death threat. If they received the message, security would be increased for all family members. She hated frightening them, but the warning was necessary.

She erased her call history, returned to the counter, and then handed the kid back his phone. "Thank you."

She reached for his phone number, folded it, and slid it into the back pocket of her jeans.

"So I'll wait for your call." He leaned against the counter like the stud he'd be in a few years. Perhaps he'd find a local beauty and have two point five kids. If she had options, she'd choose that life with Henry.

"Sounds great." A quick wave and she was out the door.

She drove a half mile away to a hidden pull-off on the side of a soybean field in order to plan her next move and rest. Several hours later, her neck ached as though someone had twisted it, a pasty film coated her mouth, and the moon had disappeared. So much for a quick escape. She had to find a more efficient means to travel to Massachusetts than driving a stolen car or boarding a plane with a stolen passport. She would use her real passport, but it had expired several years before. She'd only held on to it in case she ever required assistance from the US embassy. Using it on a plane now, she'd be pulled into security and never get home.

The drive to Charlotte, North Carolina, took four hours. Her driving skills were rusty, and the buffeting from the massive tandem trailers and big rigs screaming by her kept her wide awake for the entire journey. The adrenaline charging her system while running from the hotel decreased to a simmer. Except for a knot in her stomach, a rock in her throat, and a dagger in her heart, she felt fine.

She arrived in the parking lot of an all-night Walmart in a cookie-cutter suburb by 6:00 a.m. She fluffed her hair, put on Henry's jacket, and cruised into the store as though she was picking up a gallon of milk after a long night at work.

She found a sports duffel bag to carry her limited worldly possessions. She then made her way over to the electronics department searching for the right television, the right person. Her target wore a University of North Carolina sweatshirt. A twentysomething with a yearning for an oversized Smart TV. After leering at it for several minutes, he shrugged and moved on to a smaller version. Bingo.

"Excuse me, sir?"

He glanced at her outfit and grinned, apparently thinking she was worth speaking with for at least a few minutes. "Yes?"

"I was wondering if you could do me a huge favor? I have to

access some cash but my boyfriend seems to have emptied my bank account."

Doubt and suspicion clouded his face and lowered his eyebrows. "So you want my money? Sorry, babe, but***"

"I don't want your money. I want to use my credit card to buy that television for you." She pointed at the flat screen of his dreams. "For six hundred dollars, cash. It's a savings of over a thousand dollars, but no returns, for obvious reasons."

He stared back at the TV with a lust he'd probably never harbored for a woman. "Six hundred?"

"Cash."

"I'll need to run to the ATM."

"I can wait." She wandered around the store while she waited as though she made transactions like this all the time. The hunting department contained a few side display cases with a selection of bowie knives. She picked out one with an ivory handle and a leather case, although in reality, the ivory was a cheap laminated knockoff. It seemed shorter than the others, about a six-inch blade instead of the usual nine- or twelve-inch blade. At least it was 1095 carbon steel. Strong enough to pierce Luc's malevolent heart.

Ten minutes later, her mark arrived with a tall, muscular friend dressed for a day on a construction site in worn jeans, a faded blue T-shirt, and work boots. From the grins on their faces, they obviously thought she was desperate. She was, but she wouldn't be held hostage. She still had the car, a half tank of gas, and eighty-eight dollars and thirty-two cents.

"Jesse was waiting for me in the truck. He can help carry it," her target said in response to her lifted eyebrows.

She assisted them in moving the massive box to the checkout counter, along with help from the store stock crew. The cashier also rang through the duffel bag, the knife, a bottle of water, and a bag of Doritos. She hadn't enjoyed those since she'd left for Europe. Pulling out the credit card she'd found in Simon's closet, she held her breath, hoping the transaction went through. It did.

In the parking lot, a thick wad of twenty-dollar bills filled her pockets, providing her with her first reason to smile since seeing Luc. The two men walked away with their dream television. All in all, a good deal for everyone, except Simon.

Next item of business, she had to ditch the car. Too bad, because it was a sweet ride, but she'd never make it up the East Coast alone in a shiny red convertible with a tracking device beaming her GPS coordinates. She abandoned it in a garage a few blocks from the train station in Charlotte.

The next train departed toward Providence, Rhode Island, via Washington, DC, at 7:00 a.m. Alex purchased a coach seat and hopped aboard. Ten minutes later, the first train of her journey left the station.

CHAPTER 21

Simon hung up his phone and cursed. The conniving wood nymph had stolen his credit card and was out shopping for a television set. What the hell was she going to do with it? Sell it?

He punched the bed in his third-rate Parisian hotel room hard. Yes. She'd sell it for a fraction of the cost and walk away with the cash. Damn it to hell. He'd misjudged her over and over again, from letting her gain access to Henry's house to not searching her before leaving his bedroom, to flying her to the States, her home turf no less, with enough cash to go anywhere and a smitten earl at her beck and call. He'd never botched an assignment more in his life.

His blond conquest from the night before stirred. "Simon, ça va?" Her bronzed skin looked decadent on top of the bunched-up white sheets. His already-heated blood shifted focus. The temptress stretched her arms above her head, flexing the muscles in her chest and elongating her lean stomach. A perfect respite from the chaos brewing outside. She turned on her side and motioned him over.

His smile returned. "Yeah. Everything's fine."

One more journey in this woman's embrace would go a long way toward keeping his demons at bay. He rested his head on the pillow next to her and began to rub her lower back and the smooth skin of her ass. He'd call Henry after he had his fill of Valerie.

A knock on the door broke the moment. Simon stilled. If his competitors found him, he'd have more to worry about than a stolen credit card and Henry's painting.

The knock continued, more rapidly and aggressively. Simon placed his finger on Valerie's lips to keep her quiet and then pulled out his gun.

"Who is it?" he called out in English, stepping to the door stark naked and carrying the Beretta in his hand.

"Open up, lover boy." Nicola's voice penetrated the wood and scorched his veins.

What the hell did she want? He opened the door, knowing she'd never leave until she gained entry. Nicola, wearing black leggings, black knee-high boots, and a long gray transparent shirt, pushed her way past him without so much as a glance at his naked body until she arrived at the foot of the bed. If he had to choose a lover at that moment between Valerie and Nicola, he'd have to flip a coin. They both wore sex like a weapon.

Not one to be disturbed by his state of undress, Nicola examined him from shoulder to toe, making his manhood retreat at the indignity, and then she turned to Simon's last bit of sanity, the beautiful woman lying in the bed. "Am I interrupting anything?"

"Not anymore." He slipped on his jeans and threw Valerie her little black dress.

Nicola sat in the small, stained chair by a window overlooking the side of a brick wall and watched Simon and Valerie dress.

Valerie bolted as soon as she pulled her dress down, carrying her shoes out the door. The deadly glare she'd launched toward Nicola was received with a smirk. His partner reveled in screwing with others' lives.

"She seemed nice." Nicola opened the two-thirds-empty bottle of Russian Standard vodka on the table and took a swig.

"Piss off."

She stood and moved to his side. "Feeling frustrated?" He wished his father's beatings had knocked the morals out of him and not into him, because at that moment, he longed to entice Nicola onto the bed and finish what he'd started with Valerie.

"What the hell do you want? Shouldn't you be at Luc's house?"

She caressed his arm and smiled as he took a step back. "I needed an update and thought I'd get it firsthand."

"Your only job at present is to monitor Luc and find his contact in Kabul. Figure it out and then get the hell out of there."

"It's difficult to learn anything from him since he's still traveling around."

"He's not back?" The news couldn't have been worse. It had to be him in Atlanta. Was he going after Gabe? He clenched his fists, damning himself for not taking care of everything himself.

"I anticipate he'll return today or tomorrow morning."

She shrugged as though this was normal for Luc. She'd only spent the past six days with him, and yet her responses implied more than a week's worth of intimacy. When she embedded herself, she went all the way. Her eyes locked with his, and her expression transformed from sophisticated girlfriend to experienced operational officer. "You keep me chasing artifacts while you get to negotiate deals of steel. My skills are becoming rusty. Next case, I get the guns, you secure the collateral."

"I've had my share of shitty assignments, too. Grow some balls and do your job."

She stiffened and then glared at him. "When do you meet with Teodor?"

"Tomorrow."

"Good." She slouched onto the bed and leaned against the headboard, an awkward place to see her after everything he and

Valerie did in the same spot a few hours before. "How's Henry doing with his quest?"

"Dismally. He's too focused on Gabe's absence."

"Didn't she accompany him to Atlanta?"

"She disappeared during the auction. Henry let the painting get away in order to chase her down. He may have spotted Luc." Simon needed vodka more than Nicola did. He took the bottle Nicola hadn't bothered to recap and upturned it, letting the liquid burn his throat. After one more swig, he relaxed.

"Did we lose it?" she asked.

"I have a call in to Quinn. I want to know where the painting is at all times." Another sip, another step closer to serenity. "Who knew a piece of art could cause so much trouble?"

"You offered it. 'No bother,' you said at Secretary Hanlen's request. 'My brother will never miss it, he rarely steps foot in his gallery.'" Her snicker did nothing to diminish his concern for Henry and Gabe. They'd become caught in this web because of him. Hopefully, Henry wouldn't have his heart broken in addition to losing his heirloom.

"He's not too focused on the painting right now. Gabe has some link to Luc. Henry saw Luc's initials tattooed on her chest."

"The missing girlfriend?"

"Probably. Henry has no idea where to find her, and I haven't had any new information to offer him. All I know is he thinks he saw Luc at the auction in Atlanta. Now both Gabe and Luc are missing."

"I'll try to find out his location." Nicola stretched out her legs and crossed her arms over her chest. She appeared exhausted. Sleeping with the enemy always frayed nerves and caused insomnia.

"You look like shit. Why don't you take a nap here and then go back?"

As usual, she became an enraged adolescent at his comment about her needing anything to perform her job better. She slid off the bed. "I'm fine. Just wanted to check in."

"Consider yourself checked in. Sure you don't want to stay? My morning somehow freed up during the past twenty minutes."

"*Quel dommage.*" She grabbed her purse and opened the door. "Good luck tomorrow." She strode away without a backward glance.

***

During the long hours of her train ride, Alex slept a little, stared out the window, and nursed a severe case of melancholy. Each mile down the track separated her farther from Henry. Her heart broke in two, severed by distance and unbearable circumstances, but protecting him was paramount.

Arriving in Washington, DC, Alex had a five-and-a-half-hour wait for the next train to Providence. She wandered into the sunny afternoon, enjoying the freedom of walking around for a few hours without the fear of discovery.

At the local McDonald's, she attached the knife case to the inside of her waistband. If she angled the long knife toward her hip and under Henry's leather jacket, no one would notice it, but she could reach it with ease. It wasn't a gun, but it should work if Luc came close enough.

She purchased a bacon cheeseburger and a bottle of water. Nothing tasted quite right. Perhaps her taste buds had soured permanently. Besides eating junk food, Alex had nothing to do but regret her cowardice in running away from Luc. She should have killed him at the gallery with a broken champagne flute, a small marble statue, or a shove through the window. Forty-five stories straight down in a free fall would have killed him, but the moment had passed, and he was alive, and she was running.

She headed toward the train station, but the allure of the tattoo parlor across the street provided her a perfect time killer for the final half hour before the train left. The careful placement of three small and, hopefully, inexpensive lines would eliminate Luc's mark forever.

The train to Providence took six hours. The travel exhausted Alex, but she continued onward. She couldn't take the chance of someone getting hurt because she'd dallied. The bus out to Woods Hole in southern Cape Cod didn't cost as much as she'd expected, providing her with a few additional funds after buying a ferry ticket to Martha's Vineyard.

When she stepped foot on the ferry, she started to relax. On a clear day, the island could be seen from the mainland. If the boat went down, Alex could swim the final half mile to her parents' house. Nothing would stop her now.

Would her family be mad at her?

And her sisters. God, how she'd missed them. Despite being labeled as the odd sister, she'd always craved their approval, love, and respect. They tried to understand her, but they just didn't get her method of learning through immersion. Speaking only Spanish to the housekeeper, only French to the au pair, and only Korean to the woman at the library, she became fluent within months of beginning a new language. She only needed to learn a word once, and it would stick in her brain. The way her mind processed and decoded information didn't interest others; it scared the hell out of them, as though some demon had possessed her.

When she realized other people couldn't learn languages as quickly or distinguish the material composition of things in quite the same way she could, she tried to hide her talents. But it was impossible. She not only saw the world differently, she reacted to it differently. For years, she'd believed she'd been poisoned by a radioactive isotope and had received special powers. The powers, however, had never proven to be of the superhero variety.

She lost her father's respect, because, in her father's words, *she didn't use her God-given talents to make something of herself.* If she'd achieved high grades and graduated from college, perhaps he would have loved her more.

She went to the bathroom to brush her hair, rinse her face, and remove her "Danielle" contacts. Back to brown hair, brown eyes, old jeans, and an old T-shirt. She almost resembled the frightened young woman who had left home eight years ago with a small duffel bag and five thousand dollars cash to book a plane overseas and begin a new life. Alex Northrop, daughter of Peter and Gabrielle, sister of Anna and Julia, had disappeared that day. Today, she was going home.

CHAPTER 22

Simon drove an hour north of Paris to Betz. On the outskirts of the village, he turned onto a long driveway toward a fifteenth-century stone farmhouse surrounded by fields recently prepared for new crops.

He remained in his rented Mercedes until Teodor arrived in a chestnut Maybach.

They both exited their vehicles, meeting in the middle of the gravel drive. The familiar adrenaline rush heightened Simon's senses. Teodor would love to kill him and take over his business. Literally, cutting out the middleman. Chances were, however, he wouldn't. Simon arranged the best arms deals and had the lowest failure rate, and the majority of his arrangements worked to perfection for all sides. Besides, if he made an attempt on Simon's life, Teodor would be dead within seconds by a bullet to the brain delivered by the sniper located in the attic of the farmhouse.

"Nothing says trust like an armored vehicle." Simon tapped Teodor's arm as they shook hands.

"Too true." Teodor knocked on the Kevlar vest Simon wore under his jacket. "Where's Luc?"

"He has something brewing in the States. I have possession of all of the artifacts, so there should be no problems." A situation Simon hated. "Do you have your appraiser with you?"

"Yeah. He's good, but I'd prefer the appraiser Luc used a few months ago. Alex."

Alex? "Never met him."

Teodor threw his head back and laughed. "Not a him, a hot young thing with a keen eye for detecting forgeries." He raised his eyebrows to indicate just how lush.

Son of a bitch. All this time he'd been focused on some bloke, and Alex was in his arms, literally. "Short and elfin?"

"Yeah, Alex Lemoine, a sweet French confection. Imagine a woman who can determine authenticity on sight during the day and snuggle into bed with you at night. The perfect companion. Smart as hell, too. She greeted me in Ukrainian and spoke to some of the American dealers in fluent English. Every deal she handled for Luc went off perfectly, according to my contacts."

"What happened to her?"

"No idea. Her first mistake was trusting Luc. He'd convinced her the work was connected to the cultural office of Warsaw."

Everyone in the game profited from using gullible people. Simon, however, didn't think Alex was the type to be taken in, which explained how she ended up in Oxford and not rotting away at the bottom of a garbage dump.

Simon smiled for Teodor's sake. "Sounds like a gold mine. I never knew her name, but I remember hearing about her."

"Perhaps she learned too much. I hope he didn't kill her. It would be a waste of a good asset." Teodor shrugged, turned to his car, and waved the occupants out.

Two men emerged, one in a business suit and the other in jeans and a sweatshirt. "Simon, you've met Jarek. He'll help transfer your purchase."

The more casual man's face bore the signs of a man standing in close proximity to a mortar attack. Pock marks, streaks of scarring, and the partial loss of his ear provided him with a sinister appearance, the result of tampering with explosives without proper training. Jarek nodded his greeting and then turned away to speak on his phone.

Teodor shifted his attention to the guy in the suit. "Leonard is my newest appraiser. Stole him away from the Hermitage."

Too bad the guy didn't realize that his new lucrative paycheck would result in a shortened life span. Sometimes they lasted only a few weeks. Luckily, Alex had street-smarts and was a master of disguise. He temporarily forgave her for stealing his credit card. To survive in his fucked-up world, sometimes people needed to lie, steal, or murder.

Simon texted his contact and within five minutes, two helicopters approached and landed in adjoining fields. An Arpía Black Hawk, probably purchased by Teodor from a crooked Argentinian general, contained several green boxes full of an arms cache.

Simon's team used a Mi-17, stolen from Syria. It contained millions of dollars' worth of artifacts from Afghanistan, smuggled out by Luc's connections.

Teodor and Simon stood as sentries watching the transfer of goods.

Thirty minutes later, the helicopters took off.

The arms, now safely flying over the French countryside, would be tagged and sent on to Afghanistan. Regrettably for the Taliban, the transportation would experience roadblocks and the ISI in Pakistan would be waiting to confiscate the shipment.

Simon smiled. Nicola would be happy to hear everything went according to plan. After losing her brother to a bullet fired by Taliban forces years ago, she'd committed herself to shifting the flow of guns to the people who would have made her brother safe. She needed to be careful, however, not to lose her soul trying to right all the wrongs of the past.

***

Renting a bike and cycling across the island from the ferry

terminal, past tall dune grass and sand dunes spilling along the back roads leading to her house, Alex felt the terror of the past few days dissipate. Her father had the resources to protect the family. They'd all be safe with the added protection she'd demand they put in place. She needed to explain to them how deep the danger ran through each of their lives because of Alex's bad choices. And she wanted to be close to them.

She wanted to go home.

After another half hour pedaling, the house came into view. It hadn't changed in eight years, a noble eight-bedroom refuge on the edge of the sea. Large windows opened up to a perfect view of Nantucket Sound. Memories flooded her, like the summer her father refused to buy her a Jet Ski because she'd failed math class. She'd refused to eat until he'd relented. What a spoiled little girl she'd been. She'd never appreciated her birthright until she'd abandoned it to start over with nothing.

She turned onto a path two houses before hers, leading to the beach. It would be easier to arrive in the back, the place where everyone always congregated. Each house in the area faced the water across a huge section of private beachfront. The residents granted neighbors the use of their sections to stroll through on the way to Edgartown. Reciprocity among the wealthy, as long as the common tourists stayed away.

Alex tucked the bike into a row of bushes. It would be perfectly safe. Their section of the island was deserted at this time of year as most of the neighbors stayed on the mainland until the temperature tipped over eighty-five degrees. She pulled off her sneakers and dug her toes into the sand. No sand in the world felt as good to her. She strolled along the edge of the water, carrying her bag and sneakers, until the squeal of children in the distance caught her attention.

The heavy emotions she'd worn for the past few days lifted into a mild euphoria. Her family was here and in sight. A little girl and boy played by the edge of the water. Anna had given birth to a daughter a few years back and a son more recently. Alex could be seeing them for the first time. Too far away to get a clear look, she picked up her pace.

"Alex." The voice, low, sophisticated, and deadly, came from behind her.

Luc.

Pain and panic ripped through her chest. She almost ran toward her house, but intuition told her to freeze where she was. Glancing over her shoulder, she nearly collapsed at the sight of the man who had transformed from her beloved to her mortal enemy.

Luc strolled down the beach wearing a white blazer and navy pants, an outfit more appropriate for Saint-Tropez than the Vineyard. His hands were tucked in his pockets as though he had not a care in the world. A stranger might interpret his appearance as carefree and confident. Alex knew better. His handsome face and winsome smile hid his true intent. To kill her. Had she really been in love with him once?

"Alex. *Quelle coïncidence que nous sommes ici ensemble.* But perhaps I should be speaking English to you. Impressive for an American to convince everyone around her that she was French. Me included. Alex Lemoine, interesting name, more beautiful perhaps than Alexandra Northrop, but not as prestigious as the missing heiress to the Oak fortune."

Lemoine. The name had made sense eight years before. A favorite artist in the Boston Museum of Fine Arts, Jacques-Antoine-Marie Lemoine, provided her with a cover for her simple life working for the auction houses and living in a flat by Saint-Germain. When Luc, a handsome and mysterious art broker, had offered Alex extra income for a few short assignments, the naive girl jumped at the opportunity. She'd escaped a controlling father only to become trapped by an even more controlling lover.

His arm reached around her shoulders, and he pulled her close. If only she had Henry's gun right now, she could end this faster than the speed of sound. She did, however, have the knife and a close proximity to her target.

He switched back to French. "I'm disappointed in you. Running away, hiding your identity. You'll be punished. Or perhaps we should punish one of your newly discovered relations instead."

She refused to speak. What was the point? Action would help her more. She dropped her sneakers and bag in the sand.

Reaching for the knife with as much stealth as she could muster, she turned toward him. The handle warmed in her grip, the blade pointed toward her target. She thrust it at his heart. She moved fast enough to hit his rib, but without enough force to penetrate the beating organ that only pretended to love her.

"Bitch." Luc grabbed for the knife. Alex waved it in front of him, making a dangerous target for a hand to grasp. Tightening her grip, she took another swing, but he was prepared and threw his hand into her face to push her away. The impact knocked her back and sent a shot of pain through her nose. Her eyes stung and began to water, obstructing her vision.

Focus on the goal. Protect the family.

She stepped toward him again, swinging her arm without pause, creating a better chance at hitting him and preventing him from grabbing it. He moved like a dancer near a limbo stick. He was also bleeding through his shirt.

Oh my God, he was too fast and too strong.

She thrust toward his face, but Luc caught her wrist. Before he had time to gloat, she grabbed the knife with her other hand and tried to stab his neck.

"Enough." He pulled the arm in his grasp back hard. The force caused her to lose her balance.

This time, he held both of her wrists, kicked out her legs from under her, and fell on top of her. The body weight crushed down on her and pinned her on the sand. She continued to struggle, but one of his hands freed and pulled her hair until she released the knife. He tossed it toward the water. Searing pain burned her scalp. Tears fell across her cheeks.

His mouth covered hers to muffle any cry for help. She tried to bite him, but he went on the offense and took hold of her upper lip with his teeth until she stopped moving her head. Her heart beat rapidly against his chest. Luc's fierce presence muddled her brain, preventing her from thinking of a way out of her predicament.

She was out of breath and exhausted. He lifted his head up, and Alex saw in his eyes the flaming rage of a man who'd just fought for his life.

Despite his heavy breathing, he spoke with a chilling control that would offer no quarter to the woman under him. "Remember this, Alexandra Northrop, I will kill each and every member of your family if you ever try to hurt me again. Do you understand?"

Her nod was impeded by his hand over her windpipe.

Luc permitted her to sit up while he retrieved her weapon. He then buttoned his jacket to cover the blood leeching through his shirt.

The children farther down the beach had stopped and stared at them. Two women who may have been her sisters hustled the children into the house.

Soon, the beach was empty except for a security guard dressed in black walking toward them. Did he work for her family? They'd never had much security when she was younger. Perhaps Anna received her warning, and her father increased their presence. Thank God she had help on the way. If he could occupy Luc's attention, she could get to the house and warn her family.

Luc pulled her to her feet, placed his arm around her and squeezed. The pressure hurt her ribs, but she didn't make a noise. They both limped away from the shore and toward a row of tall dune grass that blocked the view to the house. The security guard followed. She didn't dare make an escape attempt. Yet.

The man, older with graying temples and wisdom in his eyes, was enormous compared to Luc. A hero worthy of taking down her enemy. He approached with his hand resting on a revolver hooked to his belt. "This beach is private. I'm going to have to ask you to leave."

Alex licked her dry lips and tasted blood. The guard had to notice, because his eyes narrowed on Luc and then flicked back toward her. "Are you all right, ma'am?"

"We're leaving," Luc replied, but Alex dug her heels firmly into the sand and braced herself. "Let's not make a scene, *chérie*," Luc added.

Take a chance with her family or go with Luc where he could torture her and still place her family at risk? She pulled away from Luc to get to the guard, but he tightened his hold on her.

"I need to see my father, Peter Northrop." She tried to break free of Luc's grip, but he held firm, his blood now seeping through his blazer and dripping onto her arm.

The guard reached for his weapon.

Alex saw the red light on the side of the man's head only a moment before his body recoiled and blood oozed from a hole that had shattered his skull. A dull roaring in her ears blocked all sound. Her eyes had taken over all of her senses, and the gruesome image etched itself into her mind as a permanent nightmare. The guard's expression remained stoic; his mouth hung open like he wanted to speak, despite his death. Alex's mouth opened to scream, but no sound came out.

Luc watched the man fall to the ground, shook his head, and then turned to Alex. "I've been trying to kill you for months. I'm very tempted to leave your body here with that ugly carcass, but I find the idea of interacting with the Northrops of Boston too intriguing."

Her legs gave way. She dropped next to the man who had come to rescue her. Another fatality because of her. Maybe if she struggled, Luc would kill her and leave her family alone.

He yanked her up. "Disobedience is never acceptable. The next one down is that little boy with the blond hair. My men have a perfect shot through the side window into a family room."

Anna's son. It must be. The realization that Luc stood in close proximity to her family with an armed assassin ready to kill on command crumbled her defenses and crushed her will to fight.

"No. I'll do anything. Please leave them alone."

Luc clasped her arm and pulled her toward the street, forcing her to walk away from her home for the second time in her life, this time in bare feet and under armed guard.

CHAPTER 23

———————— ✆ ————————

The trees in North Carolina had the audacity to bloom green, pink, and white, despite the fact that Henry's world had crumpled to pieces. Just to spite him, warm breezes flowed among a cluster of modern office buildings. Henry had headed to Charlotte after Simon informed him of Gabe's unusual purchase of a large television set at a Walmart. Then the rental car company had contacted him after locating the Mustang in a garage within ten miles of that same Walmart. Three days combing this small Southern city, and he'd learned nothing. Searching for her in Oxford had been one thing, but trying to find her in an entirely different country was like finding a granule of sand in a silo of grain.

His mobile rang during his walk back to the hotel room after another useless day exploring hotels, stores, museums, the railroad terminal, and the bus depot. Simon.

"Any new information? Because no one remembers her in this entire city." Henry tried to sound more upbeat than he was, but why bother? Simon had already figured out he harbored strong feelings for Gabe when Henry had willingly parted with Lady Elizabeth and the future of the women's shelter to find her.

"Actually, I did." Simon's voice reflected Henry's serious

mood. "Alex is female. Luc Perrault's ex-girlfriend. From what my source tells me, she's a native of France, although fluent in English and Ukrainian. She's also an experienced art appraiser."

Alex is Gabe? The news energized him. It made perfect sense. If she saw Luc at the auction, she'd run away as quickly as possible to avoid the man who had beaten the hell out of her and threatened to kill her.

Henry could have helped her, and he should have told her about his background. Perhaps she would have trusted him to protect her. On the other hand, his training hadn't provided him with the means to decipher the identity of the most important person in his life. What an idiot. He should have added two plus two and reached four. Instead, he ended up with a small fraction of a personality and nothing of substance.

"What's her surname?" Hopefully, it would shed light on her location.

"Lemoine, but I think it's an alias."

"Alex or Lemoine?"

"No idea."

"No idea?" Henry's voice lowered, and he squeezed the phone tighter.

"My source only knew her briefly through Luc. And don't get your hopes up too high with this information. She has more personalities than Doctor Who."

"I can't stay here any longer. As far I know, she took the first train or bus out of here or hitchhiked with a rock band to Seattle."

"Let me see if I can confirm her surname with a few art contacts in Paris. If we don't have it by morning, you might as well fly home. Talk to you soon." He hung up, leaving Henry with only a crumb of new information. Enough to make him hungry for more.

The idea of leaving Gabe in the States bothered him. That blasted hole in his heart had opened wider and deeper. It would never be filled until he saw her again. If he saw her again.

During his walk back to the hotel, he analyzed everything

she'd said to him and everything he'd subsequently learned about her. Control freak father, fleeing the United States for Europe, amazing ability in art, fluent in many languages, abusive boyfriend, hiding out in England. He was missing something important, he just didn't know what.

Once in his hotel room, he wrote "Alex Lemoine" on a piece of paper from the desk. He then wrote "Gabrielle West" and "Belinda." He sketched her acorn tattoo and "L.P."

Glancing over at the pile of luggage, he tried to think of where she would go. She didn't have much with her, except a few hundred dollars and the euros and pounds in her wallet, but she'd probably acquired more from her television transaction. Her suitcase remained by his bed, waiting for her to claim the contents. He'd already searched it over and over again, looking for secret compartments, a scrap of paper in a pair of jeans. Anything. Nothing. She'd abandoned some old dirty clothes on the floor of the Atlanta hotel room, her ingenious way of slipping past everyone at the auction.

Turning on the news, he stretched out across the bed and mustered the energy to call room service. The national news broadcast the growing violence in Afghanistan. *"Pakistan confiscated twenty weapons caches enroute to Kabul***"*

"I'd like to order a BLT on wheat bread, light on the mayo. No chips please. A pot of black tea would be good as well, with milk. Thank you." He paused as the woman in the kitchen repeated the order.

The news shifted out of Afghanistan to Boston for the funeral of a security guard killed in Martha's Vineyard. *"Peter Northrop, CEO of Oak Industries, and his wife, Gabrielle, were on the property with their family to celebrate Easter at the time of the attack."*

He glanced at the television and saw a tall, fit older man and an attractive woman who looked remarkably like***

Henry hung up the phone and stared at the screen. Gabrielle and a tattoo of a "baby oak." When the news shifted to the weather, he ran over to his laptop. As it booted up, he tapped his fingers on the desk.

Come on. I need this info three days ago.

He searched for Peter and Gabrielle Northrop and found a few articles about their family. Three daughters, Anna, Julia, and a third who was not mentioned by name. He continued searching for the third daughter using Alexandra Northrop and there, on the screen, was an image of *his* Gabe in high school. Long brown hair, elfin nose, and a smart-ass attitude evidenced by the lift of her chin and defiant smirk on her face.

"Alexandra Northrop, the youngest daughter of Peter Northrop, recently graduated from the Winsor School. She'll be attending Bowdoin College in the fall." He found no mention of her after high school.

He mentally calculated her age from the date of her high school graduation. The dates didn't quite add up, unless she'd lied. She wasn't twenty-four or twenty-six. She was closer to twenty-eight.

He wanted to contact her father immediately. The man's phone numbers, however, were unlisted, and his offices were closed until the next morning. His energy restored, Henry hustled around the room to pack his belongings while booking the next flight from Charlotte to Boston. He could fill Simon in on his discovery during his cab ride.

***

Most people would love to fly a private jet to Paris. Alex would have preferred a commercial carrier with lots of witnesses and maybe an air marshal.

After takeoff, Luc and his thugs surrounded her seat. He was still pissed about the stab wound in his chest.

"Serge, hold her arms," he said in French, refusing to speak English to her after they'd left Massachusetts. Serge pulled her arms behind her, one on each side of the airplane seat. Alex tried to stop him, but his strength outmatched hers by a hundred and fifty pounds.

"Pascal, come here. I need you to assist me with something," Luc said to his first henchman.

Pascal's physique reminded Alex of Simon's, only without the devil-may-care smile. He'd spent the afternoon shoving her place to place, generally by her hair. Causing pain seemed to be Pascal's favorite hobby. As he approached her, Alex tried to kick him away. He lifted his hand to slap her, but Luc stopped him.

"Don't damage her face." Luc then directed him to her stomach.

Despite her struggle to avoid a blow to her abdomen, he hit his mark with perfect accuracy. The impact shut her down. Her lungs struggled for breath as traitorous tears fell down her cheeks. She couldn't breathe, couldn't move, couldn't function. In order to avoid the mocking looks and twisted glances she'd be receiving, she closed her eyes.

"Have you had enough?" Luc's voice sounded almost calming. He wouldn't kill her right now. He'd torture her for a while, like a cat playing with an injured mouse.

She nodded as best as she could, but refused to open her eyes.

A man's hand, smooth and without a callous, lifted her chin and squeezed her jaw until her mouth opened. Her eyes opened as well.

"Keep your eyes open. I want you to see why you're being punished." Luc unbuttoned his shirt to reveal a solid chest with smooth muscles, and a gash under his right nipple.

She shivered at her handiwork. It had been cleaned and was covered with an ointment, but it looked painful.

"I'm sorry?" Her voice gained some strength as the impact of the punch died down.

"No, you aren't. You want me dead. I want you dead. Only one of us will succeed, and I'm betting on me."

His threat bolstered her courage. She spoke through gritted

teeth. "Maybe I'll get lucky, and you'll have a stroke and die in front of me."

He squeezed her face again. Hard enough to hurt, not hard enough to bruise. One of Luc's talents. "You get to live for at least a month or two."

"How exciting for me."

He grinned as though he'd won the lottery. "It will be. We're getting married."

The scowl fell off her face. Marriage equaled a lifetime of torture. "Married? I'd ask if you're insane, but that would be redundant."

Luc continued squeezing her jaw and tightened his grip when she tried to shake free. "We'll be married only long enough to access your trust fund."

His hand released her, but Serge pulled her arms back a bit more until they felt like they were being pulled out of her shoulders. Alex tried to imagine a painful massage therapy where they needed to pull the muscles beyond their comfort zone in order to get the best stretch. It still hurt like hell, but perhaps she was going to feel better after he released her.

"I don't have a trust fund. My father cut me off years ago."

"No, your father cut off your sister Anna and put her money in a trust for her children. Apparently, he disliked her choice of husband." Luc smirked. "He never placed any restrictions on your wealth."

Why would her father restrict Anna the golden girl's trust fund and not hers? It didn't make sense, unless Anna's husband had tried to access the family wealth. Peter protected his money more fiercely than he protected any of his children.

Still, he wouldn't have left his missing daughter with access to such an enormous amount. "I don't believe you. Where would you get that information?"

"The senior trust officer at your parents' bank became a wealth of information with the proper incentive."

She needed time to figure this out. And she'd have some.

"There's a waiting period and a residency requirement. It could take months to get married."

"You've been living with me for the past year, according to my documents. And any other waiting periods can be waived." Luc grinned.

He released her face, slapped her cheek gently, and walked toward the back bedroom. "I'm going to take a nap. Don't embarrass yourself by screaming like a little girl. I don't wish to disturb the pilots."

Her cheeks throbbed from where he'd squeezed her cheeks into her molars. The ache in her shoulders cramped up, but Serge wouldn't release her arms. Alex yawned, her body's attempt to shut down from the fright and fatigue, and trying to appear as though their treatment of her didn't matter. She shifted her shoulders to convince the idiot to free her. He wouldn't.

Pascal approached her again. Standing to her side to avoid being kicked, he gripped her left leg with one hand. His other hand secured her knee. Her arms burned from their locked position and were no help. She tried to hit him with other leg, but only succeeded in flailing it around. Besides, he was too fast.

Like watching a car accident in slow motion, Alex's body jerked back as Pascal stomped the full weight of his foot onto her shin. She could feel the break, feel the horrific pain spreading out from her leg to her whole body. Her lungs stopped functioning, her throat constricted, and she gasped for air. A second wave of pain shot through her, and her airways opened. With lungs filled to capacity, she screamed, loud and long.

CHAPTER 24

enry's cab traveled from Logan Airport through quaint New England towns filled with white steeple churches and grassy town commons to the Northrop family home in Concord, Massachusetts. He arrived a few minutes before 7:00 a.m. Dressed in a comfortable pair of jeans and an untucked black dress shirt, he'd concealed Simon's lethal present in his belt and thrown the rest of his Alex-approved wardrobe in his suitcase. During the flight, he'd stored the gun in his checked luggage. Simon conveniently provided all the documentation needed to carry a concealed weapon in all fifty states. He'd thank Simon later for taking care of him during the trip.

The Northrop estate, because it sure as hell wasn't just a house, rivaled the grounds of Ripon Manor. The enormous colonial mansion stood on a hill overlooking the Concord River. Lights, still visible in the early morning, illuminated a path down the sloping lawn to the water. Alex's mother never allowed her to have a hedge maze? Poor little rich girl. And he'd thought she'd grown up impoverished. She must have been hysterical thinking about his lectures on social graces. No wonder she fit in. She wasn't acting as a wealthy heiress. She *was* a wealthy heiress.

He paid the driver and took his suitcases. He'd call for a ride back to the airport after he'd spoken to Mr. Northrop and, hope-fully, located Alex.

When he knocked, a security guard dressed head to toe in black opened the door, stepped out, and shut the door firmly behind him. The same height as Henry, the guy puffed out his chest and sucked in his cheeks as though the presence of any guest before eight in the morning could get him and the guest terminated.

"Can I help you?"

Henry smiled to lighten the mood. "I'm looking for Alex Northrop."

"Alex?" His eyebrows furrowed.

"Yes. Is she here presently?"

The guy's eyes sighted on the bulge near Henry's hip where he'd holstered the gun. He should have left it in his suitcase.

Henry reached to take it out to hand to the guard. "I can***"

"Hands up." The guard grabbed Henry's arm, twisted him around, and shoved his face into the wall. Pain exploded near his jaw. He tasted the metallic tang of the asshole's aggressive tactics. Henry pushed back and forced the guard slightly off balance.

As Henry struggled to get free, he grabbed as much of his aggressor's hair as he could and slammed him into the wall beside him. He dodged the bloke's attempt to pummel him. Without letting go of his hair, Henry forced the guy to the ground face-first and wedged his knee into the base of his spine. Pulling out the gun that had started this confrontation, he aimed it directly behind the guard's ear.

"What the hell was that for?" His breathing was still heavy as he regained control.

Before three seconds passed, two guns punched into the back of his head from two new security guards.

"Drop it now," one of them called out.

Henry held steady for a moment. He'd seriously misjudged the security at the Northrop house.

"Drop it." Someone shoved a gun into his head again. The

barrel dug into his scalp. If he didn't turn up dead, he'd be sore for a week.

Henry loosened the grip on the gun. A large hand pulled it away from him. Another hand took the form of a large rock and connected with his cheek, shoving him against the house. The impact hammered through his face and his ear. Henry's lip was bleeding, and the back of his head stung.

Guard number one, now on his feet, kicked Henry in the gut. Every last bit of air was punched from his lungs, and the ache radiated through one of his ribs. It didn't feel broken; he'd already experienced that several times in his life and would never forget that sharp unrelenting pain.

He remained on the ground like a scarecrow that had been ransacked by crows with a vendetta. One of the guards was on the phone while the other two stood over him, guns locked, loaded, and begging for an excuse to kill him. The guard who had started the incident had blood dripping down his chin. Henry couldn't feel sympathy for the blighter.

The door cracked open and a petite woman about thirty years old peeked out. Her long brown hair with blond streaks and a pixie nose resembled Alex's. "Should I call the police?" She sounded nervous, but curious.

"Your father wants to speak with him first."

The woman disappeared, and an older man, dressed for a game of golf, appeared in her place.

Mr. Peter Northrop himself. Head of Oak Industries and the man who had caused Alex to run away. He looked different dressed in Izod golf separates rather than in the expensive black suit custom-made for a funeral. Henry disliked him immediately, but it may have had more to do with the pain spreading throughout his body than the man's demeanor.

"Who's this?"

The guards continued to aim their guns at Henry's head. "He's looking for Alex and pulled a weapon on Declan, Mr. Northrop."

Declan didn't say anything. He stood at attention, his cheek split and swelling. Blood smeared around the edges of the injury.

"I was attempting to provide him with the gun in order to enter your house unarmed. I'm not an idiot." Henry tried to defend himself.

Mr. Northrop raised his eyebrows, no doubt challenging his statement. "Let's start with a name."

"Henry Chilton." Lying on his back with blood drooling out of his mouth was not the best way to make a proper introduction, nor the best manner of meeting the parents of the woman he loved. It had to be love, because at that moment he'd have killed everyone in his vicinity to protect Alex. The longer she was out of his arms, the more fixated he became on getting her back into them. If that wasn't love, then he must be insane.

"Mr. Chilton, before I call the police, I'd like to know what you want with my daughter."

The strange history Henry shared with Alex needed to stay protected until he had a better handle on the father-daughter dynamic. He reduced their story to the basics. "We traveled to Atlanta together for an art auction, and she disappeared."

"You're an art dealer or collector?"

"I'm an anthropology lecturer at Oxford University."

"You don't dress like an anthropologist." The Alex look-alike called out over Mr. Northrop's shoulder.

Henry couldn't help but smirk at hearing a voice so similar to Alex's. "I left my tweed jacket in England."

Mr. Northrop directed his anger toward his daughter. "Julia, go in the house until this is over."

Julia disappeared immediately.

His attention returned to Henry. "Do you have identification proving this?"

"Of course." Henry reached for his wallet and realized the security detail had pinched it from him while beating him up.

Declan handed it to Mr. Northrop, who proceeded to take out

his university identification, a credit card, and his passport and read them thoroughly.

"He's telling the truth." Julia, her voice low and directed at her father, pushed past him with an iPad and showed everyone a picture of Henry from the prior year's faculty awards dinner. "Not only that, but Wikipedia claims that Dr. Henry Elliott Chilton, anthropologist, is also the Earl of Ripon. How cool is that? We haven't had royalty here since Princess Margaret stayed for a weekend to support the foundation gala."

***

Bright lights and a sterile hospital environment greeted Alex when she woke. She glanced toward her leg, wrapped in a large cast from her knee to her ankle. There should be pain, but there wasn't, only a queasy stomach and a sore throat. A medicated haze weighed her down and muddled her mind. She needed to skip a dose or two of whatever was dulling her senses in order to become coherent enough to plan Luc's murder. Maybe she'd have the time and energy to kill his minions as well, Pascal in particular.

On the subject of minions, the only other person in her room was Pascal, stretched out in a recliner with a newspaper in his hand. He lifted his head when she tried to shift her body over an inch.

"Enjoying some downtime?" She spoke with a scratchy voice in French.

"Enjoying the sight of you in a cast. Can't wait until it heals so I can break it again." A stupid chuckle rumbled out of his mouth.

They both became quiet when the nurse arrived. A younger woman, she cast her eyes away from Pascal and focused only on her job. She checked Alex's temperature and blood pressure and asked some questions in French about Alex's leg. The nurse reached for a glass of water and handed it to Alex along with an orange pill. "Take this."

Alex hesitated, took the pill, and left it under her tongue as she swallowed the water. Some would leech into her system, but she should be able to spit the rest out.

After the nurse left, Pascal walked over to the bed. "Keep it in your mouth."

She pretended to swallow and then stuck out her tongue with the pill hidden inside her cheek.

He punched at her shoulder. "If the pill comes out, I'm shoving it all the way down your throat with my finger."

He stood at her side for around fifteen minutes to make sure she didn't get rid of the pill. It was dissolving and tasted nasty. Too much of the drug had found its way into her bloodstream. She struggled to keep her eyes from closing, but eventually fell asleep.

After what seemed like two minutes, someone shook her. "Wake up, *ma chérie*."

She ignored Luc's command, partly from fatigue, partly from fear. If she was in the hospital, he couldn't hurt her. He placed a hand on her shoulder and squeezed. The pressure should hurt, but she'd become impervious to abuse. The medication protected her from the pain. Her closed eyes protected her from the hate emanating from his icy gaze.

He shook her again but caused no pain. The medicine must be working still or someone must be with him. Her eyes opened partway. A man stood next to Luc in a lab coat. After a full stretch, she opened her eyes fully. Could this man help her?

"Alex, this is Dr. Richet. He's here to release you. We don't want to miss our wedding."

Leaving the hospital would make her more vulnerable than ever. She had to stay as long as possible. "I can't leave. I'm not feeling well."

Luc brushed some of her hair from her face. The move would have been sweet if the man doing it wasn't trying to harm her. "Can I have a few minutes alone with her?"

"Absolutely. I'll be in the hall." The doctor nodded at Luc

without a glance toward Alex. Luc's money would keep him focused on his patron and not his patient.

Alex wanted to scream out to him for help, but remembered the bloody image of the last person she'd asked to help her. Too many innocent people lingered nearby.

"You disappoint me. Where's the adoration you gave me when we first met?" He pulled out his phone and typed on the screen for a few seconds. "Your future happiness is linked to my happiness and right now, I'm not happy."

He wouldn't be receiving her adoration or any positive attention. Instead, she shut her eyes and tried to drown out his image.

The sharp pinch on her arm told her he didn't appreciate being ignored. "I thought you might like to see your family." She opened her eyes again to find Luc's phone in her face. A photo on the screen showed her family dressed in mourning attire at the security guard's funeral. *"The Northrop family mourns the loss of the head of their security team, Adam Miller. A member of the Northrop staff for five years, he leaves a wife and teenage son. There have been no new leads in the murder investigation."*

Her father and mother stood side by side dressed in black. Julia, Anna, and a man that could be Anna's husband, Jason, remained behind them. Her mother appeared stoic, but the muscles in her jaw seemed strained. Tension rocked though her, and her stomach heaved. She'd caused this. It was all her fault.

Luc pulled the phone away. "How many pictures of funerals will I be showing you before you obey me?'

After a knock on the door, the doctor popped his head into the room. "Everything all right?"

Alex tried to force a smile, but couldn't fake it. "Yes. I'm ready to leave."

"Great. I'll go finish the paperwork." The doctor fled the room again without examining her leg, leaving her alone with the two malignant cancers that had caused the injury.

She pasted on her best Gabrielle countenance, the one her

mother was wearing at the guard's funeral. Alex would borrow it for her wedding.

After a painful car drive, they arrived at the *mairie*, a local government office for civil weddings, near Luxembourg Gardens. It was an impersonal place with black vinyl chairs lined up in rows. A wood podium decorated with silk flowers and vines was positioned at the front of the room for the officiate. Most girls who dream of a wedding envision white gowns, flowing bouquets, and being surrounded by family and friends. For Alex, her wedding involved a bright blue peasant skirt over her cast, two witnesses who loved to watch her cry out in pain, and a groom who would prefer to slit her throat rather than kiss her lips.

The officiate still hadn't arrived twenty minutes later. Alex continued to stand in pain next to Luc and his guards. She felt like an ugly ducking, but she remained cool by breathing in the fading scent of Henry from his jacket. Pascal and Serge wore tailored pants and nice, button-down shirts. Luc was decked out in an Armani black suit and a red silk tie. At least someone dressed for the occasion. He never held her hand or even looked in her direction. No pretending on his part.

She didn't want to be the brave one any longer. She missed Henry. She loved Henry. He, no doubt, hated her for leaving him alone in Atlanta. Leaving the engagement ring in his pocket should have convinced him she didn't want anything to do with him. As painful as that would be, she was glad he wouldn't be searching for her. She rubbed her thumb against her ring finger, remembering the feel of the engagement ring.

"Will you be putting me up in your summer home on the Riviera? I'll suffer alone there without complaint," she asked Luc.

He shook his head, as though the possibility had crossed his mind and he'd dismissed it. "Regrettably, you have to work. I need a qualified appraiser for a few transactions, and you owe me for not killing any family members, yet."

The thought that he could and would harm her family sucked the air from her lungs. She needed to stay strong. "I might be losing my touch. I'm having a hard time right now determining if those heathens standing behind me are human or ape."

"Hey." One of the apes became offended at the accuracy of her description.

"Back off, Pascal. She'll be available to you later."

"Shit." Alex stepped back, her widened eyes mocking them. "Is he going to eat me?"

Pascal closed the gap between them. "I'm going to break your other leg."

"Good luck with that. You must be embarrassed that you only made a hairline fracture of the tibia and didn't break it in two. Luc's standards must have fallen, because he used to employ only the best."

Luc pulled Pascal away from her and made him stand by the wall. Alex waved as he was placed in a time-out.

When the civil servant arrived, Luc told him to proceed directly to the vows. They had to be spoken in French. Alex almost said them in English, but realized screwing up the wedding might harm her family. She'd go through the motions in order to become a widow before Labor Day.

Committing herself to Luc as his bride bothered her more than she cared to admit. She hated breaking oaths, and yet she had no intention of keeping these vows. For now, however, she had to comply with Luc's wishes and prayed her wedding night wouldn't involve agony and humiliation. She'd be obedient until the first moment she had to rip every last bit of life from his heinous existence.

CHAPTER 25

───────────── ❧ ─────────────

Peter Northrop offered Henry the use of a bathroom to clean off the blood from his face and to change into clean clothes. Not particularly generous considering it was his overanxious security detail that had rumpled his appearance in the first place. After cleaning up, he went in search of Mr. Northrop, his wife, and his daughter Julia in their breakfast room. A pissed-off security guard followed him like a shadow on a sunny day. No doubt the fact that Henry would be sharing breakfast with the family while Declan was traveling to the hospital for a few stitches added to the man's hostility.

As Henry trekked down an endless hallway, a large portrait over the fireplace in the study came into view. The sight froze Henry in place.

Alex.

She appeared to be about fourteen or fifteen in the painting. Her long brown hair had been pulled high into a messy ponytail with random chunks falling out around her face. The artist captured her brandy-tinted eyes filled with adolescent annoyance and rolled back in aggravation at having to pose for such a long time. The young woman, attired in black jeans and a cream-colored crewneck sweater, leaned against the wall with her arms crossed, defiant and amazing. A 4-D person in a 3-D world.

How could anyone want to tone down such perfection and force her into a staid life where she'd suffocate under social restrictions and extreme expectations? She'd set herself free to display her true colors to the world. Thank God she did, or he never would have met her.

When he arrived in the breakfast room, Mrs. Northrop offered him a seat. The family held themselves aloof as was expected. He'd arrived as an armed stranger at their door, searching for their lost child.

Mrs. Northrop, the real Gabrielle, sat poised and elegant, her smooth brown hair pulled into a neat bun. Wearing a simple tan dress and a sweater, she acknowledged Henry with a tentative smile, one that reached her cheeks, but faded before engaging her eyes. She offered him her hand in greeting.

Mr. Northrop, on the other hand, regarded Henry the way a duke of old would acknowledge a footman. He seemed put out to be having a guest of such little consequence. Henry cloaked himself with the aristocratic airs of his own father, another pretentious patriarch. He leaned back in his chair and countered Mr. Northrop's attitude with a proud countenance of his own. As nonsensical as that seemed, it often worked to earn the respect of some of the blowhards in his own country.

Julia poured Henry a mug of coffee and offered him some refreshments. "Are you called Lord Ripon?" she asked while sliding the cream toward his cup. Despite watching a bevy of security guards disarm him a half an hour ago, she appeared quite at ease in his presence. Her smile seemed genuine and her demeanor welcoming.

"Please, call me Henry."

He couldn't help staring at her. Despite longer hair and a more sunny disposition, her appearance reminded him of Alex. Even as Julia held herself with the confidence that comes with a billion dollars in the bank, she acted approachable and warmhearted. He saw her approval of him, despite his airs of self-importance. Could she read his intentions so easily? Alex was a lousy judge of character, thus her current predicament.

"I haven't heard from Alex in a long time. I'm curious for any news you can give me."

"Julia, I'd prefer we refrain from discussing our personal business with Mr. Chilton." Obviously not a fan of titles, nor familiar names, Peter Northrop didn't seem to tolerate idle chitchat in front of strangers. He turned to Henry. "So how did you meet Alexandra?"

"She was a guest at a dinner party at my house. We'd decided to travel together to an art exhibition in Atlanta."

"And the last time you spoke to her?" His tone became an accusation.

Henry restricted his words to only what Mr. Northrop needed to know. "Four days ago. She disappeared from the gallery. I'm worried about her, and now with the death on your property, I'm even more concerned."

Mr. Northrop tented his fingers in front of his chin. "I find it strange that Julia loses contact with Alexandra for six months, and then Anna receives a cryptic message from her warning of a death threat. Within twenty-four hours, my head of security is gunned down on my property. And now, you arrive at her childhood home in search of her. She hasn't lived here in almost a decade. Haven't we been through enough?"

Henry couldn't temper the scowl he aimed at Mr. Northrop. The guy didn't want to help him. He wanted to minimize his bad press. "As I told you earlier, she went missing at the auction we attended together. I assumed she'd try to seek you out since she was in the States."

"What specifically is your relationship with Alexandra, Mr. Chilton?"

What was their relationship? Business associates? Boyfriend and girlfriend? Lovers? "We're engaged."

Mrs. Northrop paled, and then pulled her emotions inside,

leaving Henry to wonder whether she was more shocked by Alex's sudden reappearance and departure or her engagement.

"Engaged?" Julia shrieked and jumped up to give Henry an unexpected hug. "How wonderful. When's the wedding? We have to be invited. Tell Alex I'd travel through the nine gates of hell to see her again. Anna would, too."

Before Henry could answer, Mr. Northrop cleared his throat for attention. Julia and Henry both turned toward him.

"How long did you wait to propose after learning of Alexandra's family and the amount held for her in trust?"

"I beg your pardon? You know nothing about me and nothing about Alex, either, to speak such drivel."

Mr. Northrop shook his head. "Your type are a dime a dozen. Unlike the useless nobility in Europe, I earned my fortune." His voice deepened into a threat. "And I'll tell you this, you have a better chance of being named Miss America than you do of getting your hands on that cash."

Her father's belief that a man couldn't love Alex for anything but her wealth churned in Henry's gut. He fought hard to stay in control. This man was toxic, and Alex was better off without him.

Henry took a breath and spoke with a restrained calm. "Your opinion of me matters only to yourself. The purpose of my visit was not to kiss your arse, but to locate Alex. She's in trouble, and I'll do whatever I can to protect her. Obviously, she didn't feel the need to return to what had been her home many, *many* years ago. I now understand why. Instead of offering assistance, you show contempt toward the only person actively looking for her."

"She didn't want to be found. We never closed the door on her coming back."

"Admirable."

"I will not be insulted by some worthless gold digger."

"I can assure you I had ample opportunity to pursue a career in something significantly more profitable than anthropology. My life is not defined by my title, my bank account, or my profession. Protecting your assets instead of assisting me in finding your daughter makes you far more pathetic. And it makes me thankful Alex has not remained under your influence." Henry wiped his mouth with the napkin from his lap and stood up. "This meeting is over. I understand her family history a whole lot better now having met you in person. Good day, Mr. Northrop." Henry turned to Mrs. Northrop, her lips pinched in her emotions. "I'm sorry to leave so abruptly, but I promise to have Alex contact you when I find her."

She rose from her chair and clasped Henry's hands, ignoring her husband. "Thank you, Lord Ripon. Thank you for looking for her. I'd do anything to know she's all right."

He said good-bye to Julia and left to locate his bags.

When he arrived in the front of the house to wait for his taxi, a red Tesla stopped in front of him. Julia hopped out of the driver's seat and popped the front trunk.

"Get in. I'm taking you to the airport. I need an update on my sister. Sorry about father's outburst. He's a tyrant, but he means well. That's his traditional *welcome to the family* speech. He'll be over his insecurities by the wedding."

Henry hesitated. "I don't want to cause any rifts between you and him."

"That would never happen. We've learned to differ on just about everything in life, but still respect each other. I don't think he's ever forgiven himself for driving Alex away from home, so now he's defensive about it."

"I apologize for my rude exit, but I have little sympathy for your father."

"He doesn't want sympathy, he wants world domination. I think he'll respect you more for telling him off. Jason, Anna's husband, is such a major league suck-up the entire family has written him off as a loser. It's fitting that Alex has a warrior on her side." She handed him a piece of paper. "Anna and I were on the beach the day Adam was shot. We watched a woman fighting with a man in the same location. It sounded like two lovers having an argument. We were too far away to identify them, but the police found a duffel bag near Adam's body. It contained Alex's expired passport, a wallet, and some other stuff. Local, state, and federal law enforcement are working on the case. My father even hired a private investigator to try to locate Alex. So far, there's no evidence of her existence, except for the bag. I made a list of the contents for you. Maybe it will help you find her."

During the journey from Concord to Boston, Julia told Henry about her childhood and living under Peter Northrop's roof. Henry shared a little of what he knew about Alex eight years later, hiding the fact that he didn't know near enough. His thoughts, however, remained focused on the list in his hand.

***

Alex always hated Luc's imposing mass of stone on the right bank of Paris. Built in the year 1900, the style was reminiscent of a fairy-tale château, but the feelings and memories it evoked reminded her of a horror movie. She'd lost her virginity in a brutal and emotionless manner in the elegant master bedroom suite. Luc had cracked her rib in the spacious, modernized kitchen and pushed her down the gorgeous, curved marble staircase. Stolen art decorated the walls, and artifacts sat in display cases after being pillaged from countries that were losing their heritage under their noses. From a hidden spot on the stairway, Alex had watched Danielle and her boyfriend murdered in the art gallery under those priceless paintings and artifacts, after Danielle had argued with Luc over moving to San Francisco.

Pascal shoved Alex through the back entryway. Her crutches slid, and she lost her balance. Falling to the floor, she paused in place to catch her breath. The pain in her leg throbbed, but she didn't want medicine clouding her judgment, so she tried to ignore it. She took a quick intake of air and bit down with her back molars to suck in the scream that wanted to come out, but couldn't, in order to keep Pascal from exploiting her weakness.

"Get up." He stood over her, yet offered no assistance.

She stayed on the floor for a second too long. Pascal kicked her cast. Pain shot through her leg, causing Alex's back and neck muscles to wrench. Her gasp and the water pooling in her eyes must have provided him with enough of a response, because he backed off. She shifted her position to brace herself with the crutches and lift herself up.

Gritting through the agony coursing through her leg, she limped one step ahead of Pascal down the hall toward the kitchen, avoiding his rough grasp. A cook or someone else in the household staff might be in the kitchen. Their presence could soften Pascal's aggressive treatment of her. They wouldn't actually help her. She wasn't that optimistic. They'd be risking their own lives to save hers and, honestly, she didn't want another death on her hands. The blood she was responsible for already made Lady Macbeth's hands appear downright sterile.

Hope rushed through her at the sight of a woman by the counter until the woman's dress and demeanor came into focus. Her long straight brown hair cascaded across her shoulders, her plunging neckline exposed double Ds, and her tight skirt revealed sexy stripper legs. The kind only seen spread apart from the back as the woman bent over to present her ass to a room full of horny men. Definitely not a cook. She had an arrogant manner merely pouring hot water into a cup. This sensual woman must be Luc's latest bed partner. She was more his type than Alex was. Slutty and, most likely, easily deceived.

"Good, you're back." The stripper spoke in the Queen's English to Pascal. "I'm going to need***" She stopped talking when she noticed Alex.

A casual stroll of her eyes over Alex's pathetic wedding attire and cast caused her to smirk. "*Bonjour. Tu es qui?*" The words came out slow and pronounced in an exaggerated manner. Was she sucky at foreign languages or speaking to Alex like a child?

"Don't bother." Pascal spoke in barely conversant English. "She speaks better English than you. Her French is better than yours, too. She's American and Luc's new bride."

"New bride?" The woman's eyes widened a smidgen, but soon returned to a more relaxed exterior.

Without showing a hint of jealousy at being introduced to her husband's lover, Alex smiled and put out her hand. "Hi. I'm Alex."

The woman's eyebrows raised a fraction; perhaps she'd heard of her. She gripped Alex's hand and stared into her eyes, looking for something. "I'm Nicola. Nice to meet you. I'm a guest of Luc's."

Simon's Nicola? Alex needed more information. This connected Simon and Luc in a way she couldn't piece together. *Had Simon set her up?* She didn't know what to believe.

"Nice to meet you."

"What happened to your leg?" For a moment, Nicola appeared to send pity in Alex's direction, but as Pascal approached them, the expression turned to conceit. "You're not Luc's type at all. He tends to prefer sophistication and elegance in his girlfriends."

"Luckily, I'm not his girlfriend. Too much pressure to perform. As his wife, I'm stuck with him until one of us dies, hopefully sooner than later. Therefore, there's not much need to impress him. You, on the other hand, conform to all of Luc's specs—tall, lean, full of self-importance. He'll have replaced you by the end of the week."

Nicola ignored her digs. "This makes an interesting twist on our relationship. I'll discuss it with him tonight in bed."

"Be my guest. In fact, I'd prefer it if you kept him entertained every night until you're replaced with an eighteen-year-old centerfold."

"My dear Mrs. Perrault, he'll never be bored with me." Nicola leaned against the counter and took a sip of tea, a woman in for the duration.

The rusty gears in Pascal's pea-sized brain must have kicked in, because he stepped between them as if breaking up a bar fight. The realization that Luc's wife and mistress maybe shouldn't cross paths finally dawned on him. "You won't be seeing much of each other. Mrs. Perrault will be staying in her room until her husband returns."

He reached down and lifted Alex off the ground, clasping her crutches in one of his giant hands. A quick exit to separate the sparring women. Perhaps Pascal's mistake would cause him to end up at the bottom of the Seine. A cheerful thought.

"Tell Luc to keep out of my room when you see him." She waved to Nicola as Pascal hustled her from the kitchen.

CHAPTER 26

Simon never demanded anything from Henry. So when he told Henry to fly direct to Charles de Gaulle instead of Heathrow, Henry found the quickest route and jumped on a plane.

The taxi dropped him off at a low-budget hotel a few blocks from one of the seedier sections in Paris. A half-lit neon sign advertised the Hotel Dupré, a beige stone establishment covered in soot and grime. He scanned the deserted neighborhood for any sign of life. A lack of cafés, restaurants, and storefronts kept tourists away from this small, dark back street. After paying the driver, he lifted the two suitcases he'd been lugging around since Atlanta and headed to the entrance.

The room on the third floor appeared as dirty and gray as the outside facade of the building. Simon opened the door for his brother. He blended well into the environment in worn jeans and a black T-shirt, and carrying a cold beer in his hand.

His expression at seeing Henry's bruised face courtesy of the Northrop security team wasn't pity. It bordered on amusement. "What happened to you?"

"I met Alex's family."

Simon grinned and handed Henry the beer, grabbing another

from a cooler under the window without a view. "I'm glad you're in one piece and could make it here. We have a lot to discuss."

"Starting with Alex's true identity." Henry took a swig of the cold beer. The drink slid down his throat, giving him a needed touch of nourishment.

"Boston blue blood. It fits her profile."

Henry shook his head. "I'm supposed to be the expert on reading people, but you predicted this outcome. How the hell did I miss all the signs?"

"I was thinking with my head, and your brains had migrated below your belt, a rare occurrence for you. I, on the other hand, have years of experience thinking with my knob." Simon rummaged around near the closet and tossed a bag of chips to Henry, opening a jar of nuts for himself. "I can't believe you traveled all the way to her father's house in Massachusetts, and he gave you the cold shoulder. Although if someone had just murdered my head of security, I suppose I'd be apprehensive, too."

Sitting on the chair, Henry took another swig, put the bottle on the floor, and opened the chips. "Mr. Northrop, like the all-powerful Oz, acted a good game, but couldn't help me, or wouldn't. He thinks I'm a gold digger. Imagine that."

"Not impressed by the title?"

"He referred to me as Mr. Chilton. I guess his corporate billions trump my castle and the reproduction of a Lawrence portrait." He bit into a chip and spit it out. "What the hell is this?"

"Soft-shell-crab-flavored chips." Sitting on the unmade bed, Simon stretched his legs out and rested them on a pile of laundry.

"Dear God. Warn me when you hand me something inedible. Give me the nuts. They are regular nuts?"

Simon threw Henry the package. "Salted almonds."

"Alex's patronizing father doesn't matter in any of this. She hasn't been in touch with him since her first year in university. As far as I'm concerned, he's a nonentity in this search. My priority is Alex.

She went to Atlanta to help me and ran right into Luc. I can't believe I compromised her safety for the bloody painting. And for what? She's gone. The painting's gone. Everything's a mess." He tried to distance himself from the image of her fighting with Luc on the beach. It could have been someone else, but probably wasn't. She was right, he was no hero. He'd led her into harm without any protection.

Simon scrubbed a hand through his hair and turned his focus to his beer. "If I'd known the trouble this would cause, I never would have used it."

"Used it?"

Simon sighed. "When you transferred the painting to Oxford, I assumed you didn't care for it, so I borrowed it. The restoration company you used is known for creating reproductions. The transaction provided us the opportunity to track the authentic pieces to illegitimate auction houses and online brokers. I would have eventually returned it to your house once we'd finished with it."

"*You* switched my picture?" Henry's knuckles whitened around the beer bottle.

Simon glanced down at the floor and kicked an old sock toward the chair. "I'm trying to get it back."

Heart racing, Henry shoved back the chair and dived onto his brother. Simon tossed his beer bottle away from the bed and shifted over to avoid Henry's full assault.

Fists flew. Henry punched Simon in the gut. Simon reacted by kicking him onto the floor, where he landed on his ass and skidded into the wall shoulder-first. The pain rocketed through his body. He should stop, but Simon hadn't suffered enough yet.

Simon stood by the window. One of his hands clutched his stomach. "Don't."

Henry pushed off the wall and lunged at Simon's torso. He slammed into his older and larger brother, knocking him into the door. He was winded, but ready for more.

Simon, however, raised his hands in an unimpressive surrender. His breathing was heavy and a grimace appeared on his face. "Feel better?"

The pain in Henry's shoulder flared. "Sod off."

Simon returned to sitting on the bed. "You're allowed to be mad at me, but I'm on your side. If you'd stayed calm for one minute, I would have told you Alex's current location."

Henry's head twisted in Simon's direction, his focus returning to Alex. "Where is she?"

"She's with Luc at his house on the right bank."

In Paris?

"How the hell do you know that?" He didn't know whether to continue his grudge against his brother or give him a hug.

"I have someone on the inside who has seen her."

Henry's proximity to her destroyed his patience. His heart raced and his chest tightened.

"Is she all right? Is she there against her will?"

"We have to take this slow and investigate. Breaking down a door without all the facts will not only put her life at risk, but it will blow my cover and that of my partner."

"If Alex is at risk, she needs help now."

"As I'd said before, I have someone on the inside monitoring the situation. If she's at risk, we'll get her out. If you were leading a group in a rescue mission, would you make a plan or run in like a teenager fueled on testosterone?"

Henry rubbed sweat off his face. Simon was right. Henry had received decorations while in the Royal Navy for his well-planned and -executed missions. Acting without thinking had never been acceptable in the SBS. With a deep breath, he placed his trust in his brother again. "What do you have in mind?"

***

After a night locked in her bedroom, Alex was allowed to enjoy April in Paris in the courtyard. The warm sun provided her with additional fortitude to survive the coming weeks.

Pascal stood guard over her. She'd prefer Serge, but he'd

disappeared. He could be anywhere assisting Luc with some other deal or dead from an act of incompetence.

With her hurt leg propped up on a chair and a steaming cup of coffee in front of her, Alex could almost imagine sitting in the rose garden in Ripon annoying Henry. He must hate her for running away with no warning. Yet it was her only option if she was to protect her family. Although the physical connection was gone, emotionally, she was more tied to him than ever. Since the minute she'd stepped into the stairwell in Atlanta, she'd harbored an empty feeling in her gut that no food would ever satisfy and no drink would ever quench. If her brain could convince her heart to sever the emotional connection, she'd be stronger and more able to complete her task.

The door to the house opened. Nicola walked out carrying a cup of coffee. Her hooker outfit of the day included black stilettos and a blue wrap dress that opened enough to showcase her fake breasts. Pascal's eyes wandered over her body as though stripping her down and taking notes.

Alex pasted on her bitch smile. "Get lucky last night? I sure did. Luc never showed up in my room."

Nicola sat in the chair opposite Alex, more than an arm's length away. "I'm surprised you didn't hear me at least one of the seven or eight times he brought me over the edge. I tend to scream a lot."

"Too busy sleeping. Thank God for pain medication."

Pascal appeared amused at their hostility. He leaned against the side of the house to enjoy the show. Luc must like the idea of his wife and mistress interacting, because Pascal saw no need to separate them this morning.

Nicola took a huge guzzle of her coffee, as though she were downing a shot of tequila. "Pascal, darling, could you be a dear and get me another cup of coffee with cream."

Alex tipped her own cup toward him in a toast. "I'd ask, too, since I'm the invalid and not simply lazy, but I'd rather you not poison me today."

Pascal walked over to Nicola and ignored Alex.

Alex pushed. "Perhaps Nicky here would like to eat with the kitchen staff. She is paid by the hour, isn't she?"

"Take your time, Pascal. I find this minger quite entertaining." Nicola lounged in her chair and rested her elbow on the table.

Pascal chuckled and left for the kitchen.

Alex dropped the smile, her focus turned serious as though she were appraising a painting. She hoped her assessment of Nicola was in the ballpark of her real worth. Humans, however, rarely provided as much value as anticipated.

"Are you Simon's Nicola?"

"I'm not owned, possessed, or enslaved by anyone. I may, however, know a Simon or two." A non-answer. The sexpot had transformed into a corporate shark with negotiating skills.

"Are you Henry's Gabe?"

Bingo. She had to be Simon's Nicola, or she'd never have known about Gabe. Hearing Henry's name, however, stunned her, but she held her face emotionless. She wanted to trust her, but chickened out to protect Henry. "Gabe? Never heard of her or Henry for that matter."

"Interesting." Nicola tapped her hand on the table as if she were bored. "If you want a friend, contact me. I can help."

She couldn't risk Nicola getting hurt. "I don't need help, just some time to recuperate."

Nicola raised an eyebrow after glancing toward Alex's cast. "You're in way over your head."

"I have my reasons for staying." She looked over at the door to make sure Pascal hadn't returned. "Why are you here? Luc doesn't let his girlfriends walk away without bruises or a body bag."

"Luc's amusing and useful to me right now. And the sex with him is even worth tolerating your presence."

"I see my two ladies are enjoying each other's company. How disturbing." Luc, speaking in English, stood by the open door. Had he heard their exchange?

Alex glared at her captor's approach. "If I'd known you already had a housemate, I would have asked for my own place."

Nicola laughed. "As long as he comes to me at night, I'm not complaining."

Luc rubbed Nicola's shoulders and kissed her. Deeply. Nicola moaned. Did he think Alex would be jealous watching him stick his tongue down Nicola's throat? *Au contraire*, it made her thankful for Nicola's presence.

"It's amazing how disgusting kissing sounds when you're not actually involved. Perhaps it's your technique, Luc. You never were that good with your tongue." She watched them pull apart after her comments.

He shifted from Nicola to his wife. His hands were positioned with his thumbs on the softest area of Alex's neck. "I'd watch what you say. You don't want me to be widowed too soon."

"Don't harm the witch, sweetheart. I prefer being a mistress to a girlfriend. It has more cachet. Besides, maybe we can convince her to join us after her cast comes off," Nicola purred.

His hands loosened, and he stepped back to Nicola. "I like how you think."

"Perverted and slutty?" Alex asked.

"Sexy and alluring," Nicola replied and leaned into Luc's embrace.

Pascal returned with Nicola's coffee and placed it in front of her.

"Nicola, I must speak to my *wife* for a few minutes alone. I bought you a present during my last trip. It's hanging in the west gallery. Enjoy." Luc then turned to Pascal. "You can leave as well."

With a stiff nod, Pascal disappeared into the house. Luc pulled Nicola's chair out and kissed her good-bye. His hands lifted under her dress. How charming. Groping the girlfriend in front of the wife.

After Nicola left the patio, Luc went over to the door and shut it. He strolled back to Alex with his phone in his hand and switched to French, his preferred language with Alex. "You're not a very obedient wife. In fact, you're turning into quite the liability. If I were you, I would try harder to obey me and show me proper respect in front of others."

"It's hard to respect someone I loathe."

"You'll need to get over this dislike of me sooner rather than later. Physical punishment hasn't been effective to tame your tongue. You don't seem to care if we beat you to death." He tapped on her cast. "You're tougher than I gave you credit for, but you should think of others when deciding what toxic words will exit your mouth."

The images of Danielle and her boyfriend's brutal death flashed into her mind, the sound of bullets taking down Matt, and the red light signifying the security guard's last moment. Alex felt light-headed. She didn't want any more violence around her unless it involved Luc. She remained silent, removing all emotion from her face as well.

Luc's fingers caressed her cheek. "You give me instant compliance when I reach out to your bleeding heart. How pathetic. Too bad you didn't shut your mouth sooner." He placed the cell phone with an internet news story in front of her eyes. "Tragic about your niece."

"My niece?" The bottom fell from her stomach, and her eyes betrayed her fear by filling with tears.

Daughter of Northrop heiress hurt in hit-and-run accident. The driver has not been located. The four-year-old child was listed in critical condition at Massachusetts General Hospital.

Rachel? Bile burned her throat. Anna must be going crazy with worry.

"Alive, but who knows for how long." He smirked.

She spun on him and grabbed his hand. "Please. Leave my family alone. Please."

"Start acting like you want them to live, and no one else will get hurt." He yanked his arm away, removed the tragic news report from her view, took a sip of her coffee, and then left her alone to cry.

CHAPTER 27

Henry fell asleep in Simon's bed on a pile of dirty laundry. He woke as the sun squeezed a sliver of light through the window between the walls of the adjoining buildings. Simon was gone.

They'd spent the night working on ways to extract Alex from the house without Luc discovering them. The plan they'd devised required several days and a permanent hiding spot for Alex. It would work, if she cooperated. Henry doubted she would.

Simon had disappeared around midnight to find a bed at some woman named Valerie's flat. He'd told Henry he'd return after a lunch meeting he didn't seem particularly keen on attending. He had better refocus on helping Alex. Henry couldn't wait for information about her until that evening, when Simon attended a dinner at Luc's for a few players in the messed-up game of stolen art and illegal arms. Simon should be speaking to his contact on the inside and trying to catch a glimpse of her now, not later. Instead, at least twelve hours would elapse until Henry learned anything. Unacceptable.

He dressed quickly and stepped out into the spring air to organize his thoughts and rid his body of the stress hampering the mental acuity required to rescue her.

An hour and many blocks through Paris later, he strolled in front of Luc's residence, a monster of a house framed with a large stone wall extending to each side and protected by cameras sitting in plain view to deter outsiders. Henry glanced around, searching for his best vantage point.

The café across the street was perfect. He hustled around oncoming traffic and chose an available table tucked under a large green awning. The previous patron had left a copy of the *International New York Times* under a half-drunk cup of coffee. Henry ordered a fresh cup of tea and pretended to read. Shadowing his face from the street traffic, he set to memorizing all the entrances visible to him and considered the best approach inside.

After an hour, a black Audi with tinted windows pulled into the driveway. Luc Perrault exited the car and headed to the front door. Henry fixated on Luc's gait, his clothing, and his need for a shave. The urge to run across the street and plow his fist through the man's nearly perfect features threatened to overwhelm him. He cracked his knuckles and prepared to move closer, but took a deep breath and sipped some tea instead. Simon would kill him for being in the neighborhood, but Henry trusted his instincts, which told him to observe, and if needed, act. He threw a few euros on the table and waited.

The front door of the house opened. A large man assisted Alex down the front walk. Seeing her pulled the tension from his chest, only to have it return when he saw the cast on her leg.

Someone had hurt her again.

Short brown hair blew over her eyes as she negotiated the two stairs to the driveway with crutches. Her long pink skirt and pink flats projected a cheerful emotion, but not one spark of anything reflected in her eyes. Her face revealed no pain when she walked, but she was in her lady of the manor mode, quiet and deferential. If she drove away, Henry would miss the opportunity to know her motivation for leaving or if she had chosen to leave him voluntarily. A broken leg told him "no." He jumped to his feet, forcing a friendly smile to appear on his face, and ran toward her.

"Alex."

Her head lifted and jerked back in shock, probably at his bruised face and split lip. He continued across the street, narrowly avoided a honking car, and stopped breathless in front of the small group. Luc glared. The man with them, probably security, stepped toward Henry with a malevolent expression. Alex remained dumbstruck.

Luc held on to her elbow as more of a restraint than a support. "Can I help you?"

"I'm her cousin."

Alex winced.

"A family relation? How convenient." Luc seemed pleased to meet him. "Nice meeting you, Mr***.?"

"West. John West."

Luc shook Henry's hand, gripping it with excessive force that Henry matched. He tried to tame the anger in his eyes, leaving his handshake as the only warning he gave Luc. They released at the same time, like two boxers before the ring of the bell.

Henry focused on Alex, although it was difficult with the guard trying to step into his space. "I haven't seen you in forever. You took off after that party at Belinda's flat."

She shrugged. "Zombie apocalypse. You can't predict when those things will happen. I should have called."

"I love a good family reunion." Luc gestured to the guard to stand down, yet he still held Alex with a firm hand. "Where are you staying? Perhaps she can contact you tomorrow."

Henry faced Alex. He wouldn't release Simon's location to anyone. "Same place as before."

A slight smile sprouted on her face, until Luc wrapped his arm around her and led her toward the car.

"If you'll excuse us, my wife and I are late for a lunch meeting."

The world stopped spinning. Henry could barely breathe. "Wife?"

Luc glanced at Alex. Her eyes focused toward the ground. When she looked up, her smile was cold and arrogant.

What the hell?

"We married a few days ago. A complete whirlwind romance." She glanced toward Luc and smiled, but the smile seemed creepy and distorted.

Why would she marry the man who beat the hell out of her? Did she love him?

Glancing toward the ground again, she spoke in a breathy tone. "By marrying Luc, I fulfill all the qualifications for membership in the women's club we used to joke about as kids. Perhaps I'll join them next time I'm in England. Good-bye, John."

She tried to step away, but Luc turned her toward him and gave her a deep and thorough kiss that Alex accepted. He helped her into the back of the car, sliding the crutches across the back window. When she was settled, Luc, Alex, and their bodyguard drove away, leaving Henry standing alone.

Nothing could have prepared him for the rage threatening to explode from seeing her in another man's arms. He wanted to lash out at her and at Luc. Instead, he remained on the sidewalk staring at the taillights of the car taking away everything that mattered to him.

He couldn't get past her marrying Luc. She almost seemed pleased about it. One minute in Henry's arms and the next in the arms of someone else. And why the hell would he care that she could join a women's club? He paused.

Not a women's club, *the* women's club.

Henry had to stop underestimating her abilities. She told him all he needed to know. The son of a bitch broke her leg. What else was he threatening to do if she didn't stay married to him?

***

Alex sat propped in the backseat of the car to stretch her leg out, struggling to hold back the rush of emotion she felt upon seeing Henry. If Luc sensed she had even the slightest attraction toward Henry, let alone this aching love, her beloved earl's life would be as good as terminated. Still, he consumed her thoughts.

Henry in Paris? Her heart leaped for joy as her brain screamed in horror. He so wanted to be her hero, but the mild-mannered professor hadn't an ounce of Indiana Jones in his veins. Simon's Nicola probably alerted them to her whereabouts. His arrival was unwelcome and upsetting.

What happened to him? The bruises couldn't be older than three or four days. She wanted to remember him sexy and sweet, not beat up and despondent. Her body trembled with too much emotion, too much confusion. She just wanted this nightmare to end. Wrapping her arms around her waist to hold herself together, she stared out the window.

Luc glanced over his shoulder as Pascal drove. "Your cousin seemed surprised to see you."

"We haven't seen each other in a long time."

"An English cousin?"

She shrugged. "Second or third cousin on my mother's side. Her cousin married some viscount in Leeds and moved her family there two or three decades ago. John is her son. I've only seen him a few times."

They drove to a rural area and down a wooded road to a small stone house, a place that could be located only with knowledge of the area and a clear destination in mind.

Luc stopped his car and waited. "I've been impressed by your behavior since your niece's accident. I like this new side of you. Make sure you continue to cooperate. If you fail me, you lose a family member. I'll be generous, though—you can choose the person I'll gun down. Perhaps I can kill Mr. West. He's in the area and not immediate family."

She swallowed her fear and nodded. "You don't need to worry about me."

"Good. I'm acquiring two paintings this afternoon. You're to stay out of the way until authentication is required. Tell me the truth and then return to the car."

She nodded again.

A black Mercedes drove down the driveway and parked. A small moving van followed. The door of the Mercedes opened and***Simon? Alex tightened the hold around her waist to soothe the fear bubbling up inside her stomach. Dressed in jeans and a black blazer, he wandered toward Luc's car and waited. He wasn't wearing his usual smile; instead, tension showed in his stiff posture and slow pace. His hands rested at his sides.

Luc opened Alex's door, pulling her out. Simon's eyes widened in a flash of recognition when he saw her. He must not have expected her. Luc tossed her the crutches and then left her alone as he spoke to Simon. They seemed to know each other. Was Simon providing the paintings? She wished she could read people's intentions as well as her sister Julia could. Would Simon betray her?

The breeze through the trees muffled their conversation. Simon mentioned something about replacing Roman and a delayed flight.

A couple of men she'd never seen before opened the back of the truck and pulled out two large packages wrapped in brown paper. The paintings. The men carried them to the house. Luc motioned Alex to follow them. She hobbled across the gravel driveway, keeping an ear toward Simon and an eye on Luc.

Empty rooms and blank walls greeted her inside the main living area of the house. The men unwrapped the paintings and placed them against the wall, rough enough to chip the corner of one of the frames. She stepped closer to them.

The two paintings had never been cataloged in her vast memory. One artist had painted both of these neoclassical mytho-logical scenes. Oil on canvas with colors and markings dating them to the year 1820 or so. Alex reached out and touched the smooth strokes, looking for anything to indicate a forgery. They were authentic. She recognized the style. The artist had to be

Sophie Fremiet, known more as her husband's model for the sculpture *La Marseillaise* than for her own impressive work. Alex searched the lower corner of one of the paintings and found the artist's mark. The delicate nature of the canvases and brutal handling of them depressed her.

The destruction of art overwhelmed her senses. She remembered crying for days after learning of a thief who had burned several masterpieces rather than hand them over to the authorities. The memory of the last painting she'd admired flooded her heart and mind. Lady Elizabeth Gillett. Did Henry buy the painting or did she disturb the night enough to throw Henry off his purpose for the trip? She hoped he'd found a way to save the painting and the Ripon Women's Club.

"Well?" Luc entered the room and stood next to her.

Wiping some of the moistness from her cheeks, she nodded toward her cold and uncaring husband. "Sophie Fremiet Rude. They're authentic and made within a year of each other."

"Excellent. Go back to the car. I'll meet you in a few minutes." He left her side to approach one of the men who had carried the paintings into the house.

As Alex made her way back toward the car, she watched Pascal hand Simon a metal briefcase. It had to be the cash for the paintings. Somehow, Simon's complicity in this sale made her sick. His involvement with stolen art wasn't news to her, but seeing him take the cash tied him to a world she detested and turned her stomach. How could Henry trust someone so corrupt, brother or not? Unless he was pretending to be corrupt. She had no way of knowing.

Pascal strolled toward the farmhouse away from Simon, who seemed preoccupied with counting his money. After Simon checked the contents of the briefcase, he placed it in the trunk of his car.

He intercepted her on her way back to the car. He grasped her hand with both of his and looked into her eyes as though trying to absorb her story. "Alex, I presume."

Luc would not be kind to her if he suspected they knew each other. She pulled her hand from Simon's clasp and backed up one step.

"Yes. And you are?"

"Simon Dunn."

"Nice to meet you, Mr. Dunn."

Simon switched to Gaelic.

"He misses you."

She flinched, shocked he knew her secret with languages. She rarely used the Gaelic she'd learned from a Scottish landlord in Paris.

"He'll get over it," she replied in the same language.

"Don't underestimate the earl. He doesn't take rejection well."

She ignored his comment. "I spoke to him this morning. His face is destroyed. What happened?"

After a slight narrowing of his eyebrows at the statement, he shook his head and then beamed her a flirtatious smile. A grimace, however, hovered around the edges of his mouth. "He met a few acquaintances of your father."

Henry had seen her family? She could picture her father's poor treatment of him. He hated outsiders. She dropped her eyes to avoid his gaze. "Tell him I'm sorry."

Simon lowered his voice. "We can help you."

We? Simon and Nicola? How could they help unless they killed Luc?

"I don't want your help." She saw Luc approach and stepped away from Simon.

"Alex, go to the car." Luc spoke to Alex in French, and switched to English for Simon. "Everything looks good. You have the payment?"

Simon nodded. "I'll hand it to Roman when his flight comes in."

"Will I see you at dinner tonight?"

"I wouldn't miss it." He nodded toward Alex before she turned to walk away.

CHAPTER 28

Simon arrived among the first of about twenty guests for dinner. Luc had not materialized, but Alex greeted each guest as they entered the spacious foyer. Wearing a loose ivory gown, she leaned on her crutches near the front entrance. Luc's security guard stood behind her, more prison guard than protector.

Simon took hold of her hand. "Good evening."

"Hello, Mr. Dunn." A poorly constructed smile greeted him, and her hand trembled in his. "My husband is currently detained in his study, but drinks are at the bar. Please help yourself."

He couldn't understand why she didn't want their help, but she was getting it regardless. He continued to hold her. "Would you care to join me for a drink, Mrs. Perrault?"

"I'm afraid I have front door duty. Perhaps later." Her eyes flickered toward the guard.

"No one else will be arriving for a while—come on." He guided her to the bar.

"Mr. Perrault asked you to remain at the door. You can't leave." The security guard stepped in front of them and attempted to chastise Alex and scare Simon off with some bullshit aggressive expression. A bully over a woman a third of his size; the man should be castrated.

"You'd almost think she was under house arrest the way you're treating her." Simon laughed at his own brand of warning. "Why don't you find the lady a chair? It's obvious she's been standing too long."

Alex brushed Simon's lapel with a whisper touch. "Don't be silly, Mr. Dunn. I'm quite all right. I prefer standing." She dropped her hand to her side and returned to her station.

"As you wish. I look forward to speaking with you later." Simon nodded to her, then strolled to the bar and ordered himself vodka straight up. He greeted several acquaintances, none of whom he'd ever want to meet without the Beretta in his waistband.

While chatting with one of Luc's artifact importers from Cambodia, Simon kept his eye on the front door and his brother's obsession. She stood erect, but frequently shifted the weight off her bad leg. She should be sitting. He'd love to get that prat standing with her alone to teach him some morals.

The door opened again and Roman entered, heading directly for Alex. If he recognized her as Belinda, then Alex, Nicola, and he would all be at risk.

Simon walked as fast as he could across the foyer to shield Alex from Roman's view. He was too late. Roman had already placed his arm around her waist.

"Nice to see you again, Belinda. Still attached to Simon?"

He glanced between Alex and Simon.

Alex tilted her head and said something back to Roman in fluent Russian. Nothing submissive about this woman when she pulled out her inner warrior. Even her stance morphed into something different than Belinda's *eye candy with no brain* persona.

Roman perused her body again with a curious stare and responded to her in his native tongue. He seemed confused at the similarities the brunette shared with the blond Belinda. Alex's strength and intelligence, however, eclipsed dim-witted Belinda's personality. Good.

"Roman." He clasped his old friend on the shoulder. "I see you've met Luc's new wife, Alex."

"Alex? Alex Lemoine?" Roman stared at her face. They may have been introduced during Alex's previous life.

"Yes. Small world, isn't it? She helped Luc with a few sales, fell in love, the rest is boring. Come, let's get a drink." He gripped Roman's arm in a wrestling hold, and they walked off, leaving Alex with her bodyguard.

"Did you bring anyone tonight?" Roman asked.

"No. Belinda went to Miami to visit a sick relative. Annoying, but it keeps her happy. I don't have the patience for more drama by inviting someone else right now."

"I understand."

Luc, sporting a navy blazer, jeans, and boat shoes, ambled up to them with a drink in his hand. "Welcome. I'm glad you both could make it. Sorry you weren't at the exchange this afternoon."

Roman shook his hand and patted him on the back. "The plane was delayed in Edinburgh. Simon handled everything, I take it?"

Simon creased his brow and faced Roman. He preferred both parties in a transaction to be present to minimize his own financial and physical liability. "We'll talk later about my additional fee for the hassle of your absence."

The risks of a transaction always rose at the transfer point. Simon had never represented Roman's interests in an art-only deal, preferring to be known exclusively as an arms dealer. Risking his life for stolen art and a briefcase full of cash seemed a waste. In this case, however, he wanted to reestablish contact with Luc. Alex's presence at the transfer was a bonus.

Luc seemed uninterested in Roman and Simon's relationship, except where it made him money. "We should meet before you both fly back to the UK. I may have some interesting business developments to share."

Roman nodded toward Luc and then clasped Simon's arm in a gesture of friendship. "We look forward to it."

Several more people arrived. Simon watched Alex greet them, most likely in their native languages. She winced a few times and shifted her stance, but otherwise held herself together. Luc and Roman also watched the front door.

"I see you met my wife Alex," Luc said to Roman.

"Beautiful. Fluent in Russian. You've done well for yourself." Roman's love for beautiful women never caused too much harm. He preferred women who were willing and available, although he often began his flirtations before a woman's prior relationship ended.

"She's a gem." Luc's face showed more of a scowl than admiration until he turned his attention to the large marble staircase. Simon's eyes followed.

Dressed to kill in a black low-cut cocktail dress that flared out from midcalf, Nicola sauntered right into Luc's arms. He kissed her as though staking a claim. Ballsy move in front of the new wife. It also told Simon how disposable the women were.

"I think you both know Nicola."

Roman nodded and greeted her with a kiss on the back of the hand.

Simon glared. "We know each other intimately."

Luc slipped his hand up toward Nicola's breast. "Ah. Yes. You were together for a year or two. I remember. Should I separate you at dinner?"

"Don't bother." She waved her hand breezily. "It will make the meal much more interesting for all involved if we get to rehash his infidelities over chilled melon and prosciutto." Nicola glowered at Simon. She always looked fantastic glowering.

"Very well. Shall we head in?" Luc linked arms with Nicola and called over to Alex's guard. "Help my wife into the dining room, Pascal."

A major slight in the presence of a roomful of people, but Alex seemed content to remain aloof. Simon, on the other hand, preferred a beautiful escort on the walk to the dinner table. He drifted back to the door, maneuvered himself between Alex and Pascal, and assisted her to the dining room. Pascal followed them like an ass tethered to a horse.

"Nice evening," Simon commented in Gaelic, a language learned from his mother's Scottish relations. He walked with a slow pace so she could limp along beside him.

She nodded. "Pleasant."

"How do you like living in Paris?"

"Crowded and loud."

"Not a city girl?"

"No. But don't worry, Luc promised to place me in a small plot of my own real soon. I'm not greedy, though, I intend to share it with him." A shimmer in her eyes materialized as she spoke.

"Very considerate of you. Any place in particular?"

She sighed, her eyes drifting away to perhaps a memory. "I imagine living in a rural town, near an ancient castle, perhaps with a horn blower to close the small square on a rainy night."

"I know a town exactly like that." Simon grinned at her.

She lifted her head and pushed back her shoulders as though preparing to take on the burdens of the world. "Mine exists only in my dreams."

"Dreams are funny things. Just when your life turns into a nightmare, you wake up and realize the best is yet to come." He squeezed her arm and made a silent vow that he'd get her out of this mess. The sadness in her eyes ripped at his conscience. After all, he'd sent her directly into Luc's clutches.

Simon's own dream, the woman dressed in black, escorted an enemy to dinner. He hoped to pull Nicola away from this hellish existence as well as Alex, but Nic possessed a stubborn streak of infinite duration.

Luc seated Alex to his left. A lush redhead flanked him on the right side. He focused solely on the redhead. His wife focused solely on the dinner.

Simon sat between a French model wannabe and Nicola. Roman sat on her other side.

During the fourth course, consisting of cognac shrimp with beurre blanc sauce, Roman dominated Nicola's attention. His hand slid below the table. Despite the glowing admiration she beamed toward Roman, Simon recognized that she was reaching her limit by the tension in her neck.

He turned away from Martina something-or-other and placed his hand on Nicola's shoulder, stopping her conversation with Roman. "Roman, my friend, don't go setting your sights on Nicola. She'll be pretty well used up after her stay with Luc. If you want, I'll set you up with someone who will appreciate you."

The blaze erupting from Nicola's eyes toward him became warm and friendly as Roman's hand shifted back to his lap. The tension in her neck relaxed, and her shoulders softened under Simon's touch.

"Blonde or brunette?" Roman asked.

"Blonde. All the way, if you know what I mean."

They both laughed, and Nic grinned as though she appreciated a good joke that demoralized women.

"Are you heading to Zurich next week?" Roman asked. "I was thinking about it. I need to discuss my present requirements with Luc before I make any final decisions. If I go, I'll bring Belinda and her friend. We can double-date."

"I like how you think." Roman raised his wineglass to him and then turned away from Nicola to focus on his other dinner companion, the wife of a major donor to the Musée d'Orsay. Regrettably for the museum, her husband's tax-deductible donations included more reproductions than originals.

Nicola angled her head toward Simon and frowned. "You can unhand me now."

"I could." He rubbed his fingers across the base of her hairline. "I'm wondering what it takes to please a woman like you."

"Money, gifts. In fact, Luc gave me a present this morning. Something you never did."

"Jewels?"

Nicola grinned while trying to shift his hand off her. "Better. A painting. Some lady on a horse. He told me I could store it here indefinitely."

Good. The painting showed up earlier than he'd planned.

"He's generous. It makes sense to abandon all we've been through and run to his side." His fingers continued to massage her.

She sighed as he brushed one of his fingertips over the edge of her ear, a sound he wished he heard in his bed at night.

Turning her game on, Nicola changed her sigh to a sneer. "You and I had nothing."

"Didn't we?" Simon's hand dropped away from her skin. He tucked the lingering heat in his fist. "I seem to remember making love on the plane to Fiji and riding bareback for hours on the beach."

Their conversation drew a few stares from their neighbors, but Luc seemed intent on making the redhead his conquest for the night and missed their bantering.

"We never went horseback riding together." Shaking her head, she lifted her fork and stabbed a shrimp.

"I never said we did."

"Pig." Nicola spoke louder than proper, and most guests now looked in their direction.

Simon smirked at the audience. "You miss me, admit it."

Luc turned away from the redhead toward Simon and Nicola. "Are you all right?" he called across the table.

"Fine." Nicola flashed a smile toward Luc and waved off his question. "If you'll all excuse me, I need some fresh air." She pushed out of her chair to stand, but Simon placed a hand on her shoulder again, keeping her seated.

"Don't bother, I was just leaving." He rose and kissed her cheek. "Take care of yourself, Nic."

He walked to Luc at the head of the table and shook his hand. "Thanks for dinner. We'll talk in a few days." Then he lowered his face and spoke in a hushed tone only Luc and Alex could hear. "If you have the wife out, leave the bitch in the bedroom. She annoys me."

***

Henry had moved all of his and Simon's things to a hotel closer to Alex. The place offered room service and clean sheets, a vast improvement from Simon's hole-in-the-wall existence.

Waiting for Simon to return from dinner took patience and a quick walk past Luc's house to make sure everything appeared secure. Returning to the room, he paced, pretended to read, and watched television until Simon arrived at ten.

"You're early." He tried to sound cool and detached, but Simon had always read Henry's emotions as though they were broadcast through a megaphone.

Simon pulled off his jacket and threw it on the dresser. "I accomplished my goals."

"How is she?"

"She's putting weight on her leg, so it can't be too bad. I'm trying to pull her hospital records to see the extent of the damage."

"Did you speak with her?"

"Only briefly. I walked with her into the dining room. Luc was too busy escorting his new mistress."

"What?" Luc had to be an arrogant sod to treat women with such disrespect.

"It's obvious Alex isn't there for love. She's not even there for the sex. I think the mistress is staying in Luc's bedroom."

Simon's comments triggered an unexpected release of tension in Henry. The existence of Luc's mistress could protect Alex from Luc's abusive sexual proclivities. Yet he still couldn't understand why she went along without a fight. "He beats the hell out of her and treats her with disdain. Why would she marry him?"

"Blackmail. Have you ever met a battered woman in your life?

For a man who seems to care so much, you need some classes on the psychology of abuse."

Simon was right, as always. Luc probably aimed for a share of the Northrop fortune, exactly the son-in-law Mr. Northrop tried to protect his daughters from. Alex, on the other hand, cared only about her family. Her love for them was evident in the brightening of her facial expression when she spoke about them.

"You're right," he said. "She's sacrificing herself for her family. The security guard was killed by an assassin, maybe in front of Alex. A duffel bag containing her possessions was found at the scene. And what about her niece? I showed you the report earlier. The hit-and-run occurred outside of her house. No one's caught the suspect. Alex won't make a move or fear Luc will do more than merely hospitalize her kin."

"She's pretty tough. She'll be fine until my contact figures out a way to sneak her out."

Henry nodded, but remembered what she'd said to him in Edinburgh. It won't be over until one of them was dead. The muscles in his legs, shoulders, and neck tightened, and his heartbeat deepened into a heavy pounding. Her plan didn't involve escape.

"No. She won't leave. As long as Luc is alive, her family's at risk. Why didn't I see this before?" He found it difficult to speak the words with his throat constricting.

"What the hell are you talking about?"

"She'll protect her family no matter the cost. She's going to kill Luc or die trying." Henry jumped up. The tension moved to his chest. "I have to stop her." Grabbing a gun from the dresser, he headed toward the door.

Simon called after him. "You'll be the cause of her death if you show up guns blazing. Think. You never reacted like this in the service."

Henry paused. The reason for his actions struck him in the gut like a lead bullet wrapped in lace. "I've never had so much at stake."

CHAPTER 29

—————— ❧ ——————

When the last guest departed, Alex lumbered toward her room with Pascal close on her heels. "Can you hold my crutches a minute?"

He obliged her by pushing her into the oncoming stairs. Her wrist hit one stair and the cast slammed hard into another. The pain shot throughout her body and caused her eyes to tear up. She stayed in the awkward position, inhaling and exhaling until the stabbing ache receded. Pascal stood over her grinning like a schoolyard bully.

Her gown had ripped in the fall. It didn't matter, though. She didn't intend to wear it again. She forced herself into a sitting position and caught her breath. The marble chilled her through the thin material and sent an arctic shiver through her limbs. If Luc thought she was tormenting Pascal, he'd hurt one of her sisters or the children again. She needed to hold herself together until they were safe.

With a burst of adrenaline, she struggled to stand. The crutches remained a few feet away on the floor. Lifting the dress past her calves to prevent herself from tripping again, she climbed step by step. The pain in her leg made for a slower climb, but it also prodded her forward, a warning of things to come if she didn't buck up and fight.

Luc had left the table with some redheaded tramp named Matilde. The girl was looking for a shortcut to wealth and would find that shortcuts typically led to dead ends. But she might provide Alex a few extra hours to figure out a way to finish this game tonight.

Limping toward her room, she maintained a certain distance from Pascal. He didn't seem worried about her trying to escape. Instead, he mumbled apologies into his phone for his long absence from whatever desperate female he'd convinced to date him.

She entered her bedroom and shut the door, leaving Pascal on the other side. The lock clicked into place. Luc had arranged to keep her in, but not him out. Dragging herself over to the bed, she leaned against the headboard and elevated her leg with a pillow. After a few minutes, she shifted her foot. As much as the position helped the swelling, her leg felt as though fire ants were swarming under the cast. She kicked the pillow aside with her other leg and let her broken leg rest flat.

They'd left her with nothing in the room to use as a weapon. No lamps, statues, fireplace tools. They'd even taken her crutches. Only two Queen Anne chairs remained by the window. The heavy brocade curtains over the windows wouldn't help her, either. She had nothing.

She couldn't rely on anyone else. Were Simon and Nicola allies or enemies? She didn't know who to trust anymore. The dining room had quaked from their open hostility. After Simon had left, Luc knelt at Nicola's side and caressed her shoulders to ease her fiery emotions. She'd left dinner early, while Luc had escorted the redhead to someplace comfortable to discuss "opportunities."

For the moment, Nicola and Alex shared a common imprisonment. Luc would never allow Nicola to walk away from him, even while he was interviewing someone else for her job. They had to stay put and wait. Hopefully, Nicola would be free after Alex figured out an escape from this nightmare existence.

The handle to the door turned. Luc walked in. His blazer was gone and his shirt untucked. He looked like a man who'd just finished screwing a redhead. He shut the door behind him and wandered slowly to the bed.

"Alex, darling, you look tired." She hated when he called her darling. He'd called her darling before raping her the first time, and the word now burned her ears.

"Exhausted." Every tired muscle alerted, ready to fight.

"Feel free to fall asleep. I've decided to consummate our marriage tonight. Your body is all I need." He spoke as though molesting her was a bore, but a necessity.

Icy fear spread through her veins. She shifted to the opposite side of the bed. Rejection would infuriate him, but she couldn't convince herself to cooperate with his demands.

"Don't play hard to get. I've already had my share of dominating someone against her will tonight, and I'm not in the mood to call Pascal in to hold you down."

The thought of Pascal seeing her so vulnerable soured her stomach and stopped her retreat.

"That's my girl." He stretched over the bed and pulled her toward him. "You're mine, Alex, until your death. Never forget that."

She scanned the room again, in case a magical weapon appeared since Luc had entered. No such luck. He had the upper hand.

He brushed her hair back. "I miss your long hair. If you live long enough, you'll have to grow it out for me."

Kissing her shoulder, he slowly unzipped her gown. Alex shuddered at his touch. His fingers felt like a scorpion crawling on her skin, waiting for the right moment to sting. The gown loosened; a strap slipped off one of her shoulders. Her body began to tremble. *How do you fight a man who strips down your defenses, both physically and emotionally?*

"You're so beautiful. The perfect complement to my art collection." He kissed behind her ear and grasped a bunch of her hair to expose her neck. "If you behave, we could do amazing things together in the art world."

She tried to back away. His hand had twisted her hair through fisted fingers.

The grip on her hair tightened, and he wrenched her head back. "What the fuck is this?"

The stabbing pain he caused stole her breath. "What?"

He yanked her hair again and threw her back onto the bed. "You altered my mark." His face reddened to crimson, and his lips curled.

The tattoo. She'd forgotten about her layover in Washington, DC. "I didn't know we'd be getting back together. I guess we can change it back." She struggled to keep her voice from quavering.

"Change it back? Who the hell is ER?" He spit out the words.

He'd kill her for having another man's initials on her, even if it was only the man's title and not his name, so she reached into her memory for a woman. "Eleanor Roosevelt. She's my role model."

"You lie." He slapped her face.

She threw up her hands to press on the stinging. Her stomach twisted with fear. "The Queen of England?" The words came out between sobs.

"Wrong." He slapped her again; her ear ached as though a hammer had struck it. Tears formed in her eyes, and she struggled to get away. She wasn't ready to die. He pushed her off the bed by kicking her cast. Loud screams came from her mouth, but no one arrived to help her. Landing hard on the floor, she ignored all the pain and shuffled toward the fireplace. Not even a damn log available to launch at him.

Through her tears, she focused on the Queen Anne chairs. Twins, made of a hard oak. She couldn't break them into pieces in her condition, but maybe she could break his head with one.

Before she reached them, Luc arrived at her side and kicked her in the stomach, his shoes slicing through the thin material and scraping her skin. The wind knocked out of her, she gasped for air and coughed, barely breathing.

Blood soaked through the white dress still wrapped around her torso. A bloody bride in a macabre horror film. This was it. The final act.

She caught his next kick with her hands and tried to pull him off balance, but the beatings had weakened her. She only managed to slow him down. When he stepped back, she dived for the chair. Lifting it only halfway above her head, she swung it toward him. He evaded it with ease. She swung again.

This time he grabbed it and tossed it toward the door.

"You are a dead woman."

She reached the second chair before he turned back to her. When he raised his hands to stop her from hitting him with it, she launched the chair in the opposite direction and straight into the silver gilt mirror hung over the fireplace. The mirror shattered.

Luc stepped back to avoid the flying glass, giving Alex the chance to dive into the spraying shards. The glass cut her knees, but the agony spurred her on. She lifted a large piece in the shape of a dagger. The edges pierced her palm and lacerated her fingers, but she squeezed tighter in order to strike at him with deadly force. She rushed toward him, attempting to stab him in the neck. His size and strength made her job impossible. She managed to scrape it across his face before he threw her on the bed and knocked the weapon from her hand. His fist landed on her cheek below her eye. The impact pushed her head into the headboard. The last thing she heard was Luc calling out to Pascal.

***

Henry swallowed several shots of the cheap Irish whiskey Simon had ordered from room service. It helped dull the nagging dread that occupied all of his thoughts. He finally settled down to research Luc's location on the internet. Mapping out their operation provided the perfect distraction from his raging emotions.

Simon relaxed while Henry's analytical mind dissected and used every smidgen of information he'd gleamed from his time at the café as well as the information Simon provided on the dinner at Luc's house. More information came from Google Earth and the MI6 satellite surveillance system.

He lifted his gaze from the laptop. "I'm impressed with these programs. They would have helped us in Afghanistan at the start of the war."

Simon laughed. "You jumped ship too soon. Technology changes by the millisecond now."

"I miss it occasionally, but I'm a swot at heart. Reading books, researching. And what would I do without the Ripon Women's Group?"

"Attend more social events, I suppose."

Simon's mobile rang. He answered the call in the bathroom.

A bad feeling rose through Henry's gut. He wished he could listen in to understand the depths of the intelligence Simon had access to.

Simon shouted into the phone. His alarmed words were muffled through the door, but the message was clear. He sprinted out of the bathroom. "Henry, we have to get Alex out *now*."

Shit. If something happened to her, his world would end.

Henry's stomach twisted and cramped. Pressing a fist to his mouth, he tried to harness his growing dread at the outcome. He moved with efficient strides and focused on his sole objective.

He grabbed the gun Simon had given to him. They both secured the weapons in their waistbands, hidden from the public and the police. Within seconds, they bolted out of the hotel, jogging down the street fast enough to get there, but not so fast as to draw attention to themselves. They crossed through a side street and into the backyard of one of the houses next to Luc's. The wall was high between the properties, but a Range Rover parked near it provided the perfect means of entry.

"We only have one chance if this alarm goes off." Henry slowed and gave the area a quick once-over.

Sliding under the car, Simon reconfigured a few wires. "It should be all set. Let's go."

He bounded to the top of the vehicle. Henry climbed up behind him. They peered over the wall. The house was eerily silent. They hopped over and moved to an entryway next to a small patio.

Simon signaled Henry to stay back as a lookout while he tried the door. It was locked. "My partner is on the second floor. I'll assist there. You locate Alex. Fighting was heard on the third floor, so start there."

Simon kicked the lock on the door, but the door didn't give. This wasn't the time to wait for backup. Henry grabbed a patio chair and smashed it through the full-length window in the door. Raking the rough edges with the chair, he stepped in, gun drawn and ready. Simon followed behind.

The bottom of the house was dark, except for a few lights left illuminating a path to the kitchen and the front foyer. They crossed a large family room. A creak from the right sent them diving in different directions, avoiding a bullet aimed at one of them. He heard Simon shuffle against a wall.

They couldn't waste time down here. They needed to find Alex.

When the bastard with the gun started firing a haphazard spray of bullets and moved farther into the room, Simon fired a single bullet toward the sound. His shot ripped through a window in the dining room. Damn, he'd never been a straight shot. The gunman fired back. Neighbors would be calling the police soon. They didn't have much time.

Henry took aim, a position as natural as holding a book, and hit the assailant midforehead. The man dropped with a *thud*.

He'd let his conscience rip him apart later, after Alex was safe and in his arms.

Staying low, he crossed to the dead assailant and took his gun. He acknowledged Simon with a nod and crept out of the room.

CHAPTER 30

Henry hadn't killed anyone since leaving the service. Death still wrenched his gut and ripped out a piece of his soul, but the urgency to find Alex took priority. He climbed the stairs two at a time until he hit the second-floor landing. A quick glance to the left and right revealed long hallways of doors. The enormous house must have forty rooms in it.

Simon would be heading to his partner as soon as he picked his arse up off the floor. Henry continued up the stairs to the third-floor landing. He needed more information. The only sound came from something shuffling around on the second floor. Probably Simon.

A stream of light flowed out from under a door farther down the hall. Henry took off toward the light and paused. Not hearing anything inside, he pushed the door open, keeping his gun raised. His stomach roiled as he braced himself for whatever his instinct told him was behind the door.

"Alex?" He spoke in a loud whisper.

The opulent bedroom had a crackling fire in the fireplace filling the room with a smoky scent. By the fireplace, the room's only occupant sat in a chair with his legs crossed, pointing a gun toward Henry.

Luc.

"If it isn't cousin John. Nice to meet you again." A long, bloody laceration marked his face, and his clothes appeared disheveled and stained. His serenity, amid such a violent appearance, failed to cover his malevolent soul. He'd kill Henry without a moment's hesitation. Henry approached with caution.

"Where's Alex?" He glanced around the room with his gun trained on Luc's head. He'd have killed him immediately, but he didn't kill arbitrarily. He might require information.

"My wife? She was sleeping soundly last I saw her. *Dead to the world* as the saying goes." His arm stretched across the armrest, his aim steady and directed at Henry. "Should I be calling the police about a break-in? I'd hate to kill you, but I'm within my rights to use deadly force to protect my family."

Henry glared at the prat who'd ripped apart Alex's life. "Let me take her out of here, and I won't be forced to kill *you*." Cocky language might hold Luc back if he had the slightest hesitation to kill. He didn't.

Luc's gun went off and struck one of Henry's knuckles in his right hand. As the pain exploded across his fingers, he lost hold of the gun. A second round went over his head and he dived out the door, reached into his waistband with his left hand, and pulled out the Glock 19 he'd taken from the corpse near the back entrance.

Breathing heavily, he heard Luc throwing more wood into the fireplace. He turned back into the room. Luc was pushing burning firewood into the middle of the throw rug. The son of a bitch was going to burn the place down with Alex inside. The edges of the rug had already caught fire. Henry stayed low, catching his breath, the hatred for Luc pushing away his panic for Alex's safety.

A low growl came from Henry's throat as he aimed with his left hand and fired. His shot nicked Luc in the shoulder. Luc dived to the ground and returned the volley, missing twice, but hitting Henry on the side of his chest the third time. The force knocked him to the floor and pushed the air from his lungs. He shook the pain off and silently thanked Simon for the loan of the Kevlar vest. It still hurt like hell, but he was alive. He needed to move his position to avoid being vulnerable to a final shot in the head.

"Good-bye, Mr. West. Good luck finding your *cousin* in time to escape."

Luc clicked on an empty cartridge, paused, and then swung the butt of his gun toward Henry's face. Quick reflexes had the gun in Henry's tight grip before being pistol-whipped. He tried to pull Luc off balance, but Luc kicked his chest while pulling the gun out of his hand.

Flames had already spread up the heavy drapes. Noxious gases billowed throughout the room. Henry roused himself before the smoke and fire overtook him. By the time he pushed himself to a standing position, Luc had run.

Bracing the wall, Henry tried to ignore the blood oozing from his dominant hand. He stared at the fire and the room around him. Nothing was available to slow down the blaze. He had to get Alex out before the flames consumed the house. The hall stretched in both directions from the main staircase. Henry headed to the right first. Throwing each door open with his left hand, he glanced inside for any trace of Alex before moving on to the next room. He worked methodically, but every room sat empty.

His right hand was bleeding profusely. He wiped the blood on his shirt and refocused on locating Alex. She had to be here. Somewhere. Anywhere.

At the end of the hall, he turned and headed back toward the staircase to search the rooms in the other wing.

"Alex," he hollered.

Smoke streamed out of the fiery room and permeated the open spaces of the house. Henry held his breath trying to avoid the toxic fumes. Moving quickly, he sucked in some less smoky air and continued his search. More doors, more empty rooms. The entire hallway was getting brighter as the fire behind him flared. If she was on a different floor, he wouldn't have time to locate her.

Where was she? Henry fought the panic rising up in him. Stay calm and do the job. Another door, empty. There were only two more doors until the end of the hall.

He opened the closest and light streamed over his shoulder, revealing a macabre scene. He swallowed his scream. The room was smashed to bits. Chairs overturned, a broken mirror, and Alex.

His Alex.

He turned the light on and tried not to cry out at the state he found her in. Her face was swollen and discolored.

A white and bloody material covered her body. She looked like death. He wouldn't survive if he lost her. His heart broke apart, and the beating of those separate pieces deafened him.

"Alex. Do you hear me?" He rushed to her side.

Her pulse gave him hope. Faint hope at best, but her heart still fought for life. Moving her might worsen her injuries, but he had to risk it, or she'd die in the fire.

"Hey, Sunshine. Wake up." *Please, wake up.*

Pulling the duvet around her, he lifted her into his arms. The simple task felt awkward with his damaged hand. Her body fought him at first. Black eyes flickered open. Alex didn't seem to recognize anything. Her stare turned toward the glimmering light from the blaze out the door. She didn't react. Her muscles relaxed into his arms, and her eyes closed again.

He covered her nose and mouth with the duvet as he entered the hall and kissed her forehead. She'd lost weight since Atlanta. She was thin before, but now she seemed emaciated. Holding her as securely yet gently as possible, he shifted most of her weight to his left arm. His right hand continued to lose blood and feeling, but he had to use it to secure her to him. Tugging at the duvet again, he covered the rest of her face.

The fire had expanded across the third floor. He rushed to the stairs through the smoke filling the hall and past the flames coating the walls.

***

Simon knew exactly where to run. Second floor, third door on the right side. Nicola, the queen of procedure, had drawn Simon a map of her location on a cocktail napkin during one of their meetings. His beautiful Girl Guide always prepared.

The third door to the right stood open, waiting for him. He paused, preparing himself for an armed assailant or an empty room. Nothing, however, could have prepared him for the scene inside.

Her room, decorated in a non-Nicola pink floral theme, appeared as though it awaited a new guest. The bed was made, the dresser cleared, and Nicola's small suitcase was zipped and ready to go. She wouldn't be going anywhere.

Blood splattered the closet door and the adjoining walls. Nicola, wearing the black dress that had drawn the admiration of the men at dinner, lay in a crumpled heap on the floor. Her eyes stared toward the ceiling. No fear resided in that gaze. She stared down death the way she faced all of life's challenges, with ballsy determination.

Simon stopped feeling. An icy numbness covered his heart. His mouth froze into a frown. This was part of the game, but the game had turned sinister and foul. He no longer saw the point of it. They'd survived a long time, but both of them had ignored the risks increasing against them with each new assignment.

Only a small hole had entered her chest, but Simon knew the other side would show the true devastation of the mortal wound.

He knelt by her side. Placing his gun down next to her, he closed the eyes that touched him in his sleep, the ones he wanted looking at him every morning, the ones he wanted to see in their children. Brushing her hair back, he let his fingers absorb the waning warmth in her skin.

"I promised to have your back, sweetheart, and I let you down. I'm so sorry." A chill crept through him and sucked away that part of his soul that longed for a simple life with a complicated woman.

Footsteps at the door caught his attention. Pascal, one of Luc's boys. "Simon Dunn. Come to reconcile with your ex-girlfriend? You're too late. Unlike you, when Luc is done with a woman, he prefers not seeing them with their exes, or anyone else for that matter."

Simon slid his hand toward his gun, but the Glock pointed in his face stopped him.

Pascal stood over him with a pleased-as-shit grin on his face. "Luc will be curious to know how your dead body came to rest near the remains of his latest whore." He tapped Simon's face with the nozzle to indicate he should step away from Nicola.

Simon glanced back at her. She was dead. His frozen heart wouldn't break, so long as he left it undisturbed.

He stood slowly and walked to the door with Pascal. A flicker of light from the stairway grabbed his attention. "I hope we're meeting Luc in a less heated section of the house."

As Pascal's eyes shot a concerned glare toward the flames, Simon swung his arm and knocked the gun from the son of a bitch's hands. Punching with his left hand, he nailed Pascal in the stomach. The impact pushed him into the wall, but the bastard shot forward again, lifting Simon off the ground and slamming him across the hallway.

Simon's knee to Pascal's groin forced the asshole to drop his hold. They both stepped back to breathe. After a deep intake of air, Pascal charged him again and tried to throw Simon off balance, but his weight and height equaled Pascal's. He had Pascal on the ground without too much exertion, but Pascal kicked out his leg, shoving Simon across the landing. His head hit the railing, but he managed to right himself and pull a five-inch blade out from near his calf.

Tucking it in his palm, he closed in on Pascal. He feigned right and then plunged the knife deep into his enemy's chest. Pascal faded to the floor.

Simon kicked Pascal's face once more before pulling out the knife. "I hope you rot in hell."

Turning to retrieve Nicola's body, Simon froze at the roadblock before him. The fire had spread through the venting system into Nicola's room. The curtains ignited and dropped embers across the floor. He stood helpless as Nicola's dress caught fire and within seconds, she disappeared behind a wall of flames.

***

The stairs seemed to descend forever. Ash and smoke flowed around Henry, hindering his view of the solid marble floor in the main foyer. With Alex wrapped up and passed out in his arms, he ran toward the front door, but Luc stepped from the main parlor, blocking their escape. He waved his gun toward them, wearing a smirk that needed to be beaten off his face. There may have been enough time to reload, but something in Luc's bravado told Henry he was bluffing.

Luc stepped toward them. "I'm afraid you can't help Mrs. Perrault. As the story goes, she dies in the fire and her husband, who tried to save her, didn't make it to her in time."

"You seem to be mixing up a tragedy for a comedy. You're the pathetic loser who dies in a fire you set yourself, leaving Alex, the happy widow, to dance on your grave."

"A funny man." Luc pointed the gun at Henry. "Take her to the other room."

Henry couldn't reach his own gun. "I'd prefer to take her out the door."

"I can shoot you now and drag your bloody corpse into the gallery."

Henry's eyes narrowed. "Go ahead, ace, shoot me."

The gun clicked. Luc threw it at his head. Henry ducked and rested Alex next to the front door as Luc charged him.

Luc tried a right jab, but Henry caught his fist in his left hand and returned a right elbow into his face.

Blood sprayed from Luc's nose, but didn't slow his attack. He kicked up at Henry and hit him in the gut. The thickness of the vest softened the blow. Henry pushed forward. The venom racing through his veins powered his left hand into a crunching punch at Luc's chest. The strike was hard enough to break a rib.

"That's for Alex's broken rib."

Henry's long arm span proved advantageous against the short-limbed Luc, allowing his left fist to connect with Luc's face. More blood splattered from his nose. They continued swinging at each other. Henry propelled Luc into the gallery and away from Alex.

Luc tried to fight back, but Henry was stronger. He rammed his foot into Luc's knee until it popped. Luc fell to the floor with a bellow.

"That's for Alex's leg."

Henry leaned against the wall, chest heaving and lungs aching from the smoke. Staring at him from no more than twenty feet away, Lady Elizabeth graced the smoldering walls. Son of a bitch. Smoke filled the space as the fire rushed through the adjacent rooms. Getting Alex to safety was his main priority, not getting revenge or even the painting. He turned to leave Luc to die in the fire.

Stupid move. Luc grabbed a statue and flung it toward Henry's head. He ducked, but a corner of it nicked his temple. The pain pushed him off balance and into the wall next to an iron trident hung on loose pegs. Limping, Luc loomed closer, throwing anything within his reach. Eyes wild with anger, Luc lifted a large marble bust over his head. Henry executed a roundhouse kick to Luc's face, swiping at his arms in the process. The bust fell to the floor, but Luc stood upright on the broken leg and ten gallons of adrenaline.

Henry reached for the trident and spun the staff toward Luc. "Hurry up. I have a widow to console."

Luc rushed him, but Henry sidestepped the assault, spun

around, and speared him through the side of his neck. When he pulled the spear back, Luc fell to the floor, dead.

Henry stumbled through the gallery toward the front door. He didn't want to be a hero. He wanted a brandy, a good book, and a woman named Alex.

Simon, looking beat-up himself, strode into the gallery, holding her. "We need to leave now."

Henry glanced back at the portrait on the verge of being swallowed up in the fire and nodded.

Staring at the blood pooling from the back of Henry's hand, Simon furrowed his eyebrows. "Are you okay?"

"I will be when Alex gets to the hospital." Henry followed his brother to the door, watching several strands of Alex's hair that had fallen out of the blanket sway with each of Simon's steps. "Where's your contact?"

With a stone-cold face, Simon signaled with a nod toward the upstairs. "Dead. Let's go."

CHAPTER 31

The trip back to the house in Oxford took two weeks. Alex required surgery on her leg and time to allow the rest of her injuries to improve before attempting the journey. Henry and Alex made the trip without Simon. He'd disappeared after getting them both to the hospital. He told Henry he'd be in touch. So far, he hadn't even sent a text.

With Simon gone, Alex adopted his recliner as her favorite place to prop up her feet. Henry stood in the doorway of the den and enjoyed the sight of her healing and growing whole again. Immersed in a book, she hummed Vivaldi between sips of tea, while wearing a baggy Oxford sweatshirt. Her loose skirt hung over the edge of the footrest and a small fleece blanket covered her lap.

"Henry, if you're going to stare at me and get all sentimental and sappy, I'm going to have to check into a hotel. You're becoming pathetic."

He loved her attitude. "It's nice to see you home finally."

She shut the book and placed it on the table next to her. "Remember, this is only a resting stop for me. I have bigger and better things to do than sit around all day sipping tea. You're an anchor on my ambitions."

He would support any decision she made, but would do everything in his power to convince her that her place was with him. "Really? You have ambitions?"

"I was thinking of finding a new job."

"A job?" After all the suffering she went through, she needed to rest.

"Unlike the aristocracy of England, some people need to work."

Henry laughed. "An heiress to a biotech fortune needs the money less than I do."

"It's not always about the money. Perhaps my father should donate my trust fund to your family foundation, or maybe I'll start a foundation here to help organizations like the Ripon Women's Group. If you let me, my first priority will be to renovate the wing."

He'd let her redesign the entire castle in fluorescent colors if she stayed.

"You also have to contend with Luc's inheritance. What will you do with several million euros?"

"That one is easy. I'm donating the money to the countries that have had their treasures stolen from pirates like Luc. I hope it helps return some of them to their rightful owners."

"I'm proud of you."

"I'm proud of you, too. You rescued me, despite the dangers, although I'm glad Simon was there with you."

"I more than held my own." He lifted his hand. It was still wrapped up, and to be determined if it would ever be one hundred percent again.

"From what Simon told me, you saved my life and his, too. Not bad for a navy medic."

"Don't forget my stint in food preparation."

"How could I forget?"

"Simon needs credit, too, for providing the weapons and keeping me sane enough to rescue you."

"He'd be even more heroic if he didn't disappear after telling me all the amazing things you did to save me."

Simon's job required him to disappear now and then. In this case, he also needed to separate himself from the three bodies found in Luc's house. Henry would miss his companionship and his cooking. "He'll be back after he ties up some loose ends."

"I hope so, but I'm keeping the chair until I leave."

"Agreed." Henry patted his pocket. She couldn't leave him. They were both capable of surviving alone, but were far better together, like bangers and mash. He sat on the edge of the recliner and brushed his good fingers through her hair. She leaned into his caress, and they both existed in each other's company for a few moments.

"You left something with me a few weeks ago. It belongs to you." He reached into his pocket and pulled out the engagement ring, lifted her hand, and slid it onto her finger.

She stared at it. "I love this ring, but I can't wear it."

"Why not?" Henry's heartbeat raced. He wanted to marry her for real. With her in his life, everything made sense. Everything had more depth and meaning and fun.

She held her hand out and continued to examine the ring. She shook her head. "It belongs to the Countess of Ripon. Mr. Baum will implode if he knows you've handed it over to some American commoner."

"You're not common. Besides, my uncle used a few of his political connections to remove Mr. Baum from his post."

"Powerful family. Perhaps the next trustee will care about the Ripon Women's Group. It almost makes me want to stay and help out. Transforming back into a Northrop instead of a Lemoine means I can't live in sin with my boyfriend. I should have something more permanent. Bostonians are far more conservative than Parisians."

Henry grimaced at how difficult Alex was being, but then his smile broke through as he realized what she'd said. "Since marriage to me would be as permanent as it gets, will you agree to be my countess?" The hole in his heart filled completely. Alex wanted to marry him.

"No." She sighed and continued to assess the ring. "I've agreed to be your wife. I'm not some damsel in a Regency novel. This is the twenty-first century, and I don't particularly want an earl."

"If you hate earls so much, why do you have ER tattooed here?" He brushed his hand over her breast and let it linger. She slid her hand up his arm and rested her head on his shoulder. "For practical reasons. They were the only letters I could make out of L and P without missing the train to New England."

"To me, it'll always mean your undying love and devotion." Henry kissed her temple.

She sighed in response. "Whatever. We still need to negotiate this whole title thing. It would ruin my creative reputation to be a stuffy countess. Perhaps you could abdicate."

"One doesn't abdicate a title, only a throne. You must have missed that when reading your books in the barn."

"The barn was pretty small. Why don't you give the title to your uncle?"

"If you'd like, but we'd have to give up the castle and the hedge maze. They go along with the title. And he'd never allow the Ripon's Women Group to use the east wing."

Henry could see Alex figuring out the algebraic computation that made an heiress into a countess from a rebel goddess minus the castle and maze multiplied by the joy she'd give to the families in need.

She quirked her mouth to the side and shrugged her shoulders. "I guess I could accept the title for the opportunity to work with your little charity thing."

Henry laughed and squeezed her as tightly as he could without hurting her broken ribs. "My aunt and uncle think you'd be a *brilliant* countess."

"They also think your position at the university is *cute*. Not the people I'd rely upon for my self-worth."

"Come. I've made dinner. We can discuss what everyone will call you while we eat." Henry helped her out of the chair and placed her crutches in her hands.

On the way to the kitchen, they wandered through the gallery. Lady Elizabeth sat on her horse and peered down her nose at the earl.

Alex stared ahead at a small landscape Henry had acquired from a local artist when visiting the Isle of Skye several years ago. "See the way the artist melded the oils with the acrylic paint. It adds a depth you can't achieve with one type of medium."

Henry moved toward her. "As interesting as that may be, I like it because it reminds me of a trip my mother and I took to the ocean, away from my father. My mother laughed the entire week. I'd never been so happy, until now. I love you, Alex."

Placing both crutches in her left arm, Alex tightened her grip on Henry. "I think I've loved you since that first kiss in the maze, Lord Henry."

He leaned over and kissed her, closing his eyes, savoring her taste. Careful to not hurt the broken bone in her cheek or harm the many bruises that had faded to shadows of her injuries, he breathed in the scent of jasmine tea and a cinnamon roll she'd purchased at the local bakery. It would have been a perfect moment, if she'd reciprocated the kiss. Her mouth, however, remained on his, frozen in one position, a frown. He glanced down to see Alex gaping at Lady Elizabeth.

"That's Lady Elizabeth," she announced.

"We should call this version *Lady Elizabeth Gillett, the Second*."

Alex shook her head. "No, the real Lady Elizabeth."

Henry continued to hold her, but turned his attention to the painting. Sure enough, the blue eyes had faded to a softer hue.

It didn't make sense. "I saw the painting catch fire in Paris."

"Which version?" She limped over to the portrait and brushed a finger over the muzzle of the horse.

"I didn't stop to analyze the colors in the painting while fending off Luc." How could the painting have been switched again, unless*** *Simon.* His brother had better contact him soon.

"Sorry." She hugged him and rested her head on his shoulder. "I wish I saw you all heroic and masculine."

"I'm masculine enough to not have to show you how heroic I am."

"Yet another reason I love you."

***

Alex hobbled out of Ripon Manor and walked through the rose garden, carrying a single orange rose. Her limp was less pronounced, and her leg felt much better since her final surgery a few weeks before. Her gown, made of white organza tied with an orange satin sash around her waist, blew in the crisp autumn air.

Julia and Anna strolled in front of her wearing tea-length tangerine dresses, while Rachel rushed into the maze in a white dress decorated with orange polka dots. The little girl didn't look as though a car had struck her six months ago. She'd made a much quicker recovery from her ordeal than her aunt did from Luc's rage.

Peter Northrop met his daughter at the entrance and tucked her arm into his. His pace slowed to assist her. "It's nice to see you so happy. You're a beautiful bride, although I think something a bit more traditional would have been preferable."

"I'm wearing mostly white." She brushed her hand across her orange sash.

Peter shook his head. "Having a title will place your life under more scrutiny than you ever had with us."

He still didn't get it. Henry wasn't marrying her for her fortune, and she wasn't marrying him for his title, although the castle was a nice bonus. They respected each other. They cared about each other's past, present, and future. They loved each other. And they both desired to start a family, no matter what form that family might take.

"Trust me, becoming the Countess of Ripon will be a cakewalk compared to living as Peter Northrop's daughter. At least Henry likes me no matter what I wear or do."

One of his eyebrows arched up. "Orange hair included?"

"Orange hair included. Although if you want to be technical, it's only a couple of orange extensions."

They turned the final corner. The few guests invited to the ceremony, immediate family and a local minister, stood in the middle of the maze near the spot Henry had first kissed her. There would be a large reception for everyone else later in the afternoon.

The real Gabrielle, her elegant mother, stood next to Alex's sisters and Jason. Alex released her father and stepped carefully to her mother's side. Her father had only taken her so far in life. He'd only escort her on part of this journey as well. Someday, they might try to work out their differences, but not on her wedding day.

Her mother clasped her hands. A rare tear cascaded down her cheek. "You look unique and incredibly beautiful. Thank you for including us in this special day."

"I'm glad you're all here."

They hugged. Alex had lost years with her family due to the stubborn streak she'd inherited from her father. No longer. She wanted them all back in her life.

She released her mother as her sisters pushed their way into her arms. When she finished greeting her family and Henry's aunt and uncle, she turned her attention to the sexy gentleman attired in a black tuxedo. Henry Elliott Chilton, Earl of Ripon, anthropologist, professor, and hero of her heart. Henry took her hands and pulled her into her comfort zone.

"I feel the need to say some incredibly sentimental drivel that will cause your eyes to roll to the back of your head," Henry said.

"Go ahead. It's a wedding, after all." She brushed a kiss across his lips and sighed. He tasted like hot chocolate savored by a roaring fire in the great hall.

He cleared his throat and tugged her closer. "I never believed I'd find a perfect someone with intelligence, humor, integrity, and beauty to spend my life with, but you crashed my dinner party and my heart. Thank you for agreeing to marry me, despite my title and boring profession."

When he kissed her, he dominated her senses and clouded her mind with silly hearts and songs and butterfly wings. She surrendered. If he didn't stop soon, they'd never get to the *'til death do us part* part. He pulled back, his eyes glinting with a mischievous expression. The separation left her wanting and needy. He'd kissed her to oblivion.

Alex could barely breathe. "A man could get lucky with fancy words like that."

"That's my intent, Sunshine. That's my intent."

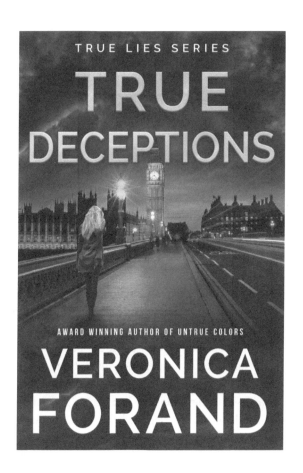

TRUE LIES SERIES

TRUE DECEPTIONS

AWARD WINNING AUTHOR OF UNTRUE COLORS

VERONICA FORAND

Turn the page for a sneak peek of
True Deceptions, Simon's story.

CHAPTER ONE

―――――――――――― ❧ ――――――――――――

Simon didn't want to know what the future held, and he didn't want to acknowledge the past. At this exact moment, however, he wanted Anna Marie from Wisconsin, an all-American blue-eyed, blonde pharmaceutical sales representative looking to experience everything life offered. During dinner, he'd given her his usual warning that people weren't always what they seemed, but she'd ignored his words and stroked the length of his leg with her foot, requesting some private time with him.

"Listen love, I think we should call it a night. I'm leaving Bermuda soon and so are you, and, at this point, I don't have room in my life for a relationship."

She laughed and reached across the table for his hand. "I'm looking for company for one night only. I have to return home tomorrow, and so far, I have nothing to take home with me but memories of business meetings and a tour of the local hospital."

She caressed the top of his hand and weaved her fingers between his. How could he turn down such an offer?

He lifted her fingers to his lips and kissed them. His gaze rested on full lips painted blood red to entice and seduce. "I'm sure I can provide you with some far more interesting memories to take home."

"Good." She stood up and encouraged him to the door of the restaurant. "I bet I can leave you with a few as well."

Once they were alone in his hotel suite, Anna Marie poured them each some champagne, bending over enough to reveal an amazing pair of breasts about to cascade out of her floral sundress. Biting her bottom lip, she lifted her gaze to peek at him through golden hair. Seductive energy swirled around her. Simon read her intentions like the cover of a tabloid.

He stood on his balcony. The view overlooked Castle Harbor at night, but he faced his dinner companion who continued to pour them each a drink. Dinner had dragged for two hours, and he was ready for dessert. Her eyes lifted from her task. Her smile reminded him of the carefree and happy life he'd enjoyed before Nicola had died in a blaze of heroism.

"This is the most luxurious hotel I've ever seen. It's four stars up from the hotel I'm staying in." Looking like a child in a candy store, she'd probably sacrifice everything to live in Simon's world. She had no idea how costly it could be. And he'd never allow her to find out.

"I'm glad you like it." He sat on the couch and stretched his legs under the bleached wood and glass coffee table.

"Wisconsin is beautiful in April, but there's no ocean breezes like here. Even the smell of the water is nice. Bermuda must be totally different from England, too."

"True."

"Have you ever met anyone with a title?"

Besides his father and half brother? "No. The British aristocracy doesn't lower itself into my social circles."

She laughed and whipped her hair over her shoulder. "I love the royal family. The dresses. The hats. It's all so glamorous."

"Come here." He had the perfect cure for her prattle.

She carried the crystal flutes to the couch and handed him one. He placed it on the table and focused his attention on her. Her blue eyes could swallow a man whole and keep him hypnotized. He had difficulty looking away.

She sipped the champagne too fast, without seeming to enjoy the taste, only the exclusivity of the beverage. "I haven't had champagne since my sister's wedding. I usually drink cosmos. What do you usually drink?"

"Vodka."

"Most of the guys I know drink beer." She took a few more sips. Her eyelashes fluttered, and her tongue peeked out of those perfect lips to lick a leftover drop of her beverage.

Simon reached his conversational limit. He took her glass and placed it next to his. Her smile became demure, but seductive. She placed her hand on his leg, both an offer and an acceptance. That was all he needed. Tonight, nothing mattered but the beautiful woman in his arms. He pulled her toward him, his hand caressing her back. Straight blonde hair fell across her shoulders. He brushed it aside in order to taste the salty air flavoring her neck. A sigh escaped her lips. He wanted all of her, all night.

When he pulled the straps of her dress down and claimed an exposed breast, she sighed again and spurred him on by brushing her fingers though his hair. His thumb played with her nipple until her sighs turned into moans. Soon he had her sprawled across the couch, topless and begging for attention. He complied with her wishes and provided her with pleasures small town farm boys had probably never shown her.

His kisses moved up her neck, stopping to nibble her earlobe. She turned toward him, demanding his attention on her soft, full lips. His mouth feathered over hers until she parted her lips, and their tongues met. She tasted like champagne mixed with nuts. Almonds. Bitter almonds. *Shit.*

Her eyes widened, and she gasped for breath. He pulled away just before her body began to convulse. Five to ten minutes since the last sip—someone must have spiked the hell out of the champagne for the poison to hit her so quickly. It didn't help that she'd spent dinner flirting instead of eating. She had nothing in her system to stop the cyanide from killing her.

Simon turned away from Anna Marie and spit out her saliva. He wiped his tongue on his shirt and then spit again. He'd be fine, but she wouldn't be. He knelt next to the couch and brushed her hair back. Her body rocked, and he held her steady by her shoulders, whispering stupid nothings, but the horror reflected in her eyes didn't subside. Her convulsions had slowed, and tears fell fast down her cheeks. She would die in the arms of a stranger who didn't know her, love her, or have the capacity to mourn for her.

Anger rushed through him. *Another woman dies because of me.* "I'm so sorry. I didn't know."

Struggling to breathe, she stared at him as though he was a monster, until her eyes shut, and she faded away from Bermuda and the glamorous life she'd never have.

No one was supposed to know his location. He'd stayed hidden for the past eight months. It was time to relocate and hide somewhere new.

The next few hours involved moving her body to a vacant room in his hotel. The task was easily handled with the help of a laundry cart and knowledge of the security cameras. He cleaned off the champagne bottle and left it by her side for the local authorities to play with.

When he returned to his suite, he had a visitor. An unexpected and unwanted visitor.

"Simon Dunn. On a stakeout, are you?" Dressed in white trousers and a pink polo shirt, Tucker Magee looked like a pretty boy on a modeling assignment instead of a spineless intelligence officer.

"I'm on vacation."

"For eight months?"

"How the hell did you find me, Tucker?"

"The problem with shagging every sexy woman on the island

is their love of social media. The boys at headquarters have had the facial recognition program scanning for you for months."

"Glad to know the vast resources of the Secret Intelligence Service are used for employee retention instead of actually protecting the commonwealth. You could simply offer more vacation time and a better benefits package."

Tucker glanced at the back of his hand. No doubt he'd just had a manicure and was admiring the handiwork. His image had always taken priority over his actual job requirements. "Her name was Sarah, here on break from university."

"I don't remember her."

"A picture of her in a bar with her friends showed your ugly face in the background. They tagged you 'hot guy.'" He smiled, the snotty prat.

"What the hell do you want?"

"My assignment is to bring you back to London."

"I'm not ready."

Tucker's eyebrows rose. "Word on the street is you killed Luc Perrault after he stole away your latest piece of ass. They even say you snuffed Nicola in a rage of passion."

His accusation fueled Simon's anger. "I didn't kill her."

"Doesn't matter. The rumor will increase your influence brokering arms deals. Everyone's going to mind you now that you're a known murderer, and that makes it even more important that you return to your post."

"I'm done."

"I don't think you understand your options. Come back immediately or stay here and face a murder conviction. Your choice." Tucker tapped his fingers together beneath his chin and grinned. "Choose wisely."

Simon's heart accelerated to full speed, drugged by adrenaline and fury. The bastard had framed him, killing a beautiful someone in order to punish him for leaving a job that burned away his soul. He stormed over to Tucker's chair, intent on ripping his heart out. Before he reached him, Tucker pulled out a 9mm Ruger and pointed it directly at Simon's crotch. His eyes narrowed, and he waved Simon back with the barrel of the gun.

"What makes you so sure I won't disappear again?" Simon asked.

"You've always hated collateral damage. It's your biggest weakness. We don't have time to insert anyone else into the game right now. Return to work or we'll create a bloody trail behind you so deep you'll drown in it." Tucker rose from his seat and strode to the door. "I expect to see you back in your flat by tomorrow." He left the room without looking back.

CHAPTER TWO

One transatlantic flight later, Simon paused in the hallway outside of his flat. Nicola had lived with him there for five years as his pretend lover. He'd spent too much time working there, hoping she'd become his real lover. It never happened. She'd died first.

The muscles in his face tightened. He needed a strong drink to get through the night. Alcohol and women were his panacea. Female companionship, however, would only remind him of Anna Marie, and that was a memory best left alone for a while.

He flicked the lights on and made his way to the kitchen. The flat smelled like window cleaner and furniture polish—too clean after being vacant and locked up for months.

Fresh food and beer filled the refrigerator. Probably compliments of the lying rat bastards at MI6 who were blackmailing him to return to his former position. He grabbed a bottle and went to decompress in an old leather recliner. One refreshing sip cooled his throat. He shut his eyes to filter out the lingering memories of his former partner who gave everything for her country and received permanent anonymity in return.

The click of a gun and a tap against the back of his head woke him up. Usually, he'd be prepared to counterattack. This time, however, he didn't care. *Go ahead, asshole. Kill me.*

"Don't move." A voice, soft and unsure, revealed all Simon needed to know. *How wonderful, more estrogen.*

"If you're going to kill me, do it now. If not, get the hell out of my flat."

She hesitated. The fool.

He reached behind him, grabbed her hair, and pulled her over the back of the recliner. She squeaked as she flipped forward into his lap. The gun flew out of her hand and skidded across the floor, landing under the coffee table. His fist kept a secure hold on her hair, and he tugged her face where he could see it—as wholesome and innocent as Anna Marie's. Blonde hair, blue eyes, American accent. She looked exactly like the future collateral damage Tucker had warned him about. Beautiful until poisoned with cyanide and left to die.

Maybe this was a nightmare and the blonde would disappear after a few minutes.

"Simon?" she whispered.

"Have I ever shagged you?" He brushed his hand over her jeans to the top of her thigh. Her rock-solid muscles tensed.

She shook her head.

He would have remembered. Model pretty, but not as thin. Long denim covered legs ended in bare feet with blue nail polish decorated with daisies.

His hand slid over her shoulder and rubbed the back of her neck. Her shiver shot across his limbs and into places Simon didn't want awakened. "Will I ever?"

She shook her head again and proved how useless she was to him at the moment. He pushed her off his lap, sending her to the floor.

"Then get the hell out of my flat." If someone wanted him dead, they'd hired an imbecile to handle the job.

His aggressive actions sent her fleeing from the room. She had five minutes to pick up her things and leave before he picked her up and tossed her out the door. Distractions would delay him from finishing his assignment and disappearing again permanently. His hand rested on his holster in case she decided to try to kill him again. Part of him hoped she'd succeed.

A minute later she returned from the kitchen with a glass of wine instead of her suitcase. Why the hell would she stay if he'd threatened her? The liquid rippled in her shaky hand. She wore a brave face—chin tilted up, lips closed and frowning—but if he yelled "boo," she'd hit the floor face first. He was certain of it.

"Why are you still here?"

"I'm Cassie Watson." She sat on the couch, all six feet something of her, dressed in loose jeans and a pink T-shirt. "They told me you'd be a jerk, but I thought they were kidding. They weren't." She took a deep breath and a swig of wine. "Anyway, I'm your new partner."

"I work alone."

She took another sip. "I was told to report to your flat and wait. They said it would be weeks until you arrived." She frowned, probably in response to *his* frown. "I understand if you don't want me, but—"

"I *don't* want you."

She ignored him and drank more wine. "I have no place to live except here. I was told that, once embedded, I wouldn't be coming out for a while. So if we're not colleagues, perhaps we can be roommates?"

"You want to be my chum? Are you daft?"

She swallowed hard. "The service won't let me return to my old job until I complete whatever assignment they placed me here to do."

She was right. In his world, you succeeded and moved to the next assignment or you died.

"You're American."

"No. I'm British. My father and mother divorced when I was five. Mom moved me to Southern California soon after. The service said sounding American would be better, because you wouldn't want an English woman after your last partner died."

He overlooked her comment about Nicola. It was in the past— a past he wanted to forget.

He phoned a contact at MI6 to confirm her identity, and that she had, indeed, been assigned as his new partner, on an assignment the service wasn't ready to reveal. She remained on the couch, drinking wine and trembling. It was like they were now recruiting Sunday school teachers to be spooks. She spoke too softly, acted too timid, and drank her wine as though it was soda. She had nothing on Nicola, who was focused, smart, and sexy as hell. There was only way out of this situation—murder Tucker. He must be laughing his ass off. If Simon didn't accept this Cassie person, they'd eliminate her and send over some other annoying neophyte.

He stood up and stretched to his full six feet, five inches. In two steps he stood over her. Her earrings sparkled the same color as her eyes. Aquamarines. He leaned forward and rested his hands on the back of the couch, one on each side of her shoulders. She tried to pull back, but the couch kept her blocked in. His nose stopped an inch from hers.

"*If* you insist on staying here, you are under my control at all times. You do as I say, go where I tell you to go, and *never* talk to headquarters without my permission. Screw with me once, and I'll throw you and all your pretty things onto the sidewalk, embedded or not." Obedience and perseverance were the two most useful skills a new agent could possess, especially when lacking competence.

She nodded and held her glass almost steady. "I understand. I've trained for months. I'm ready."

Her gaze focused on his chin. Neophyte. She'd never convince anyone they were lovers. Her training must have consisted of watching James Bond movies and playing Risk, the game of world domination.

"How many assignments have you worked on?"

"Including this one?"

"Sure."

"One."

"You have a lot of catching up to do." He could smell merlot on her breath. So damn tempting, but thoughts of Anna Marie and her final kiss stopped him cold.

"I learn fast." She lifted her glass to take another sip, forcing him to pull his face away from hers. "Do you have our assignment?"

Even if he knew, he wouldn't tell her until she'd earned his trust. "I have no idea. I'll be told within the week. Can you stay out of my way until I learn why you're here?"

"Absolutely." She placed her hand on his chest to push him back. Her confidence growing. "I guess I'll be going to bed now."

He didn't move. He hadn't thought this far. "There's only one bed, and I don't sleep on the couch. Ever."

"Fine. I'll sleep on the couch," she said, making him feel like a callous idiot.

But he couldn't back down. She'd think he cared. He didn't.

"Fine." Pushing away from her, he stormed out of the room.

***

ACKNOWLEDGMENTS

Thanks to:

Jim, for love, support, and the beautiful writing space with a view.

Sophia, for not only reading and editing my work before anyone else, but for also inspiring me to write about a clever heroine who loves bacon.

Vivienne, for using her amazing imagination to help name characters and challenge each scene.

Mom, Dad, Stephen, Linda, Adrienne, Deb, and Jodi, for taking the time to read the story for flaws.

Michelle Grajkowski, my agent, for believing in this story.

Candace Havens, my editor, for taking my writing, my plot, and my character-building to a higher level.

Susan Scott Shelley, Jacqueline Jayne, Kate Forest, Betty Bolte, and Stephanie Julian, for critiquing the book and helping me through the highs and lows of being a new author.

ACKNOWLEDGMENTS

ABOUT THE AUTHOR

Veronica Forand is the award-winning writer of romantic suspense. Among her many awards, she won the Golden Pen Award and the Bookseller's Best.

Her experience includes: attorney, international corporate tax manager, college professor, university track and field coach, United Nations intern, homeschool mom, barista, waitress, and road crew. When she isn't writing, she's a canine search and rescue handler with her dog Max.

Did you enjoy this book? Reviews help other readers find books. I appreciate all reviews, whether positive or negative.

Sign up for my newsletter and be the first to receive information about new releases, sales, and bonus materials at www.veronicaforand.com

Thank you for reading.

Made in United States
Troutdale, OR
12/26/2024